C000225979

Henry James OM (15 April 1843 – 28 February 1916) was an American-British author regarded as a key transitional figure between literary realism and literary modernism, and is considered by many to be among the greatest novelists in the English language. He was the son of Henry James Sr. and the brother of renowned philosopher and psychologist William James and diarist Alice James.

He is best known for a number of novels dealing with the social and marital interplay between émigré Americans, English people, and continental Europeans. Examples of such novels include The Portrait of a Lady, The Ambassadors, and The Wings of the Dove. His later works were increasingly experimental. In describing the internal states of mind and social dynamics of his characters, James often made use of a style in which ambiguous or contradictory motives and impressions were overlaid or juxtaposed in the discussion of a character's psyche.(Source: Wikipedia)

Literary works:
Watch and Ward (1871)
Roderick Hudson (1875)
The American (1877)
The Europeans (1878)
Confidence (1879)
Washington Square (1880)
The Portrait of a Lady (1881)
The Bostonians (1886)
The Princess Casamassima (1886)
The Reverberator (1888)
The Tragic Muse (1890)
The Other House (1896)
The Spoils of Poynton (1897)
What Maisie Knew (1897)

PRINCE CLASSICS

THE
TWO MAGICS

HENRY JAMES

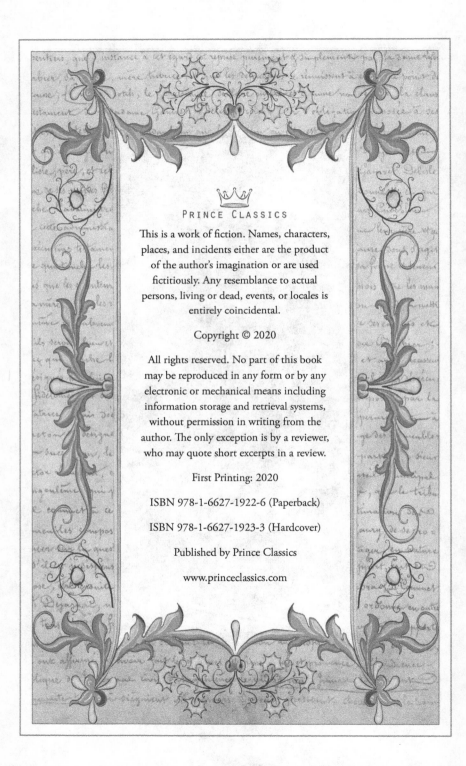

PRINCE CLASSICS

First Printing: 2020

ISBN 978-1-6627-1922-6 (Paperback)

ISBN 978-1-6627-1923-3 (Hardcover)

Published by Prince Classics

www.princeclassics.com

Contents

THE
TWO MAGICS

THE TURN OF THE SCREW

THE story had held us, round the fire, sufficiently breathless, but except the obvious remark that it was gruesome, as, on Christmas eve in an old house, a strange tale should essentially be, I remember no comment uttered till somebody happened to say that it was the only case he had met in which such a visitation had fallen on a child. The case, I may mention, was that of an apparition in just such an old house as had gathered us for the occasion—an appearance, of a dreadful kind, to a little boy sleeping in the room with his mother and waking her up in the terror of it; waking her not to dissipate his dread and soothe him to sleep again, but to encounter also, herself, before she had succeeded in doing so, the same sight that had shaken him. It was this observation that drew from Douglas—not immediately, but later in the evening—a reply that had the interesting consequence to which I call attention. Someone else told a story not particularly effective, which I saw he was not following. This I took for a sign that he had himself something to produce and that we should only have to wait. We waited in fact till two nights later; but that same evening, before we scattered, he brought out what was in his mind.

"I quite agree—in regard to Griffin's ghost, or whatever it was—that its appearing first to the little boy, at so tender an age, adds a particular touch. But it's not the first occurrence of its charming kind that I know to have involved a child. If the child gives the effect another turn of the screw, what do you say to *two* children——?"

"We say, of course," somebody exclaimed, "that they give two turns! Also that we want to hear about them."

I can see Douglas there before the fire, to which he had got up to present his back, looking down at his interlocutor with his hands in his pockets. "Nobody but me, till now, has ever heard. It's quite too horrible." This, naturally, was declared by several voices to give the thing the utmost price, and our friend, with quiet art, prepared his triumph by turning his eyes over the rest of us and going on: "It's beyond everything. Nothing at all that I know touches it."

"For sheer terror?" I remember asking.

He seemed to say it was not so simple as that; to be really at a loss how to qualify it. He passed his hand over his eyes, made a little wincing grimace. "For dreadful—dreadfulness!"

"Oh, how delicious!" cried one of the women.

He took no notice of her; he looked at me, but as if, instead of me, he saw what he spoke of. "For general uncanny ugliness and horror and pain."

"Well then," I said, "just sit right down and begin."

He turned round to the fire, gave a kick to a log, watched it an instant. Then as he faced us again: "I can't begin. I shall have to send to town." There was a unanimous groan at this, and much reproach; after which, in his preoccupied way, he explained. "The story's written. It's in a locked drawer— it has not been out for years. I could write to my man and enclose the key; he could send down the packet as he finds it." It was to me in particular that he appeared to propound this—appeared almost to appeal for aid not to hesitate. He had broken a thickness of ice, the formation of many a winter; had had his reasons for a long silence. The others resented postponement, but it was just his scruples that charmed me. I adjured him to write by the first post and to agree with us for an early hearing; then I asked him if the experience in question had been his own. To this his answer was prompt. "Oh, thank God, no!"

"And is the record yours? You took the thing down?"

"Nothing but the impression. I took that *here*"—he tapped his heart. "I've never lost it."

"Then your manuscript——?"

"Is in old, faded ink, and in the most beautiful hand." He hung fire again. "A woman's. She has been dead these twenty years. She sent me the pages in question before she died." They were all listening now, and of course there was somebody to be arch, or at any rate to draw the inference. But if he put the inference by without a smile it was also without irritation. "She was a most charming person, but she was ten years older than I. She was my sister's governess," he quietly said. "She was the most agreeable woman I've ever known in her position; she would have been worthy of any whatever. It was long ago, and this episode was long before. I was at Trinity, and I found her at home on my coming down the second summer. I was much there that year—it was a beautiful one; and we had, in her off-hours, some strolls and talks in the garden—talks in which she struck me as awfully clever and nice. Oh yes; don't grin: I liked her extremely and am glad to this day to think she liked me too. If she hadn't she wouldn't have told me. She had never told anyone. It wasn't simply that she said so, but that I knew she hadn't. I was sure; I could see. You'll easily judge why when you hear."

"Because the thing had been such a scare?"

He continued to fix me. "You'll easily judge," he repeated: "*you* will."

I fixed him too. "I see. She was in love."

He laughed for the first time. "You *are* acute. Yes, she was in love. That is, she had been. That came out—she couldn't tell her story without its coming out. I saw it, and she saw I saw it; but neither of us spoke of it. I remember the time and the place—the corner of the lawn, the shade of the great beeches and the long, hot summer afternoon. It wasn't a scene for a shudder; but oh——!" He quitted the fire and dropped back into his chair.

"You'll receive the packet Thursday morning?" I inquired.

"Probably not till the second post."

"Well then; after dinner——"

"You'll all meet me here?" He looked us round again. "Isn't anybody going?" It was almost the tone of hope.

"Everybody will stay!"

"*I* will—and *I* will!" cried the ladies whose departure had been fixed. Mrs. Griffin, however, expressed the need for a little more light. "Who was it she was in love with?"

"The story will tell," I took upon myself to reply.

"Oh, I can't wait for the story!"

"The story *won't* tell," said Douglas; "not in any literal, vulgar way."

"More's the pity, then. That's the only way I ever understand."

"Won't *you* tell, Douglas?" somebody else inquired.

He sprang to his feet again. "Yes—tomorrow. Now I must go to bed. Good-night." And quickly catching up a candlestick, he left us slightly bewildered. From our end of the great brown hall we heard his step on the stair; whereupon Mrs. Griffin spoke. "Well, if I don't know who she was in love with, I know who *he* was."

"She was ten years older," said her husband.

"*Raison de plus*—at that age! But it's rather nice, his long reticence."

"Forty years!" Griffin put in.

"With this outbreak at last."

"The outbreak," I returned, "will make a tremendous occasion of Thursday night;" and everyone so agreed with me that, in the light of it, we lost all attention for everything else. The last story, however incomplete and like the mere opening of a serial, had been told; we handshook and "candlestuck," as somebody said, and went to bed.

I knew the next day that a letter containing the key had, by the first post, gone off to his London apartments; but in spite of—or perhaps just on account of—the eventual diffusion of this knowledge we quite let him alone till after dinner, till such an hour of the evening, in fact, as might best accord with the kind of emotion on which our hopes were fixed. Then he became as communicative as we could desire and indeed gave us his best reason for being so. We had it from him again before the fire in the hall, as we had had our mild wonders of the previous night. It appeared that the narrative he had promised to read us really required for a proper intelligence a few words of prologue. Let me say here distinctly, to have done with it, that this narrative, from an exact transcript of my own made much later, is what I shall presently give. Poor Douglas, before his death—when it was in sight— committed to me the manuscript that reached him on the third of these days and that, on the same spot, with immense effect, he began to read to our hushed little circle on the night of the fourth. The departing ladies who had said they would stay didn't, of course, thank heaven, stay: they departed, in consequence of arrangements made, in a rage of curiosity, as they professed, produced by the touches with which he had already worked us up. But that only made his little final auditory more compact and select, kept it, round the hearth, subject to a common thrill.

The first of these touches conveyed that the written statement took up the tale at a point after it had, in a manner, begun. The fact to be in possession of was therefore that his old friend, the youngest of several daughters of a poor country parson, had, at the age of twenty, on taking service for the first time in the schoolroom, come up to London, in trepidation, to answer in person an advertisement that had already placed her in brief correspondence with the advertiser. This person proved, on her presenting herself, for judgment, at a house in Harley Street, that impressed her as vast and imposing— this prospective patron proved a gentleman, a bachelor in the prime of life, such a figure as had never risen, save in a dream or an old novel, before a fluttered, anxious girl out of a Hampshire vicarage. One could easily fix his type; it never, happily, dies out. He was handsome and bold and pleasant, off- hand and gay and kind. He struck her, inevitably, as gallant and splendid, but what took her most of all and gave her the courage she afterwards showed was that he put the whole thing to her as a kind of favour, an obligation he should gratefully incur. She conceived him as rich, but as fearfully extravagant— saw him all in a glow of high fashion, of good looks, of expensive habits, of charming ways with women. He had for his own town residence a big house filled with the spoils of travel and the trophies of the chase; but it was to his country home, an old family place in Essex, that he wished her immediately to proceed.

He had been left, by the death of their parents in India, guardian to a small nephew and a small niece, children of a younger, a military brother, whom he had lost two years before. These children were, by the strangest of chances for a man in his position,—a lone man without the right sort of experience or a grain of patience,—very heavily on his hands. It had all been a great worry and, on his own part doubtless, a series of blunders, but he immensely pitied the poor chicks and had done all he could; had in particular sent them down to his other house, the proper place for them being of course the country, and kept them there, from the first, with the best people he could find to look after them, parting even with his own servants to wait on them and going down himself, whenever he might, to see how they were doing. The awkward thing was that they had practically no other relations and that his own affairs took up all his time. He had put them in possession of Bly, which was healthy and secure, and had placed at the head of their little establishment—but below stairs only—an excellent woman, Mrs. Grose, whom he was sure his visitor would like and who had formerly been maid to his mother. She was now housekeeper and was also acting for the time as superintendent to the little girl, of whom, without children of her own, she was, by good luck, extremely fond. There were plenty of people to help, but of course the young lady who should go down as governess would be in supreme authority. She would also have, in holidays, to look after the small boy, who had been for a term at school—young as he was to be sent, but what else could be done?—and who, as the holidays were about to begin, would be back from one day to the other. There had been for the two children at first a young lady whom they had had the misfortune to lose. She had done for them quite beautifully—she was a most respectable person—till her death, the great awkwardness of which had, precisely, left no alternative but the school for little Miles. Mrs. Grose, since then, in the way of manners and things, had done as she could for Flora; and there were, further, a cook, a housemaid, a dairywoman, an old pony, an old groom, and an old gardener, all likewise thoroughly respectable.

So far had Douglas presented his picture when someone put a question. "And what did the former governess die of?—of so much respectability?"

Our friend's answer was prompt. "That will come out. I don't anticipate."

"Excuse me—I thought that was just what you *are* doing."

"In her successor's place," I suggested, "I should have wished to learn if the office brought with it——"

"Necessary danger to life?" Douglas completed my thought. "She did wish to learn, and she did learn. You shall hear tomorrow what she learnt. Meanwhile, of course, the prospect struck her as slightly grim. She was young, untried, nervous: it was a vision of serious duties and little company, of really great loneliness. She hesitated—took a couple of days to consult and consider. But the salary offered much exceeded her modest measure, and on a second interview she faced the music, she engaged." And Douglas, with this, made a pause that, for the benefit of the company, moved me to throw in—

"The moral of which was of course the seduction exercised by the splendid young man. She succumbed to it."

He got up and, as he had done the night before, went to the fire, gave a stir to a log with his foot, then stood a moment with his back to us. "She saw him only twice."

"Yes, but that's just the beauty of her passion."

A little to my surprise, on this, Douglas turned round to me. "It *was* the beauty of it. There were others," he went on, "who hadn't succumbed. He told her frankly all his difficulty—that for several applicants the conditions had been prohibitive. They were, somehow, simply afraid. It sounded dull—it sounded strange; and all the more so because of his main condition."

"Which was——?"

"That she should never trouble him—but never, never: neither appeal nor complain nor write about anything; only meet all questions herself, receive all moneys from his solicitor, take the whole thing over and let him alone. She promised to do this, and she mentioned to me that when, for a moment, disburdened, delighted, he held her hand, thanking her for the sacrifice, she already felt rewarded."

"But was that all her reward?" one of the ladies asked.

"She never saw him again."

"Oh!" said the lady; which, as our friend immediately left us again, was the only other word of importance contributed to the subject till, the next night, by the corner of the hearth, in the best chair, he opened the faded red cover of a thin old-fashioned gilt-edged album. The whole thing took indeed more nights than one, but on the first occasion the same lady put another question. "What is your title?"

"I haven't one."

"Oh, *I* have!" I said. But Douglas, without heeding me, had begun to read with a fine clearness that was like a rendering to the ear of the beauty of his author's hand.

I

I REMEMBER the whole beginning as a succession of flights and drops, a little see-saw of the right throbs and the wrong. After rising, in town, to meet his appeal, I had at all events a couple of very bad days—found myself doubtful again, felt indeed sure I had made a mistake. In this state of mind I spent the long hours of bumping, swinging coach that carried me to the stopping-place at which I was to be met by a vehicle from the house. This convenience, I was told, had been ordered, and I found, toward the close of the June afternoon, a commodious fly in waiting for me. Driving at that hour, on a lovely day, through a country to which the summer sweetness seemed to offer me a friendly welcome, my fortitude mounted afresh and, as we turned into the avenue, encountered a reprieve that was probably but a proof of the point to which it had sunk. I suppose I had expected, or had dreaded, something so melancholy that what greeted me was a good surprise. I remember as a most pleasant impression the broad, clear front, its open windows and fresh curtains and the pair of maids looking out; I remember the lawn and the bright flowers and the crunch of my wheels on the gravel and the clustered treetops over which the rooks circled and cawed in the golden sky. The scene had a greatness that made it a different affair from my own scant home, and there immediately appeared at the door, with a little girl in her hand, a civil person who dropped me as decent a curtsey as if I had been the mistress or a distinguished visitor. I had received in Harley Street a narrower notion of the place, and that, as I recalled it, made me think the proprietor still more of a gentleman, suggested that what I was to enjoy might be something beyond his promise.

I had no drop again till the next day, for I was carried triumphantly through the following hours by my introduction to the younger of my pupils. The little girl who accompanied Mrs. Grose appeared to me on the spot a creature so charming as to make it a great fortune to have to do with her. She was the most beautiful child I had ever seen, and I afterwards wondered that my employer had not told me more of her. I slept little that night—I was too much excited; and this astonished me too, I recollect, remained with me, adding to my sense of the liberality with which I was treated. The large, impressive room, one of the best in the house, the great state bed, as I almost felt it, the full, figured draperies, the long glasses in which, for the first time, I could see myself from head to foot, all struck me—like the extraordinary charm of my small charge—as so many things thrown in. It was thrown in as well, from the first moment, that I should get on with Mrs. Grose in a relation over which, on my way, in the coach, I fear I had rather brooded. The only thing indeed that in this early outlook might have made me shrink again was the clear circumstance of her being so glad to see me. I perceived within half an hour that she was so glad—stout, simple, plain, clean, wholesome woman—as to be positively on her guard against showing it too much. I wondered even then a little why she should wish not to show it, and that, with reflection, with suspicion, might of course have made me uneasy.

But it was a comfort that there could be no uneasiness in a connection with anything so beatific as the radiant image of my little girl, the vision of whose angelic beauty had probably more than anything else to do with the restlessness that, before morning, made me several times rise and wander about my room to take in the whole picture and prospect; to watch, from my open window, the faint summer dawn, to look at such portions of the rest of the house as I could catch, and to listen, while, in the fading dusk, the first birds began to twitter, for the possible recurrence of a sound or two, less natural and not without, but within, that I had fancied I heard. There had been a moment when I believed I recognised, faint and far, the cry of a child; there had been another when I found myself just consciously starting as at the passage, before my door, of a light footstep. But these fancies were not marked enough not to be thrown off, and it is only in the light, or the gloom, I should rather say, of other and subsequent matters that they now come back to me. To watch, teach, "form" little Flora would too evidently be the making of a happy and useful life. It had been agreed between us downstairs that after this first occasion I should have her as a matter of course at night, her small white bed being already arranged, to that end, in my room. What I had undertaken was the whole care of her, and she had remained, just this last time, with Mrs. Grose only as an effect of our consideration for my inevitable strangeness and her natural timidity. In spite of this timidity—which the child herself, in the oddest way in the world, had been perfectly frank and brave about, allowing it, without a sign of uncomfortable consciousness, with the deep, sweet serenity indeed of one of Raphael's holy infants, to be discussed, to be imputed to her and to determine us—I felt quite sure she would presently like me. It was part of what I already liked Mrs. Grose herself for, the pleasure I could see her feel in my admiration and wonder as I sat at supper with four tall candles and with my pupil, in a high chair and a bib, brightly facing me, between them, over bread and milk. There were naturally things that in Flora's presence could pass between us only as prodigious and gratified looks, obscure and roundabout allusions.

"And the little boy—does he look like her? Is he too so very remarkable?"

One wouldn't flatter a child. "Oh, Miss, *most* remarkable. If you think well of this one!"—and she stood there with a plate in her hand, beaming at our companion, who looked from one of us to the other with placid heavenly eyes that contained nothing to check us.

"Yes; if I do——?"

"You *will* be carried away by the little gentleman!"

"Well, that, I think, is what I came for—to be carried away. I'm afraid, however," I remember feeling the impulse to add, "I'm rather easily carried away. I was carried away in London!"

I can still see Mrs. Grose's broad face as she took this in. "In Harley Street?"

"In Harley Street."

"Well, Miss, you're not the first—and you won't be the last."

"Oh, I've no pretension," I could laugh, "to being the only one. My other pupil, at any rate, as I understand, comes back tomorrow?"

"Not tomorrow—Friday, Miss. He arrives, as you did, by the coach, under care of the guard, and is to be met by the same carriage."

I forthwith expressed that the proper as well as the pleasant and friendly thing would be therefore that on the arrival of the public conveyance I should be in waiting for him with his little sister; an idea in which Mrs. Grose concurred so heartily that I somehow took her manner as a kind of comforting pledge—never falsified, thank heaven!—that we should on every question be quite at one. Oh, she was glad I was there!

What I felt the next day was, I suppose, nothing that could be fairly called a reaction from the cheer of my arrival; it was probably at the most only a slight oppression produced by a fuller measure of the scale, as I walked round them, gazed up at them, took them in, of my new circumstances. They had, as it were, an extent and mass for which I had not been prepared and in the presence of which I found myself, freshly, a little scared as well as a little proud. Lessons, in this agitation, certainly suffered some delay; I reflected that my first duty was, by the gentlest arts I could contrive, to win the child into the sense of knowing me. I spent the day with her out of doors; I arranged with her, to her great satisfaction, that it should be she, she only,

21

who might show me the place. She showed it step by step and room by room and secret by secret, with droll, delightful, childish talk about it and with the result, in half an hour, of our becoming immense friends. Young as she was, I was struck, throughout our little tour, with her confidence and courage with the way, in empty chambers and dull corridors, on crooked staircases that made me pause and even on the summit of an old machicolated square tower that made me dizzy, her morning music, her disposition to tell me so many more things than she asked, rang out and led me on. I have not seen Bly since the day I left it, and I dare say that to my older and more informed eyes it would now appear sufficiently contracted. But as my little conductress, with her hair of gold and her frock of blue, danced before me round corners and pattered down passages, I had the view of a castle of romance inhabited by a rosy sprite, such a place as would somehow, for diversion of the young idea, take all colour out of storybooks and fairy-tales. Wasn't it just a storybook over which I had fallen a-doze and a-dream? No; it was a big, ugly, antique, but convenient house, embodying a few features of a building still older, half replaced and half utilised, in which I had the fancy of our being almost as lost as a handful of passengers in a great drifting ship. Well, I was, strangely, at the helm!

II

THIS came home to me when, two days later, I drove over with Flora to meet, as Mrs. Grose said, the little gentleman; and all the more for an incident that, presenting itself the second evening, had deeply disconcerted me. The first day had been, on the whole, as I have expressed, reassuring; but I was to see it wind up in keen apprehension. The postbag, that evening,—it came late,—contained a letter for me, which, however, in the hand of my employer, I found to be composed but of a few words enclosing another, addressed to himself, with a seal still unbroken. "This, I recognise, is from the head-master, and the head-master's an awful bore. Read him, please; deal with him; but mind you don't report. Not a word. I'm off!" I broke the seal with a great effort—so great a one that I was a long time coming to it; took the unopened missive at last up to my room and only attacked it just before going to bed. I had better have let it wait till morning, for it gave me a second sleepless night. With no counsel to take, the next day, I was full of distress; and it finally got so the better of me that I determined to open myself at least to Mrs. Grose.

"What does it mean? The child's dismissed his school."

She gave me a look that I remarked at the moment; then, visibly, with a quick blankness, seemed to try to take it back. "But aren't they all——?"

"Sent home—yes. But only for the holidays. Miles may never go back at all."

Consciously, under my attention, she reddened. "They won't take him?"

"They absolutely decline."

At this she raised her eyes, which she had turned from me; I saw them fill with good tears. "What has he done?"

I hesitated; then I judged best simply to hand her my letter—which, however, had the effect of making her, without taking it, simply put her hands behind her. She shook her head sadly. "Such things are not for me, Miss."

My counsellor couldn't read! I winced at my mistake, which I attenuated as I could, and opened my letter again to repeat it to her; then, faltering in the act and folding it up once more, I put it back in my pocket. "Is he really *bad*?"

The tears were still in her eyes. "Do the gentlemen say so?"

"They go into no particulars. They simply express their regret that it should be impossible to keep him. That can have only one meaning." Mrs. Grose listened with dumb emotion; she forbore to ask me what this meaning might be; so that, presently, to put the thing with some coherence and with the mere aid of her presence to my own mind, I went on: "That he's an injury to the others."

At this, with one of the quick turns of simple folk, she suddenly flamed up. "Master Miles! *him* an injury?"

There was such a flood of good faith in it that, though I had not yet seen the child, my very fears made me jump to the absurdity of the idea. I found myself, to meet my friend the better, offering it, on the spot, sarcastically. "To his poor little innocent mates!"

"It's too dreadful," cried Mrs. Grose, "to say such cruel things! Why, he's scarce ten years old."

"Yes, yes; it would be incredible."

She was evidently grateful for such a profession. "See him, Miss, first. *Then* believe it!" I felt forthwith a new impatience to see him; it was the beginning of a curiosity that, for all the next hours, was to deepen almost to pain. Mrs. Grose was aware, I could judge, of what she had produced in me, and she followed it up with assurance. "You might as well believe it of the little lady. Bless her," she added the next moment—"*look* at her!"

I turned and saw that Flora, whom, ten minutes before, I had established in the schoolroom with a sheet of white paper, a pencil, and a copy of nice "round O's," now presented herself to view at the open door. She expressed in her little way an extraordinary detachment from disagreeable duties, looking to me, however, with a great childish light that seemed to offer it as a mere result of the affection she had conceived for my person, which had rendered necessary that she should follow me. I needed nothing more than this to feel the full force of Mrs. Grose's comparison, and, catching my pupil in my arms, covered her with kisses in which there was a sob of atonement.

None the less, the rest of the day, I watched for further occasion to approach my colleague, especially as, toward evening, I began to fancy she rather sought to avoid me. I overtook her, I remember, on the staircase; we went down together, and at the bottom I detained her, holding her there with a hand on her arm. "I take what you said to me at noon as a declaration that *you've* never known him to be bad."

She threw back her head; she had clearly, by this time, and very honestly, adopted an attitude. "Oh, never known him—I don't pretend *that*!"

I was upset again. "Then you *have* known him——?"

"Yes indeed, Miss, thank God!"

On reflection I accepted this. "You mean that a boy who never is——?"

"Is no boy for *me*!"

I held her tighter. "You like them with the spirit to be naughty?" Then, keeping pace with her answer, "So do I!" I eagerly brought out. "But not to the degree to contaminate——"

"To contaminate?"—my big word left her at a loss. I explained it. "To corrupt."

She stared, taking my meaning in; but it produced in her an odd laugh. "Are you afraid he'll corrupt *you*?" She put the question with such a fine bold humour that, with a laugh, a little silly doubtless, to match her own, I gave way for the time to the apprehension of ridicule.

But the next day, as the hour for my drive approached, I cropped up in another place. "What was the lady who was here before?"

"The last governess? She was also young and pretty—almost as young and almost as pretty, Miss, even as you."

"Ah, then, I hope her youth and her beauty helped her!" I recollect throwing off. "He seems to like us young and pretty!"

"Oh, he *did*," Mrs. Grose assented: "it was the way he liked everyone!" She had no sooner spoken indeed than she caught herself up. "I mean that's *his* way—the master's."

I was struck. "But of whom did you speak first?"

She looked blank, but she coloured. "Why, of *him*."

"Of the master?"

"Of who else?"

There was so obviously no one else that the next moment I had lost my impression of her having accidentally said more than she meant; and I merely asked what I wanted to know. "Did *she* see anything in the boy——?"

"That wasn't right? She never told me."

I had a scruple, but I overcame it. "Was she careful—particular?"

Mrs. Grose appeared to try to be conscientious. "About some things—yes."

"But not about all?"

Again she considered. "Well, Miss—she's gone. I won't tell tales."

"I quite understand your feeling," I hastened to reply; but I thought it, after an instant, not opposed to this concession to pursue: "Did she die here?"

"No—she went off."

I don't know what there was in this brevity of Mrs. Grose's that struck me as ambiguous. "Went off to die?" Mrs. Grose looked straight out of the window, but I felt that, hypothetically, I had a right to know what young persons engaged for Bly were expected to do. "She was taken ill, you mean, and went home?"

"She was not taken ill, so far as appeared, in this house. She left it, at the end of the year, to go home, as she said, for a short holiday, to which the time she had put in had certainly given her a right. We had then a young woman—a nursemaid who had stayed on and who was a good girl and clever; and *she* took the children altogether for the interval. But our young lady never came back, and at the very moment I was expecting her I heard from the master that she was dead."

I turned this over. "But of what?"

"He never told me! But please, Miss," said Mrs. Grose, "I must get to my work."

III

HER thus turning her back on me was fortunately not, for my just preoccupations, a snub that could check the growth of our mutual esteem. We met, after I had brought home little Miles, more intimately than ever on the ground of my stupefaction, my general emotion: so monstrous was I then ready to pronounce it that such a child as had now been revealed to me should be under an interdict. I was a little late on the scene, and I felt, as he stood wistfully looking out for me before the door of the inn at which the coach had put him down, that I had seen him, on the instant, without and within, in the great glow of freshness, the same positive fragrance of purity, in which I had, from the first moment, seen his little sister. He was incredibly beautiful, and Mrs. Grose had put her finger on it: everything but a sort of passion of tenderness for him was swept away by his presence. What I then and there took him to my heart for was something divine that I have never found to the same degree in any child—his indescribable little air of knowing nothing in the world but love. It would have been impossible to carry a bad name with a greater sweetness of innocence, and by the time I had got back to Bly with him I remained merely bewildered—so far, that is, as I was not outraged—by the sense of the horrible letter locked up in my room, in a drawer. As soon as I could compass a private word with Mrs. Grose I declared to her that it was grotesque.

She promptly understood me. "You mean the cruel charge——?"

"It doesn't live an instant. My dear woman, *look* at him!"

She smiled at my pretension to have discovered his charm. "I assure you, Miss, I do nothing else! What will you say, then?" she immediately added.

"In answer to the letter?" I had made up my mind. "Nothing."

"And to his uncle?"

I was incisive. "Nothing."

"And to the boy himself?"

I was wonderful. "Nothing."

She gave with her apron a great wipe to her mouth. "Then I'll stand by you. We'll see it out."

"We'll see it out!" I ardently echoed, giving her my hand to make it a vow.

She held me there a moment, then whisked up her apron again with her detached hand. "Would you mind, Miss, if I used the freedom——"

"To kiss me? No!" I took the good creature in my arms and, after we had embraced like sisters, felt still more fortified and indignant.

This, at all events, was for the time: a time so full that, as I recall the way it went, it reminds me of all the art I now need to make it a little distinct. What I look back at with amazement is the situation I accepted. I had undertaken, with my companion, to see it out, and I was under a charm, apparently, that could smooth away the extent and the far and difficult connections of such an effort. I was lifted aloft on a great wave of infatuation and pity. I found it simple, in my ignorance, my confusion, and perhaps my conceit, to assume that I could deal with a boy whose education for the world was all on the point of beginning. I am unable even to remember at this day what proposal I framed for the end of his holidays and the resumption of his studies. Lessons with me, indeed, that charming summer, we all had a theory that he was to have; but I now feel that, for weeks, the lessons must have been rather my own. I learnt something—at first certainly—that had not been one of the teachings of my small, smothered life; learnt to be amused, and even amusing, and not to think for the morrow. It was the first time, in a manner, that I had known space and air and freedom, all the music of summer and all the mystery of nature. And then there was consideration—and consideration was sweet. Oh, it was a trap—not designed, but deep—to my imagination, to my delicacy, perhaps to my vanity; to whatever, in me, was most excitable. The best way to picture it all is to say that I was off my guard. They gave me so little trouble—they were of a gentleness so extraordinary. I used to

28

speculate—but even this with a dim disconnectedness—as to how the rough future (for all futures are rough!) would handle them and might bruise them. They had the bloom of health and happiness; and yet, as if I had been in charge of a pair of little grandees, of princes of the blood, for whom everything, to be right, would have to be enclosed and protected, the only form that, in my fancy, the after-years could take for them was that of a romantic, a really royal extension of the garden and the park. It may be, of course, above all, that what suddenly broke into this gives the previous time a charm of stillness— that hush in which something gathers or crouches. The change was actually like the spring of a beast.

In the first weeks the days were long; they often, at their finest, gave me what I used to call my own hour, the hour when, for my pupils, tea-time and bed-time having come and gone, I had, before my final retirement, a small interval alone. Much as I liked my companions, this hour was the thing in the day I liked most; and I liked it best of all when, as the light faded—or rather, I should say, the day lingered and the last calls of the last birds sounded, in a flushed sky, from the old trees—I could take a turn into the grounds and enjoy, almost with a sense of property that amused and flattered me, the beauty and dignity of the place. It was a pleasure at these moments to feel myself tranquil and justified; doubtless, perhaps, also to reflect that by my discretion, my quiet good sense and general high propriety, I was giving pleasure—if he ever thought of it!—to the person to whose pressure I had responded. What I was doing was what he had earnestly hoped and directly asked of me, and that I *could*, after all, do it proved even a greater joy than I had expected. I dare say I fancied myself, in short, a remarkable young woman and took comfort in the faith that this would more publicly appear. Well, I needed to be remarkable to offer a front to the remarkable things that presently gave their first sign.

It was plump, one afternoon, in the middle of my very hour: the children were tucked away and I had come out for my stroll. One of the thoughts that, as I don't in the least shrink now from noting, used to be with me in these wanderings was that it would be as charming as a charming story suddenly to meet someone. Someone would appear there at the turn of a path and would stand before me and smile and approve. I didn't ask more than that—I only asked that he should *know*; and the only way to be sure he knew would be to see it, and the kind light of it, in his handsome face. That was exactly present to me—by which I mean the face was—when, on the first of these occasions, at the end of a long June day, I stopped short on emerging from one of the plantations and coming into view of the house. What arrested me on the spot—and with a shock much greater than any vision had allowed for—was the sense that my imagination had, in a flash, turned real. He did stand there!—but high up, beyond the lawn and at the very top of the tower to which, on that first morning, little Flora had conducted me. This tower was one of a pair—square, incongruous, crenelated structures—that were distinguished, for some reason, though I could see little difference, as the new and the old. They flanked opposite ends of the house and were probably architectural absurdities, redeemed in a measure indeed by not being wholly disengaged nor of a height too pretentious, dating, in their gingerbread antiquity, from a romantic revival that was already a respectable past. I admired them, had fancies about them, for we could all profit in a degree, especially when they loomed through the dusk, by the grandeur of their actual battlements; yet it was not at such an elevation that the figure I had so often invoked seemed most in place.

It produced in me, this figure, in the clear twilight, I remember, two distinct gasps of emotion, which were, sharply, the shock of my first and that of my second surprise. My second was a violent perception of the mistake of my first: the man who met my eyes was not the person I had precipitately supposed. There came to me thus a bewilderment of vision of which, after these years, there is no living view that I can hope to give. An unknown man in a lonely place is a permitted object of fear to a young woman privately bred; and the figure that faced me was—a few more seconds assured me—as little anyone else I knew as it was the image that had been in my mind. I had not seen it in Harley Street—I had not seen it anywhere. The place, moreover, in the strangest way in the world, had, on the instant, and by the very fact of its appearance, become a solitude. To me at least, making my statement here with a deliberation with which I have never made it, the whole feeling of the moment returns. It was as if, while I took in—what I did take in—all the rest of the scene had been stricken with death. I can hear again, as I write, the intense hush in which the sounds of evening dropped. The rooks stopped cawing in the golden sky and the friendly hour lost, for the minute, all its voice. But there was no other change in nature, unless indeed it were a change that I saw with a stranger sharpness. The gold was still in the sky, the clearness in the air, and the man who looked at me over the battlements was as definite as a picture in a frame. That's how I thought, with extraordinary quickness, of each person that he might have been and that he was not. We were confronted across our distance quite long enough for me to ask myself with intensity who then he was and to feel, as an effect of my inability to say, a wonder that in a few instants more became intense.

The great question, or one of these, is, afterwards, I know, with regard to certain matters, the question of how long they have lasted. Well, this matter of mine, think what you will of it, lasted while I caught at a dozen possibilities, none of which made a difference for the better, that I could see, in there having been in the house—and for how long, above all?—a person of whom I was in ignorance. It lasted while I just bridled a little with the sense that my office demanded that there should be no such ignorance and no such person. It lasted while this visitant, at all events,—and there was a touch of the strange freedom, as I remember, in the sign of familiarity of his wearing no hat,—seemed to fix me, from his position, with just the question, just the scrutiny through the fading light, that his own presence provoked. We were too far apart to call to each other, but there was a moment at which, at shorter range, some challenge between us, breaking the hush, would have been the right result of our straight mutual stare. He was in one of the angles, the one away from the house, very erect, as it struck me, and with both hands on the ledge. So I saw him as I see the letters I form on this page; then, exactly, after a minute, as if to add to the spectacle, he slowly changed his place—passed, looking at me hard all the while, to the opposite corner of the platform. Yes, I had the sharpest sense that during this transit he never took his eyes from me, and I can see at this moment the way his hand, as he went, passed from one of the crenelations to the next. He stopped at the other corner, but less long, and even as he turned away still markedly fixed me. He turned away; that was all I knew.

IV

It was not that I didn't wait, on this occasion, for more, for I was rooted as deeply as I was shaken. Was there a "secret" at Bly—a mystery of Udolpho or an insane, an unmentionable relative kept in unsuspected confinement? I can't say how long I turned it over, or how long, in a confusion of curiosity and dread, I remained where I had had my collision; I only recall that when I re-entered the house darkness had quite closed in. Agitation, in the interval, certainly had held me and driven me, for I must, in circling about the place, have walked three miles; but I was to be, later on, so much more overwhelmed that this mere dawn of alarm was a comparatively human chill. The most singular part of it in fact—singular as the rest had been—was the part I became, in the hall, aware of in meeting Mrs. Grose. This picture comes back to me in the general train—the impression, as I received it on my return, of the wide white panelled space, bright in the lamplight and with its portraits and red carpet, and of the good surprised look of my friend, which immediately told me she had missed me. It came to me straightway, under her contact, that, with plain heartiness, mere relieved anxiety at my appearance, she knew nothing whatever that could bear upon the incident I had there ready for her. I had not suspected in advance that her comfortable face would pull me up, and I somehow measured the importance of what I had seen by my thus finding myself hesitate to mention it. Scarce anything in the whole history seems to me so odd as this fact that my real beginning of fear was one, as I may say, with the instinct of sparing my companion. On the spot, accordingly, in the pleasant hall and with her eyes on me, I, for a reason that I couldn't then have phrased, achieved an inward revolution—offered a vague pretext for my lateness and, with the plea of the beauty of the night and of the heavy dew and wet feet, went as soon as possible to my room.

Here it was another affair; here, for many days after, it was a queer affair enough. There were hours, from day to day,—or at least there were moments, snatched even from clear duties,—when I had to shut myself up to think. It was not so much yet that I was more nervous than I could bear to be as that

I was remarkably afraid of becoming so; for the truth I had now to turn over was, simply and clearly, the truth that I could arrive at no account whatever of the visitor with whom I had been so inexplicably and yet, as it seemed to me, so intimately concerned. It took little time to see that I could sound without forms of inquiry and without exciting remark any domestic complication. The shock I had suffered must have sharpened all my senses; I felt sure, at the end of three days and as the result of mere closer attention, that I had not been practised upon by the servants nor made the object of any "game." Of whatever it was that I knew nothing was known around me. There was but one sane inference: someone had taken a liberty rather gross. That was what, repeatedly, I dipped into my room and locked the door to say to myself. We had been, collectively, subject to an intrusion; some unscrupulous traveller, curious in old houses, had made his way in unobserved, enjoyed the prospect from the best point of view, and then stolen out as he came. If he had given me such a bold hard stare, that was but a part of his indiscretion. The good thing, after all, was that we should surely see no more of him.

This was not so good a thing, I admit, as not to leave me to judge that what, essentially, made nothing else much signify was simply my charming work. My charming work was just my life with Miles and Flora, and through nothing could I so like it as through feeling that I could throw myself into it in trouble. The attraction of my small charges was a constant joy, leading me to wonder afresh at the vanity of my original fears, the distaste I had begun by entertaining for the probable grey prose of my office. There was to be no grey prose, it appeared, and no long grind; so how could work not be charming that presented itself as daily beauty? It was all the romance of the nursery and the poetry of the schoolroom. I don't mean by this, of course, that we studied only fiction and verse; I mean I can express no otherwise the sort of interest my companions inspired. How can I describe that except by saying that instead of growing used to them—and it's a marvel for a governess: I call the sisterhood to witness!—I made constant fresh discoveries. There was one direction, assuredly, in which these discoveries stopped: deep obscurity continued to cover the region of the boy's conduct at school. It had been promptly given me, I have noted, to face that mystery without a pang. Perhaps even it would be nearer the truth to say that—without a word—he himself had cleared it up. He had made the whole charge absurd. My conclusion bloomed there with the real rose-flush of his innocence: he was only too fine and fair for the little horrid, unclean school-world, and he had paid a price for it. I reflected acutely that the sense of such differences, such superiorities of quality, always, on the part of the majority—which could include even stupid, sordid head-masters—turns infallibly to the vindictive.

Both the children had a gentleness (it was their only fault, and it never made Miles a muff) that kept them—how shall I express it?—almost impersonal and certainly quite unpunishable. They were like the cherubs of the anecdote, who had—morally, at any rate—nothing to whack! I remember feeling with Miles in especial as if he had had, as it were, no history. We expect of a small child a scant one, but there was in this beautiful little boy something extraordinarily sensitive, yet extraordinarily happy, that, more than in any creature of his age I have seen, struck me as beginning anew each day. He had never for a second suffered. I took this as a direct disproof of his having really been chastised. If he had been wicked he would have "caught" it, and I should have caught it by the rebound—I should have found the trace. I found nothing at all, and he was therefore an angel. He never spoke of his school, never mentioned a comrade or a master; and I, for my part, was quite too much disgusted to allude to them. Of course I was under the spell, and the wonderful part is that, even at the time, I perfectly knew I was. But I gave myself up to it; it was an antidote to any pain, and I had more pains than one. I was in receipt in these days of disturbing letters from home, where things were not going well. But with my children, what things in the world mattered? That was the question I used to put to my scrappy retirements. I was dazzled by their loveliness.

There was a Sunday—to get on—when it rained with such force and for so many hours that there could be no procession to church; in consequence of which, as the day declined, I had arranged with Mrs. Grose that, should the evening show improvement, we would attend together the late service. The rain happily stopped, and I prepared for our walk, which, through the park and by the good road to the village, would be a matter of twenty minutes. Coming downstairs to meet my colleague in the hall, I remembered a pair of gloves that had required three stitches and that had received them—with a publicity perhaps not edifying—while I sat with the children at their tea, served on Sundays, by exception, in that cold, clean temple of mahogany and brass, the "grown-up" dining-room. The gloves had been dropped there, and I turned in to recover them. The day was grey enough, but the afternoon light still lingered, and it enabled me, on crossing the threshold, not only to recognise, on a chair near the wide window, then closed, the articles I wanted, but to become aware of a person on the other side of the window and looking straight in. One step into the room had sufficed; my vision was instantaneous; it was all there. The person looking straight in was the person who had already appeared to me. He appeared thus again with I won't say greater distinctness, for that was impossible, but with a nearness that represented a forward stride in our intercourse and made me, as I met him, catch my breath and turn cold. He was the same—he was the same, and seen, this time, as he had been seen before, from the waist up, the window, though the dining-room was on the ground-floor, not going down to the terrace on which he stood. His face was close to the glass, yet the effect of this better view was, strangely, only to show me how intense the former had been. He remained but a few seconds— long enough to convince me he also saw and recognised; but it was as if I had been looking at him for years and had known him always. Something, however, happened this time that had not happened before; his stare into my face, through the glass and across the room, was as deep and hard as then, but it quitted me for a moment during which I could still watch it, see it fix successively several other things. On the spot there came to me the added shock of a certitude that it was not for me he had come there. He had come for someone else.

The flash of this knowledge—for it was knowledge in the midst of dread—produced in me the most extraordinary effect, started, as I stood there, a sudden vibration of duty and courage. I say courage because I was beyond all doubt already far gone. I bounded straight out of the door again, reached that of the house, got, in an instant, upon the drive, and, passing along the terrace as fast as I could rush, turned a corner and came full in sight. But it was in sight of nothing now—my visitor had vanished. I stopped, I almost dropped, with the real relief of this; but I took in the whole scene—I gave him time to reappear. I call it time, but how long was it? I can't speak to the purpose today of the duration of these things. That kind of measure must have left me: they couldn't have lasted as they actually appeared to me to last. The terrace and the whole place, the lawn and the garden beyond it, all I could see of the park, were empty with a great emptiness. There were shrubberies and big trees, but I remember the clear assurance I felt that none of them concealed him. He was there or was not there: not there if I didn't see him. I got hold of this; then, instinctively, instead of returning as I had come, went to the window. It was confusedly present to me that I ought to place myself where he had stood. I did so; I applied my face to the pane and looked, as he had looked, into the room. As if, at this moment, to show me exactly what his range had been, Mrs. Grose, as I had done for himself just before, came in from the hall. With this I had the full image of a repetition of what had already occurred. She saw me as I had seen my own visitant; she pulled up short as I had done; I gave her something of the shock that I had received. She turned white, and this made me ask myself if I had blanched as much. She stared, in short, and retreated on just *my* lines, and I knew she had then passed out and come round to me and that I should presently meet her. I remained where I was, and while I waited I thought of more things than one. But there's only one I take space to mention. I wondered why *she* should be scared.

<h1 style="text-align:center">V̲</h1>

OH, she let me know as soon as, round the corner of the house, she loomed again into view. "What in the name of goodness is the matter——?" She was now flushed and out of breath.

I said nothing till she came quite near. "With me?" I must have made a wonderful face. "Do I show it?"

"You're as white as a sheet. You look awful."

I considered; I could meet on this, without scruple, any innocence. My need to respect the bloom of Mrs. Grose's had dropped, without a rustle, from my shoulders, and if I wavered for the instant it was not with what I kept back. I put out my hand to her and she took it; I held her hard a little, liking to feel her close to me. There was a kind of support in the shy heave of her surprise. "You came for me for church, of course, but I can't go."

"Has anything happened?"

"Yes. You must know now. Did I look very queer?"

"Through this window? Dreadful!"

"Well," I said, "I've been frightened." Mrs. Grose's eyes expressed plainly that *she* had no wish to be, yet also that she knew too well her place not to be ready to share with me any marked inconvenience. Oh, it was quite settled that she *must* share! "Just what you saw from the dining-room a minute ago was the effect of that. What *I* saw—just before—was much worse."

Her hand tightened. "What was it?"

"An extraordinary man. Looking in."

"What extraordinary man?"

"I haven't the least idea."

Mrs. Grose gazed round us in vain. "Then where is he gone?"

"I know still less."

"Have you seen him before?"

"Yes—once. On the old tower."

She could only look at me harder. "Do you mean he's a stranger?"

"Oh, very much!"

"Yet you didn't tell me?"

"No—for reasons. But now that you've guessed——"

Mrs. Grose's round eyes encountered this charge. "Ah, I haven't guessed!" she said very simply. "How can I if *you* don't imagine?"

"I don't in the very least."

"You've seen him nowhere but on the tower?"

"And on this spot just now."

Mrs. Grose looked round again. "What was he doing on the tower?"

"Only standing there and looking down at me."

She thought a minute. "Was he a gentleman?"

I found I had no need to think. "No." She gazed in deeper wonder. "No."

"Then nobody about the place? Nobody from the village?"

"Nobody—nobody. I didn't tell you, but I made sure."

She breathed a vague relief: this was, oddly, so much to the good. It only went indeed a little way. "But if he isn't a gentleman——"

"What *is* he? He's a horror."

"A horror?"

"He's—God help me if I know *what* he is!"

Mrs. Grose looked round once more; she fixed her eyes on the duskier distance, then, pulling herself together, turned to me with abrupt inconsequence. "It's time we should be at church."

"Oh, I'm not fit for church!"

"Won't it do you good?"

"It won't do *them*——!" I nodded at the house.

"The children?"

"I can't leave them now."

"You're afraid——?"

I spoke boldly. "I'm afraid of *him*."

Mrs. Grose's large face showed me, at this, for the first time, the far-away faint glimmer of a consciousness more acute: I somehow made out in it the delayed dawn of an idea I myself had not given her and that was as yet quite obscure to me. It comes back to me that I thought instantly of this as something I could get from her; and I felt it to be connected with the desire she presently showed to know more. "When was it—on the tower?"

"About the middle of the month. At this same hour."

"Almost at dark," said Mrs. Grose.

"Oh no, not nearly. I saw him as I see you."

"Then how did he get in?"

"And how did he get out?" I laughed. "I had no opportunity to ask him! This evening, you see," I pursued, "he has not been able to get in."

"He only peeps?"

"I hope it will be confined to that!" She had now let go my hand; she turned away a little. I waited an instant; then I brought out: "Go to church. Good-bye. I must watch."

Slowly she faced me again. "Do you fear for them?"

We met in another long look. "Don't *you*?" Instead of answering she came nearer to the window and, for a minute, applied her face to the glass. "You see how he could see," I meanwhile went on.

She didn't move. "How long was he here?"

"Till I came out. I came to meet him."

Mrs. Grose at last turned round, and there was still more in her face. "*I* couldn't have come out."

"Neither could I!" I laughed again. "But I did come. I have my duty."

"So have I mine," she replied; after which she added: "What is he like?"

"I've been dying to tell you. But he's like nobody."

"Nobody?" she echoed.

"He has no hat." Then seeing in her face that she already, in this, with a deeper dismay, found a touch of picture, I quickly added stroke to stroke. "He has red hair, very red, close-curling, and a pale face, long in shape, with straight, good features and little, rather queer whiskers that are as red as his hair. His eyebrows are, somehow, darker; they look particularly arched and as if they might move a good deal. His eyes are sharp, strange—awfully; but I only know clearly that they're rather small and very fixed. His mouth's wide, and his lips are thin, and except for his little whiskers he's quite clean-shaven. He gives me a sort of sense of looking like an actor."

"An actor!" It was impossible to resemble one less, at least, than Mrs. Grose at that moment.

"I've never seen one, but so I suppose them. He's tall, active, erect," I continued, "but never—no, never!—a gentleman."

My companion's face had blanched as I went on; her round eyes started and her mild mouth gaped. "A gentleman?" she gasped, confounded, stupefied: "a gentleman *he*?"

"You know him then?"

She visibly tried to hold herself. "But he *is* handsome?"

I saw the way to help her. "Remarkably!"

"And dressed——?"

"In somebody's clothes. They're smart, but they're not his own."

She broke into a breathless affirmative groan. "They're the master's!"

I caught it up. "You *do* know him?"

She faltered but a second. "Quint!" she cried.

"Quint?"

"Peter Quint—his own man, his valet, when he was here!"

"When the master was?"

Gaping still, but meeting me, she pieced it all together. "He never wore his hat, but he did wear—well, there were waistcoats missed! They were both here—last year. Then the master went, and Quint was alone."

I followed, but halting a little. "Alone?"

"Alone with *us*." Then, as from a deeper depth, "In charge," she added.

"And what became of him?"

She hung fire so long that I was still more mystified. "He went too," she brought out at last.

"Went where?"

Her expression, at this, became extraordinary. "God knows where! He died."

"Died?" I almost shrieked.

She seemed fairly to square herself, plant herself more firmly to utter the wonder of it. "Yes. Mr. Quint is dead."

VI

IT took of course more than that particular passage to place us together in presence of what we had now to live with as we could—my dreadful liability to impressions of the order so vividly exemplified, and my companion's knowledge, henceforth,—a knowledge half consternation and half compassion,—of that liability. There had been, this evening, after the revelation that left me, for an hour, so prostrate—there had been, for either of us, no attendance on any service but a little service of tears and vows, of prayers and promises, a climax to the series of mutual challenges and pledges that had straightway ensued on our retreating together to the schoolroom and shutting ourselves up there to have everything out. The result of our having everything out was simply to reduce our situation to the last rigour of its elements. She herself had seen nothing, not the shadow of a shadow, and nobody in the house but the governess was in the governess's plight; yet she accepted without directly impugning my sanity the truth as I gave it to her, and ended by showing me, on this ground, an awe-stricken tenderness, an expression of the sense of my more than questionable privilege, of which the very breath has remained with me as that of the sweetest of human charities.

What was settled between us, accordingly, that night, was that we thought we might bear things together; and I was not even sure that, in spite of her exemption, it was she who had the best of the burden. I knew at this hour, I think, as well as I knew later what I was capable of meeting to shelter my pupils; but it took me some time to be wholly sure of what my honest ally was prepared for to keep terms with so compromising a contract. I was queer company enough—quite as queer as the company I received; but as I trace over what we went through I see how much common ground we must have found in the one idea that, by good fortune, *could* steady us. It was the idea, the second movement, that led me straight out, as I may say, of the inner chamber of my dread. I could take the air in the court, at least, and there Mrs. Grose could join me. Perfectly can I recall now the particular way strength came to me before we separated for the night. We had gone over and over every feature of what I had seen.

"He was looking for someone else, you say—someone who was not you?"

"He was looking for little Miles." A portentous clearness now possessed me. "*That's* whom he was looking for."

42

"But how do you know?"

"I know, I know, I know!" My exaltation grew. "And *you* know, my dear!"

She didn't deny this, but I required, I felt, not even so much telling as that. She resumed in a moment, at any rate: "What if *he* should see him?"

"Little Miles? That's what he wants!"

She looked immensely scared again. "The child?"

"Heaven forbid! The man. He wants to appear to *them*." That he might was an awful conception, and yet, somehow, I could keep it at bay; which, moreover, as we lingered there, was what I succeeded in practically proving. I had an absolute certainty that I should see again what I had already seen, but something within me said that by offering myself bravely as the sole subject of such experience, by accepting, by inviting, by surmounting it all, I should serve as an expiatory victim and guard the tranquillity of my companions. The children, in especial, I should thus fence about and absolutely save. I recall one of the last things I said that night to Mrs. Grose.

"It does strike me that my pupils have never mentioned———"

She looked at me hard as I musingly pulled up. "His having been here and the time they were with him?"

"The time they were with him, and his name, his presence, his history, in any way."

"Oh, the little lady doesn't remember. She never heard or knew."

"The circumstances of his death?" I thought with some intensity. "Perhaps not. But Miles would remember—Miles would know."

"Ah, don't try him!" broke from Mrs. Grose.

I returned her the look she had given me. "Don't be afraid." I continued to think. "It is rather odd."

"That he has never spoken of him?"

"Never by the least allusion. And you tell me they were 'great friends'?"

"Oh, it wasn't *him*!" Mrs. Grose with emphasis declared. "It was Quint's own fancy. To play with him, I mean—to spoil him." She paused a moment; then she added: "Quint was much too free."

This gave me, straight from my vision of his face—*such* a face!—a sudden sickness of disgust. "Too free with *my* boy?"

"Too free with everyone!"

I forbore, for the moment, to analyse this description further than by the reflection that a part of it applied to several of the members of the household, of the half-dozen maids and men who were still of our small colony. But there was everything, for our apprehension, in the lucky fact that no discomfortable legend, no perturbation of scullions, had ever, within anyone's memory, attached to the kind old place. It had neither bad name nor ill fame, and Mrs. Grose, most apparently, only desired to cling to me and to quake in silence. I even put her, the very last thing of all, to the test. It was when, at midnight, she had her hand on the schoolroom door to take leave. "I have it from you then—for it's of great importance—that he was definitely and admittedly bad?"

"Oh, not admittedly. *I* knew it—but the master didn't."

"And you never told him?"

"Well, he didn't like tale-bearing—he hated complaints. He was terribly short with anything of that kind, and if people were all right to *him*——"

"He wouldn't be bothered with more?" This squared well enough with my impression of him: he was not a trouble-loving gentleman, nor so very particular perhaps about some of the company *he* kept. All the same, I pressed my interlocutress. "I promise you *I* would have told!"

She felt my discrimination. "I dare say I was wrong. But, really, I was afraid."

44

"Afraid of what?"

"Of things that man could do. Quint was so clever—he was so deep."

I took this in still more than, probably, I showed. "You weren't afraid of anything else? Not of his effect——?"

"His effect?" she repeated with a face of anguish and waiting while I faltered.

"On innocent little precious lives. They were in your charge."

"No, they were not in mine!" she roundly and distressfully returned. "The master believed in him and placed him here because he was supposed not to be well and the country air so good for him. So he had everything to say. Yes"—she let me have it—"even about *them*."

"Them—that creature?" I had to smother a kind of howl. "And you could bear it!"

"No. I couldn't—and I can't now!" And the poor woman burst into tears.

A rigid control, from the next day, was, as I have said, to follow them; yet how often and how passionately, for a week, we came back together to the subject! Much as we had discussed it that Sunday night, I was, in the immediate later hours in especial—for it may be imagined whether I slept—still haunted with the shadow of something she had not told me. I myself had kept back nothing, but there was a word Mrs. Grose had kept back. I was sure, moreover, by morning, that this was not from a failure of frankness, but because on every side there were fears. It seems to me indeed, in retrospect, that by the time the morrow's sun was high I had restlessly read into the facts before us almost all the meaning they were to receive from subsequent and more cruel occurrences. What they gave me above all was just the sinister figure of the living man—the dead one would keep awhile!—and of the months he had continuously passed at Bly, which, added up, made a formidable stretch. The limit of this evil time had arrived only when, on the dawn of a winter's morning, Peter Quint was found, by a labourer going to early work, stone dead on the road from the village: a catastrophe explained—superficially at least—by a visible wound to his head; such a wound as might have been produced—and as, on the final evidence, *had* been—by a fatal slip, in the dark and after leaving the public house, on the steepish icy slope, a wrong path altogether, at the bottom of which he lay. The icy slope, the turn mistaken at night and in liquor, accounted for much—practically, in the end and after the inquest and boundless chatter, for everything; but there had been matters in his life—strange passages and perils, secret disorders, vices more than suspected—that would have accounted for a good deal more.

I scarce know how to put my story into words that shall be a credible picture of my state of mind; but I was in these days literally able to find a joy in the extraordinary flight of heroism the occasion demanded of me. I now saw that I had been asked for a service admirable and difficult; and there would be a greatness in letting it be seen—oh, in the right quarter!—that I could succeed where many another girl might have failed. It was an immense help to me—I confess I rather applaud myself as I look back!—that I saw my service so strongly and so simply. I was there to protect and defend the little creatures in the world the most bereaved and the most loveable, the appeal of whose helplessness had suddenly become only too explicit, a deep, constant ache of one's own committed heart. We were cut off, really, together; we were united in our danger. They had nothing but me, and I—well, I had *them*. It was in short a magnificent chance. This chance presented itself to me in an image richly material. I was a screen—I was to stand before them. The more I saw, the less they would. I began to watch them in a stifled suspense, a disguised excitement that might well, had it continued too long, have turned to something like madness. What saved me, as I now see, was that it turned to something else altogether. It didn't last as suspense—it was superseded by horrible proofs. Proofs, I say, yes—from the moment I really took hold.

This moment dated from an afternoon hour that I happened to spend in the grounds with the younger of my pupils alone. We had left Miles indoors, on the red cushion of a deep window-seat; he had wished to finish a book, and I had been glad to encourage a purpose so laudable in a young man whose only defect was an occasional excess of the restless. His sister, on the contrary, had been alert to come out, and I strolled with her half an hour, seeking the shade, for the sun was still high and the day exceptionally warm. I was aware afresh, with her, as we went, of how, like her brother, she contrived—it was the charming thing in both children—to let me alone without appearing to drop me and to accompany me without appearing to surround. They were never importunate and yet never listless. My attention to them all really went to seeing them amuse themselves immensely without me: this was a spectacle they seemed actively to prepare and that engaged me as an active admirer. I walked in a world of their invention—they had no occasion whatever to draw upon mine; so that my time was taken only with being, for them, some remarkable person or thing that the game of the moment required and that was merely, thanks to my superior, my exalted stamp, a happy and highly distinguished sinecure. I forget what I was on the present occasion; I only remember that I was something very important and very quiet and that Flora was playing very hard. We were on the edge of the lake, and, as we had lately begun geography, the lake was the Sea of Azof.

Suddenly, in these circumstances, I became aware that, on the other side of the Sea of Azof, we had an interested spectator. The way this knowledge gathered in me was the strangest thing in the world—the strangest, that is, except the very much stranger in which it quickly merged itself. I had sat down with a piece of work—for I was something or other that could sit—on the old stone bench which overlooked the pond; and in this position I began to take in with certitude, and yet without direct vision, the presence, at a distance, of a third person. The old trees, the thick shrubbery, made a great and pleasant shade, but it was all suffused with the brightness of the hot, still hour. There was no ambiguity in anything; none whatever, at least, in the conviction I from one moment to another found myself forming as to what I should see straight before me and across the lake as a consequence of raising my eyes. They were attached at this juncture to the stitching in which I was engaged, and I can feel once more the spasm of my effort not to move them till I should so have steadied myself as to be able to make up my mind what to do. There was an alien object in view—a figure whose right of presence I instantly, passionately questioned. I recollect counting over perfectly the possibilities, reminding myself that nothing was more natural, for instance, than the appearance of one of the men about the place, or even of a messenger, a postman or a tradesman's boy, from the village. That reminder had as little effect on my practical certitude as I was conscious—still even without looking—of its having upon the character and attitude of our visitor. Nothing was more natural than that these things should be the other things that they absolutely were not.

Of the positive identity of the apparition I would assure myself as soon as the small clock of my courage should have ticked out the right second; meanwhile, with an effort that was already sharp enough, I transferred my eyes straight to little Flora, who, at the moment, was about ten yards away. My heart had stood still for an instant with the wonder and terror of the question whether she too would see; and I held my breath while I waited for what a cry from her, what some sudden innocent sign either of interest or of alarm, would tell me. I waited, but nothing came; then, in the first place— and there is something more dire in this, I feel, than in anything I have to relate—I was determined by a sense that, within a minute, all sounds from her had previously dropped; and, in the second, by the circumstance that, also within the minute, she had, in her play, turned her back to the water. This was her attitude when I at last looked at her—looked with the confirmed conviction that we were still, together, under direct personal notice. She had picked up a small flat piece of wood, which happened to have in it a little hole that had evidently suggested to her the idea of sticking in another fragment that might figure as a mast and make the thing a boat. This second morsel, as I watched her, she was very markedly and intently attempting to tighten in its place. My apprehension of what she was doing sustained me so that after some seconds I felt I was ready for more. Then I again shifted my eyes—I faced what I had to face.

VII

I GOT hold of Mrs. Grose as soon after this as I could; and I can give no intelligible account of how I fought out the interval. Yet I still hear myself cry as I fairly threw myself into her arms: "They *know*—it's too monstrous: they know, they know!"

"And what on earth——?" I felt her incredulity as she held me.

"Why, all that *we* know—and heaven knows what else besides!" Then, as she released me, I made it out to her, made it out perhaps only now with full coherency even to myself. "Two hours ago, in the garden"—I could scarce articulate—"Flora *saw*!"

Mrs. Grose took it as she might have taken a blow in the stomach. "She has told you?" she panted.

"Not a word—that's the horror. She kept it to herself! The child of eight, *that* child!" Unutterable still, for me, was the stupefaction of it.

Mrs. Grose, of course, could only gape the wider. "Then how do you know?"

"I was there—I saw with my eyes: saw that she was perfectly aware."

"Do you mean aware of *him*?"

"No—of *her*." I was conscious as I spoke that I looked prodigious things, for I got the slow reflection of them in my companion's face. "Another person—this time; but a figure of quite as unmistakeable horror and evil: a woman in black, pale and dreadful—with such an air also, and such a face!— on the other side of the lake. I was there with the child—quiet for the hour; and in the midst of it she came."

"Came how—from where?"

"From where they come from! She just appeared and stood there—but not so near."

"And without coming nearer?"

"Oh, for the effect and the feeling, she might have been as close as you!"

My friend, with an odd impulse, fell back a step. "Was she someone you've never seen?"

"Yes. But someone the child has. Someone *you* have." Then, to show how I had thought it all out: "My predecessor—the one who died."

"Miss Jessel?"

"Miss Jessel. You don't believe me?" I pressed.

She turned right and left in her distress. "How can you be sure?"

This drew from me, in the state of my nerves, a flash of impatience. "Then ask Flora—*she's* sure!" But I had no sooner spoken than I caught myself up. "No, for God's sake, *don't*! She'll say she isn't—she'll lie!"

Mrs. Grose was not too bewildered instinctively to protest. "Ah, how *can* you?"

"Because I'm clear. Flora doesn't want me to know."

"It's only then to spare you."

"No, no—there are depths, depths! The more I go over it, the more I see in it, and the more I see in it the more I fear. I don't know what I *don't* see— what I *don't* fear!"

Mrs. Grose tried to keep up with me. "You mean you're afraid of seeing her again?"

"Oh, no; that's nothing—now!" Then I explained. "It's of *not* seeing her."

But my companion only looked wan. "I don't understand you."

"Why, it's that the child may keep it up—and that the child assuredly *will*—without my knowing it."

At the image of this possibility Mrs. Grose for a moment collapsed, yet presently to pull herself together again, as if from the positive force of the sense of what, should we yield an inch, there would really be to give way to. "Dear, dear—we must keep our heads! And after all, if she doesn't mind it——!" She even tried a grim joke. "Perhaps she likes it!"

"Likes *such* things—a scrap of an infant!"

"Isn't it just a proof of her blessed innocence?" my friend bravely inquired.

She brought me, for the instant, almost round. "Oh, we must clutch at *that*—we must cling to it! If it isn't a proof of what you say, it's a proof of—God knows what! For the woman's a horror of horrors."

Mrs. Grose, at this, fixed her eyes a minute on the ground; then at last raising them, "Tell me how you know," she said.

"Then you admit it's what she was?" I cried.

"Tell me how you know," my friend simply repeated.

"Know? By seeing her! By the way she looked."

"At you, do you mean—so wickedly?"

"Dear me, no—I could have borne that. She gave me never a glance. She only fixed the child."

Mrs. Grose tried to see it. "Fixed her?"

"Ah, with such awful eyes!"

She stared at mine as if they might really have resembled them. "Do you mean of dislike?"

"God help us, no. Of something much worse."

"Worse than dislike?"—this left her indeed at a loss.

"With a determination—indescribable. With a kind of fury of intention."

I made her turn pale. "Intention?"

"To get hold of her." Mrs. Grose—her eyes just lingering on mine—gave a shudder and walked to the window; and while she stood there looking out I completed my statement. "*That's* what Flora knows."

After a little she turned round. "The person was in black, you say?"

"In mourning—rather poor, almost shabby. But—yes—with extraordinary beauty." I now recognised to what I had at last, stroke by stroke, brought the victim of my confidence, for she quite visibly weighed this. "Oh, handsome—very, very," I insisted; "wonderfully handsome. But infamous."

She slowly came back to me. "Miss Jessel—*was* infamous." She once more took my hand in both her own, holding it as tight as if to fortify me against the increase of alarm I might draw from this disclosure. "They were both infamous," she finally said.

So, for a little, we faced it once more together; and I found absolutely a degree of help in seeing it now so straight. "I appreciate," I said, "the great decency of your not having hitherto spoken; but the time has certainly come to give me the whole thing." She appeared to assent to this, but still only in silence; seeing which I went on: "I must have it now. Of what did she die? Come, there was something between them."

"There was everything."

"In spite of the difference——?"

"Oh, of their rank, their condition"—she brought it woefully out. "*She* was a lady."

I turned it over; I again saw. "Yes—she was a lady."

"And he so dreadfully below," said Mrs. Grose.

I felt that I doubtless needn't press too hard, in such company, on the place of a servant in the scale; but there was nothing to prevent an acceptance of my companion's own measure of my predecessor's abasement. There was a way to deal with that, and I dealt; the more readily for my full vision—on the evidence—of our employer's late clever, good-looking "own" man; impudent, assured, spoiled, depraved. "The fellow was a hound."

Mrs. Grose considered as if it were perhaps a little a case for a sense of shades. "I've never seen one like him. He did what he wished."

"With *her*?"

"With them all."

It was as if now in my friend's own eyes Miss Jessel had again appeared. I seemed at any rate, for an instant, to see their evocation of her as distinctly as I had seen her by the pond; and I brought out with decision: "It must have been also what *she* wished!"

Mrs. Grose's face signified that it had been indeed, but she said at the same time: "Poor woman—she paid for it!"

"Then you do know what she died of?" I asked.

"No—I know nothing. I wanted not to know; I was glad enough I didn't; and I thanked heaven she was well out of this!"

"Yet you had, then, your idea——"

"Of her real reason for leaving? Oh, yes—as to that. She couldn't have stayed. Fancy it here—for a governess! And afterwards I imagined—and I still imagine. And what I imagine is dreadful."

"Not so dreadful as what *I* do," I replied; on which I must have shown her—as I was indeed but too conscious—a front of miserable defeat. It brought out again all her compassion for me, and at the renewed touch of her kindness my power to resist broke down. I burst, as I had, the other time, made her burst, into tears; she took me to her motherly breast, and my lamentation overflowed. "I don't do it!" I sobbed in despair; "I don't save or shield them! It's far worse than I dreamed—they're lost!"

VIII

WHAT I had said to Mrs. Grose was true enough: there were in the matter I had put before her depths and possibilities that I lacked resolution to sound; so that when we met once more in the wonder of it we were of a common mind about the duty of resistance to extravagant fancies. We were to keep our heads if we should keep nothing else—difficult indeed as that might be in the face of what, in our prodigious experience, was least to be questioned. Late that night, while the house slept, we had another talk in my room, when she went all the way with me as to its being beyond doubt that I had seen exactly what I had seen. To hold her perfectly in the pinch of that, I found I had only to ask her how, if I had "made it up," I came to be able to give, of each of the persons appearing to me, a picture disclosing, to the last detail, their special marks—a portrait on the exhibition of which she had instantly recognised and named them. She wished, of course,—small blame to her!—to sink the whole subject; and I was quick to assure her that my own interest in it had now violently taken the form of a search for the way to escape from it. I encountered her on the ground of a probability that with recurrence—for recurrence we took for granted—I should get used to my danger, distinctly professing that my personal exposure had suddenly become the least of my discomforts. It was my new suspicion that was intolerable; and yet even to this complication the later hours of the day had brought a little ease.

On leaving her, after my first outbreak, I had of course returned to my pupils, associating the right remedy for my dismay with that sense of their charm which I had already found to be a thing I could positively cultivate and which had never failed me yet. I had simply, in other words, plunged afresh into Flora's special society and there become aware—it was almost a luxury!— that she could put her little conscious hand straight upon the spot that ached. She had looked at me in sweet speculation and then had accused me to my face of having "cried." I had supposed I had brushed away the ugly signs: but I could literally—for the time, at all events—rejoice, under this fathomless charity, that they had not entirely disappeared. To gaze into the depths of blue of the child's eyes and pronounce their loveliness a trick of premature cunning was to be guilty of a cynicism in preference to which I naturally preferred to abjure my judgment and, so far as might be, my agitation. I couldn't abjure for merely wanting to, but I could repeat to Mrs. Grose—as I did there, over and over, in the small hours—that with their voices in the air, their pressure on one's heart and their fragrant faces against one's cheek, everything fell to the ground but their incapacity and their beauty. It was a pity that, somehow, to settle this once for all, I had equally to re-enumerate the signs of subtlety that, in the afternoon, by the lake, had made a miracle of my show of self-possession. It was a pity to be obliged to re-investigate the certitude of the moment itself and repeat how it had come to me as a revelation that the inconceivable communion I then surprised was a matter, for either party, of habit. It was a pity that I should have had to quaver out again the reasons for my not having, in my delusion, so much as questioned that the little girl saw our visitant even as I actually saw Mrs. Grose herself, and that she wanted, by just so much as she did thus see, to make me suppose she didn't, and at the same time, without showing anything, arrive at a guess as to whether I myself did! It was a pity that I needed once more to describe the portentous little activity by which she sought to divert my attention—the perceptible increase of movement, the greater intensity of play, the singing, the gabbling of nonsense, and the invitation to romp.

Yet if I had not indulged, to prove there was nothing in it, in this review, I should have missed the two or three dim elements of comfort that still remained to me. I should not for instance have been able to asseverate to my friend that I was certain—which was so much to the good—that *I* at least had not betrayed myself. I should not have been prompted, by stress of need, by desperation of mind,—I scarce know what to call it,—to invoke such further aid to intelligence as might spring from pushing my colleague fairly to the wall. She had told me, bit by bit, under pressure, a great deal; but a small shifty spot on the wrong side of it all still sometimes brushed my brow like the wing of a bat; and I remember how on this occasion—for the sleeping house and the concentration alike of our danger and our watch seemed to help—I felt the importance of giving the last jerk to the curtain. "I don't believe anything so horrible," I recollect saying; "no, let us put it definitely, my dear, that I don't. But if I did, you know, there's a thing I should require now, just without sparing you the least bit more—oh, not a scrap, come!—to get out of you. What was it you had in mind when, in our distress, before Miles came back, over the letter from his school, you said, under my insistence, that you didn't pretend for him that he had not literally *ever* been 'bad'? He has *not* literally 'ever,' in these weeks that I myself have lived with him and so closely watched him; he has been an imperturbable little prodigy of delightful, loveable goodness. Therefore you might perfectly have made the claim for him if you had not, as it happened, seen an exception to take. What was your exception, and to what passage in your personal observation of him did you refer?"

It was a dreadfully austere inquiry, but levity was not our note, and, at any rate, before the grey dawn admonished us to separate I had got my answer. What my friend had had in mind proved to be immensely to the purpose. It was neither more nor less than the circumstance that for a period of several months Quint and the boy had been perpetually together. It was in fact the very appropriate truth that she had ventured to criticise the propriety, to hint at the incongruity, of so close an alliance, and even to go so far on the subject as a frank overture to Miss Jessel. Miss Jessel had, with a most strange manner, requested her to mind her business, and the good woman had, on this, directly approached little Miles. What she had said to him, since I pressed, was that *she* liked to see young gentlemen not forget their station.

I pressed again, of course, at this. "You reminded him that Quint was only a base menial?"

"As you might say! And it was his answer, for one thing, that was bad."

"And for another thing?" I waited. "He repeated your words to Quint?"

"No, not that. It's just what he *wouldn't*!" she could still impress upon me. "I was sure, at any rate," she added, "that he didn't. But he denied certain occasions."

"What occasions?"

"When they had been about together quite as if Quint were his tutor—and a very grand one—and Miss Jessel only for the little lady. When he had gone off with the fellow, I mean, and spent hours with him."

"He then prevaricated about it—he said he hadn't?" Her assent was clear enough to cause me to add in a moment: "I see. He lied."

"Oh!" Mrs. Grose mumbled. This was a suggestion that it didn't matter; which indeed she backed up by a further remark. "You see, after all, Miss Jessel didn't mind. She didn't forbid him."

I considered. "Did he put that to you as a justification?"

At this she dropped again. "No, he never spoke of it."

"Never mentioned her in connection with Quint?"

She saw, visibly flushing, where I was coming out. "Well, he didn't show anything. He denied," she repeated; "he denied."

Lord, how I pressed her now! "So that you could see he knew what was between the two wretches?"

"I don't know—I don't know!" the poor woman groaned.

"You do know, you dear thing," I replied; "only you haven't my dreadful boldness of mind, and you keep back, out of timidity and modesty and delicacy, even the impression that, in the past, when you had, without my aid, to flounder about in silence, most of all made you miserable. But I shall get it out of you yet! There was something in the boy that suggested to you," I continued, "that he covered and concealed their relation."

"Oh, he couldn't prevent——"

"Your learning the truth? I dare say! But, heavens," I fell, with vehemence, a-thinking, "what it shows that they must, to that extent, have succeeded in making of him!"

"Ah, nothing that's not nice *now*!" Mrs. Grose lugubriously pleaded.

"I don't wonder you looked queer," I persisted, "when I mentioned to you the letter from his school!"

"I doubt if I looked as queer as you!" she retorted with homely force. "And if he was so bad then as that comes to, how is he such an angel now?"

"Yes, indeed—and if he was a fiend at school! How, how, how? Well," I said in my torment, "you must put it to me again, but I shall not be able to tell you for some days. Only, put it to me again!" I cried in a way that made my friend stare. "There are directions in which I must not for the present let myself go." Meanwhile I returned to her first example—the one to which she had just previously referred—of the boy's happy capacity for an occasional slip. "If Quint—on your remonstrance at the time you speak of—was a base menial, one of the things Miles said to you, I find myself guessing, was that you were another." Again her admission was so adequate that I continued: "And you forgave him that?"

"Wouldn't *you*?"

"Oh, yes!" And we exchanged there, in the stillness, a sound of the oddest amusement. Then I went on: "At all events, while he was with the man——"

"Miss Flora was with the woman. It suited them all!"

It suited me too, I felt, only too well; by which I mean that it suited exactly the particularly deadly view I was in the very act of forbidding myself to entertain. But I so far succeeded in checking the expression of this view that I will throw, just here, no further light on it than may be offered by the mention of my final observation to Mrs. Grose. "His having lied and been impudent are, I confess, less engaging specimens than I had hoped to have from you of the outbreak in him of the little natural man. Still," I mused, "they must do, for they make me feel more than ever that I must watch."

It made me blush, the next minute, to see in my friend's face how much more unreservedly she had forgiven him than her anecdote struck me as presenting to my own tenderness an occasion for doing. This came out when, at the schoolroom door, she quitted me. "Surely you don't accuse *him*——"

"Of carrying on an intercourse that he conceals from me? Ah, remember that, until further evidence, I now accuse nobody." Then, before shutting her out to go, by another passage, to her own place, "I must just wait," I wound up.

IX

I WAITED and waited, and the days, as they elapsed, took something from my consternation. A very few of them, in fact, passing, in constant sight of my pupils, without a fresh incident, sufficed to give to grievous fancies and even to odious memories a kind of brush of the sponge. I have spoken of the surrender to their extraordinary childish grace as a thing I could actively cultivate, and it may be imagined if I neglected now to address myself to this source for whatever it would yield. Stranger than I can express, certainly, was the effort to struggle against my new lights; it would doubtless have been, however, a greater tension still had it not been so frequently successful. I used to wonder how my little charges could help guessing that I thought strange things about them; and the circumstance that these things only made them more interesting was not by itself a direct aid to keeping them in the dark. I trembled lest they should see that they *were* so immensely more interesting. Putting things at the worst, at all events, as in meditation I so often did, any clouding of their innocence could only be—blameless and foredoomed as they were—a reason the more for taking risks. There were moments when, by an irresistible impulse, I found myself catching them up and pressing them to my heart. As soon as I had done so I used to say to myself: "What will they think of that? Doesn't it betray too much?" It would have been easy to get into a sad, wild tangle about how much I might betray; but the real account, I feel, of the hours of peace that I could still enjoy was that the immediate charm of my companions was a beguilement still effective even under the shadow of the possibility that it was studied. For if it occurred to me that I might occasionally excite suspicion by the little outbreaks of my sharper passion for them, so too I remember wondering if I mightn't see a queerness in the traceable increase of their own demonstrations.

They were at this period extravagantly and preternaturally fond of me; which, after all, I could reflect, was no more than a graceful response in children perpetually bowed over and hugged. The homage of which they were so lavish succeeded, in truth, for my nerves, quite as well as if I never appeared to myself, as I may say, literally to catch them at a purpose in it. They had never, I think, wanted to do so many things for their poor protectress; I mean—though they got their lessons better and better, which was naturally what would please her most—in the way of diverting, entertaining, surprising her; reading her passages, telling her stories, acting her charades, pouncing out at her, in disguises, as animals and historical characters, and above all astonishing her by the "pieces" they had secretly got by heart and could interminably recite. I should never get to the bottom—were I to let myself go even now—of the prodigious private commentary, all under still more private correction, with which, in these days, I overscored their full hours. They had shown me from the first a facility for everything, a general faculty which, taking a fresh start, achieved remarkable flights. They got their little tasks as if they loved them, and indulged, from the mere exuberance of the gift, in the most unimposed little miracles of memory. They not only popped out at me as tigers and as Romans, but as Shakespeareans, astronomers, and navigators. This was so singularly the case that it had presumably much to do with the fact as to which, at the present day, I am at a loss for a different explanation: I allude to my unnatural composure on the subject of another school for Miles. What I remember is that I was content not, for the time, to open the question, and that contentment must have sprung from the sense of his perpetually striking show of cleverness. He was too clever for a bad governess, for a parson's daughter, to spoil; and the strangest if not the brightest thread in the pensive embroidery I just spoke of was the impression I might have got, if I had dared to work it out, that he was under some influence operating in his small intellectual life as a tremendous incitement.

If it was easy to reflect, however, that such a boy could postpone school, it was at least as marked that for such a boy to have been "kicked out" by a school-master was a mystification without end. Let me add that in their company now—and I was careful almost never to be out of it—I could follow no scent very far. We lived in a cloud of music and love and success and private theatricals. The musical sense in each of the children was of the quickest, but the elder in especial had a marvellous knack of catching and repeating. The schoolroom piano broke into all gruesome fancies; and when that failed there were confabulations in corners, with a sequel of one of them going out in the highest spirits in order to "come in" as something new. I had had brothers myself, and it was no revelation to me that little girls could be slavish idolaters of little boys. What surpassed everything was that there was a little boy in the world who could have for the inferior age, sex, and intelligence so fine a consideration. They were extraordinarily at one, and to say that they never either quarrelled or complained is to make the note of praise coarse for their quality of sweetness. Sometimes, indeed, when I dropped into coarseness, I perhaps came across traces of little understandings between them by which one of them should keep me occupied while the other slipped away. There is a *naïf* side, I suppose, in all diplomacy; but if my pupils practised upon me, it was surely with the minimum of grossness. It was all in the other quarter that, after a lull, the grossness broke out.

I find that I really hang back; but I must take my plunge. In going on with the record of what was hideous at Bly, I not only challenge the most liberal faith—for which I little care; but—and this is another matter—I renew what I myself suffered, I again push my way through it to the end. There came suddenly an hour after which, as I look back, the affair seems to me to have been all pure suffering; but I have at least reached the heart of it, and the straightest road out is doubtless to advance. One evening—with nothing to lead up or to prepare it—I felt the cold touch of the impression that had breathed on me the night of my arrival and which, much lighter then, as I have mentioned, I should probably have made little of in memory had my subsequent sojourn been less agitated. I had not gone to bed; I sat reading by a couple of candles. There was a roomful of old books at Bly—last-century fiction, some of it, which, to the extent of a distinctly deprecated renown, but never to so much as that of a stray specimen, had reached the sequestered home and appealed to the unavowed curiosity of my youth. I remember that the book I had in my hand was Fielding's *Amelia*; also that I was wholly awake. I recall further both a general conviction that it was horribly late and a particular objection to looking at my watch. I figure, finally, that the white curtain draping, in the fashion of those days, the head of Flora's little bed, shrouded, as I had assured myself long before, the perfection of childish rest. I recollect in short that, though I was deeply interested in my author, I found myself, at the turn of a page and with his spell all scattered, looking straight up from him and hard at the door of my room. There was a moment during which I listened, reminded of the faint sense I had had, the first night, of there being something undefineably astir in the house, and noted the soft breath of the open casement just move the half-drawn blind. Then, with all the marks of a deliberation that must have seemed magnificent had there been anyone to admire it, I laid down my book, rose to my feet, and, taking a candle, went straight out of the room and, from the passage, on which my light made little impression, noiselessly closed and locked the door.

I can say now neither what determined nor what guided me, but I went straight along the lobby, holding my candle high, till I came within sight of the tall window that presided over the great turn of the staircase. At this point I precipitately found myself aware of three things. They were practically simultaneous, yet they had flashes of succession. My candle, under a bold flourish, went out, and I perceived, by the uncovered window, that the yielding dusk of earliest morning rendered it unnecessary. Without it, the next instant, I saw that there was someone on the stair. I speak of sequences, but I required no lapse of seconds to stiffen myself for a third encounter with Quint. The apparition had reached the landing half-way up and was therefore on the spot nearest the window, where at sight of me, it stopped short and fixed me exactly as it had fixed me from the tower and from the garden. He knew me as well as I knew him; and so, in the cold, faint twilight, with a glimmer in the high glass and another on the polish of the oak stair below, we faced each other in our common intensity. He was absolutely, on this occasion, a living, detestable, dangerous presence. But that was not the wonder of wonders; I reserve this distinction for quite another circumstance: the circumstance that dread had unmistakeably quitted me and that there was nothing in me there that didn't meet and measure him.

I had plenty of anguish after that extraordinary moment, but I had, thank God, no terror. And he knew I had not—I found myself at the end of an instant magnificently aware of this. I felt, in a fierce rigour of confidence, that if I stood my ground a minute I should cease—for the time, at least—to have him to reckon with; and during the minute, accordingly, the thing was as human and hideous as a real interview: hideous just because it *was* human, as human as to have met alone, in the small hours, in a sleeping house, some enemy, some adventurer, some criminal. It was the dead silence of our long gaze at such close quarters that gave the whole horror, huge as it was, its only note of the unnatural. If I had met a murderer in such a place and at such an hour, we still at least would have spoken. Something would have passed, in life, between us; if nothing had passed one of us would have moved. The moment was so prolonged that it would have taken but little more to make me doubt if even *I* were in life. I can't express what followed it save by saying that the silence itself—which was indeed in a manner an attestation of my strength—became the element into which I saw the figure disappear; in which I definitely saw it turn as I might have seen the low wretch to which it had once belonged turn on receipt of an order, and pass, with my eyes on the villainous back that no hunch could have more disfigured, straight down the staircase and into the darkness in which the next bend was lost.

X

I REMAINED awhile at the top of the stair, but with the effect presently of understanding that when my visitor had gone, he had gone: then I returned to my room. The foremost thing I saw there by the light of the candle I had left burning was that Flora's little bed was empty; and on this I caught my breath with all the terror that, five minutes before, I had been able to resist. I dashed at the place in which I had left her lying and over which (for the small silk counterpane and the sheets were disarranged) the white curtains had been deceivingly pulled forward; then my step, to my unutterable relief, produced an answering sound: I perceived an agitation of the window-blind, and the child, ducking down, emerged rosily from the other side of it. She stood there in so much of her candour and so little of her nightgown, with her pink bare feet and the golden glow of her curls. She looked intensely grave, and I had never had such a sense of losing an advantage acquired (the thrill of which had just been so prodigious) as on my consciousness that she addressed me with a reproach. "You naughty: where *have* you been?"—instead of challenging her own irregularity I found myself arraigned and explaining.

She herself explained, for that matter, with the loveliest, eagerest simplicity. She had known suddenly, as she lay there, that I was out of the room, and had jumped up to see what had become of me. I had dropped, with the joy of her reappearance, back into my chair—feeling then, and then only, a little faint; and she had pattered straight over to me, thrown herself upon my knee, given herself to be held with the flame of the candle full in the wonderful little face that was still flushed with sleep. I remember closing my eyes an instant, yieldingly, consciously, as before the excess of something beautiful that shone out of the blue of her own. "You were looking for me out of the window?" I said. "You thought I might be walking in the grounds?"

"Well, you know, I thought someone was"—she never blanched as she smiled out that at me.

Oh, how I looked at her now! "And did you see anyone?"

"Ah, *no!*" she returned, almost with the full privilege of childish inconsequence, resentfully, though with a long sweetness in her little drawl of the negative.

At that moment, in the state of my nerves, I absolutely believed she lied; and if I once more closed my eyes it was before the dazzle of the three or four possible ways in which I might take this up. One of these, for a moment, tempted me with such singular intensity that, to withstand it, I must have gripped my little girl with a spasm that, wonderfully, she submitted to without a cry or a sign of fright. Why not break out at her on the spot and have it all over?—give it to her straight in her lovely little lighted face? "You see, you see, you *know* that you do and that you already quite suspect I believe it; therefore why not frankly confess it to me, so that we may at least live with it together and learn perhaps, in the strangeness of our fate, where we are and what it means?" This solicitation dropped, alas, as it came: if I could immediately have succumbed to it I might have spared myself——well you'll see what. Instead of succumbing I sprang again to my feet, looked at her bed, and took a helpless middle way. "Why did you pull the curtain over the place to make me think you were still there?"

Flora luminously considered; after which, with her little divine smile: "Because I don't like to frighten you!"

"But if I had, by your idea, gone out——?"

She absolutely declined to be puzzled; she turned her eyes to the flame of the candle as if the question were as irrelevant, or at any rate as impersonal, as Mrs. Marcet or nine-times-nine. "Oh, but you know," she quite adequately answered, "that you might come back, you dear, and that you *have*!" And after a little, when she had got into bed, I had, for a long time, by almost sitting on her to hold her hand, to prove that I recognised the pertinence of my return.

You may imagine the general complexion, from that moment, of my nights. I repeatedly sat up till I didn't know when; I selected moments when my room-mate unmistakeably slept, and, stealing out, took noiseless turns in the passage and even pushed as far as to where I had last met Quint. But I never met him there again; and I may as well say at once that I on no other occasion saw him in the house. I just missed, on the staircase, on the other hand, a different adventure. Looking down it from the top I once recognised the presence of a woman seated on one of the lower steps with her back presented to me, her body half bowed and her head, in an attitude of woe, in her hands. I had been there but an instant, however, when she vanished without looking round at me. I knew, none the less, exactly what dreadful face she had to show; and I wondered whether, if instead of being above I had been below, I should have had, for going up, the same nerve I had lately shown Quint. Well, there continued to be plenty of chance for nerve. On the eleventh night after my latest encounter with that gentleman—they were all numbered now—I had an alarm that perilously skirted it and that indeed, from the particular quality of its unexpectedness, proved quite my sharpest shock. It was precisely the first night during this series that, weary with watching, I had felt that I might again without laxity lay myself down at my old hour. I slept immediately and, as I afterwards knew, till about one o'clock; but when I woke it was to sit straight up, as completely roused as if a hand had shook me. I had left a light burning, but it was now out, and I felt an instant certainty that Flora had extinguished it. This brought me to my feet and straight, in the darkness, to her bed, which I found she had left. A glance at the window enlightened me further, and the striking of a match completed the picture.

The child had again got up—this time blowing out the taper, and had again, for some purpose of observation or response, squeezed in behind the blind and was peering out into the night. That she now saw—as she had not, I had satisfied myself, the previous time—was proved to me by the fact that she was disturbed neither by my re-illumination nor by the haste I made to get into slippers and into a wrap. Hidden, protected, absorbed, she evidently rested on the sill—the casement opened forward—and gave herself up. There was a great still moon to help her, and this fact had counted in my quick decision. She was face to face with the apparition we had met at the lake, and could now communicate with it as she had not then been able to do. What I, on my side, had to care for was, without disturbing her, to reach, from the corridor, some other window in the same quarter. I got to the door without her hearing me; I got out of it, closed it and listened, from the other side, for some sound from her. While I stood in the passage I had my eyes on her brother's door, which was but ten steps off and which, indescribably, produced in me a renewal of the strange impulse that I lately spoke of as my temptation. What if I should go straight in and march to *his* window?—what if, by risking to his boyish bewilderment a revelation of my motive, I should throw across the rest of the mystery the long halter of my boldness?

This thought held me sufficiently to make me cross to his threshold and pause again. I preternaturally listened; I figured to myself what might portentously be; I wondered if his bed were also empty and he too were secretly at watch. It was a deep, soundless minute, at the end of which my impulse failed. He was quiet; he might be innocent; the risk was hideous; I turned away. There was a figure in the grounds—a figure prowling for a sight, the visitor with whom Flora was engaged; but it was not the visitor most concerned with my boy. I hesitated afresh, but on other grounds and only a few seconds; then I had made my choice. There were empty rooms at Bly, and it was only a question of choosing the right one. The right one suddenly presented itself to me as the lower one—though high above the gardens—in the solid corner of the house that I have spoken of as the old tower. This was a large, square chamber, arranged with some state as a bedroom, the extravagant size of which made it so inconvenient that it had not for years, though kept by Mrs. Grose in exemplary order, been occupied. I had often admired it and I knew my way about in it; I had only, after just faltering at the first chill gloom of its disuse, to pass across it and unbolt as quietly as I could one of the shutters. Achieving this transit, I uncovered the glass without a sound and, applying my face to the pane, was able, the darkness without being much less than within, to see that I commanded the right direction. Then I saw something more. The moon made the night extraordinarily penetrable and showed me on the lawn a person, diminished by distance, who stood there motionless and as if fascinated, looking up to where I had appeared—looking, that is, not so much straight at me as at something that was apparently above me. There was clearly another person above me—there was a person on the tower; but the presence on the lawn was not in the least what I had conceived and had confidently hurried to meet. The presence on the lawn—I felt sick as I made it out—was poor little Miles himself.

XI

It was not till late next day that I spoke to Mrs. Grose; the rigour with which I kept my pupils in sight making it often difficult to meet her privately, and the more as we each felt the importance of not provoking—on the part of the servants quite as much as on that of the children—any suspicion of a secret flurry or of a discussion of mysteries. I drew a great security in this particular from her mere smooth aspect. There was nothing in her fresh face to pass on to others my horrible confidences. She believed me, I was sure, absolutely: if she hadn't I don't know what would have become of me, for I couldn't have borne the business alone. But she was a magnificent monument to the blessing of a want of imagination, and if she could see in our little charges nothing but their beauty and amiability, their happiness and cleverness, she had no direct communication with the sources of my trouble. If they had been at all visibly blighted or battered, she would doubtless have grown, on tracing it back, haggard enough to match them; as matters stood, however, I could feel her, when she surveyed them, with her large white arms folded and the habit of serenity in all her look, thank the Lord's mercy that if they were ruined the pieces would still serve. Flights of fancy gave place, in her mind, to a steady fireside glow, and I had already begun to perceive how, with the development of the conviction that—as time went on without a public accident—our young things could, after all, look out for themselves, she addressed her greatest solicitude to the sad case presented by their instructress. That, for myself, was a sound simplification: I could engage that, to the world, my face should tell no tales, but it would have been, in the conditions, an immense added strain to find myself anxious about hers.

At the hour I now speak of she had joined me, under pressure, on the terrace, where, with the lapse of the season, the afternoon sun was now agreeable; and we sat there together while, before us, at a distance, but within call if we wished, the children strolled to and fro in one of their most manageable moods. They moved slowly, in unison, below us, over the lawn, the boy, as they went, reading aloud from a storybook and passing his arm round his sister to keep her quite in touch. Mrs. Grose watched them with positive placidity; then I caught the suppressed intellectual creak with which she conscientiously turned to take from me a view of the back of the tapestry. I had made her a receptacle of lurid things, but there was an odd recognition of my superiority—my accomplishments and my function—in her patience under my pain. She offered her mind to my disclosures as, had I wished to mix a witch's broth and proposed it with assurance, she would have held out a large clean saucepan. This had become thoroughly her attitude by the time that, in my recital of the events of the night, I reached the point of what Miles had said to me when, after seeing him, at such a monstrous hour, almost on the very spot where he happened now to be, I had gone down to bring him in; choosing then, at the window, with a concentrated need of not alarming the house, rather that method than a signal more resonant. I had left her meanwhile in little doubt of my small hope of representing with success even to her actual sympathy my sense of the real splendour of the little inspiration with which, after I had got him into the house, the boy met my final articulate challenge. As soon as I appeared in the moonlight on the terrace, he had come to me as straight as possible; on which I had taken his hand without a word and led him, through the dark spaces, up the staircase where Quint had so hungrily hovered for him, along the lobby where I had listened and trembled, and so to his forsaken room.

Not a sound, on the way, had passed between us, and I had wondered— oh, *how* I had wondered!—if he were groping about in his little mind for something plausible and not too grotesque. It would tax his invention, certainly, and I felt, this time, over his real embarrassment, a curious thrill of triumph. It was a sharp trap for the inscrutable! He couldn't play any longer at innocence; so how the deuce would he get out of it? There beat in me indeed, with the passionate throb of this question, an equal dumb appeal as to how the deuce *I* should. I was confronted at last, as never yet, with all the risk attached even now to sounding my own horrid note. I remember in fact that as we pushed into his little chamber, where the bed had not been slept in at all and the window, uncovered to the moonlight, made the place so clear that there was no need of striking a match—I remember how I suddenly dropped, sank upon the edge of the bed from the force of the idea that he must know how he really, as they say, "had" me. He could do what he liked, with all his cleverness to help him, so long as I should continue to defer to the old tradition of the criminality of those caretakers of the young who minister to superstitions and fears. He "had" me indeed, and in a cleft stick; for who would ever absolve me, who would consent that I should go unhung, if, by the faintest tremor of an overture, I were the first to introduce into our perfect intercourse an element so dire? No, no: it was useless to attempt to convey to Mrs. Grose, just as it is scarcely less so to attempt to suggest here, how, in our short, stiff brush in the dark, he fairly shook me with admiration. I was of course thoroughly kind and merciful; never, never yet had I placed on his little shoulders hands of such tenderness as those with which, while I rested against the bed, I held him there well under fire. I had no alternative but, in form at least, to put it to him.

"You must tell me now—and all the truth. What did you go out for? What were you doing there?"

I can still see his wonderful smile, the whites of his beautiful eyes, and the uncovering of his little teeth shine to me in the dusk. "If I tell you why, will you understand?" My heart, at this, leaped into my mouth. *Would* he tell me why? I found no sound on my lips to press it, and I was aware of replying only with a vague, repeated, grimacing nod. He was gentleness itself, and while I wagged my head at him he stood there more than ever a little fairy prince. It was his brightness indeed that gave me a respite. Would it be so great if he were really going to tell me? "Well," he said at last, "just exactly in order that you should do this."

"Do what?"

"Think me—for a change—*bad*!" I shall never forget the sweetness and gaiety with which he brought out the word, nor how, on top of it, he bent forward and kissed me. It was practically the end of everything. I met his kiss and I had to make, while I folded him for a minute in my arms, the most stupendous effort not to cry. He had given exactly the account of himself that permitted least of my going behind it, and it was only with the effect of confirming my acceptance of it that, as I presently glanced about the room, I could say—

"Then you didn't undress at all?"

He fairly glittered in the gloom. "Not at all. I sat up and read."

"And when did you go down?"

"At midnight. When I'm bad I *am* bad!"

"I see, I see—it's charming. But how could you be sure I would know it?"

"Oh, I arranged that with Flora." His answers rang out with a readiness! "She was to get up and look out."

"Which is what she did do." It was I who fell into the trap!

"So she disturbed you, and, to see what she was looking at, you also looked—you saw."

"While you," I concurred, "caught your death in the night air!"

He literally bloomed so from this exploit that he could afford radiantly to assent. "How otherwise should I have been bad enough?" he asked. Then, after another embrace, the incident and our interview closed on my recognition of all the reserves of goodness that, for his joke, he had been able to draw upon.

<u>XII</u>

THE particular impression I had received proved in the morning light, I repeat, not quite successfully presentable to Mrs. Grose, though I reinforced it with the mention of still another remark that he had made before we separated. "It all lies in half-a-dozen words," I said to her, "words that really settle the matter. 'Think, you know, what I *might* do!' He threw that off to show me how good he is. He knows down to the ground what he 'might' do. That's what he gave them a taste of at school."

"Lord, you do change!" cried my friend.

"I don't change—I simply make it out. The four, depend upon it, perpetually meet. If on either of these last nights you had been with either child, you would clearly have understood. The more I've watched and waited the more I've felt that if there were nothing else to make it sure it would be made so by the systematic silence of each. *Never*, by a slip of the tongue, have they so much as alluded to either of their old friends, any more than Miles has alluded to his expulsion. Oh yes, we may sit here and look at them, and they may show off to us there to their fill; but even while they pretend to be lost in their fairy-tale they're steeped in their vision of the dead restored. He's not reading to her," I declared; "they're talking of *them*—they're talking horrors! I go on, I know, as if I were crazy; and it's a wonder I'm not. What I've seen would have made *you* so; but it has only made me more lucid, made me get hold of still other things."

My lucidity must have seemed awful, but the charming creatures who were victims of it, passing and repassing in their interlocked sweetness, gave my colleague something to hold on by; and I felt how tight she held as, without stirring in the breath of my passion, she covered them still with her eyes. "Of what other things have you got hold?"

"Why, of the very things that have delighted, fascinated, and yet, at bottom, as I now so strangely see, mystified and troubled me. Their more than earthly beauty, their absolutely unnatural goodness. It's a game," I went on; "it's a policy and a fraud!"

"On the part of little darlings———?"

"As yet mere lovely babies? Yes, mad as that seems!" The very act of bringing it out really helped me to trace it—follow it all up and piece it all together. "They haven't been good—they've only been absent. It has been easy to live with them, because they're simply leading a life of their own. They're not mine—they're not ours. They're his and they're hers!"

"Quint's and that woman's?"

"Quint's and that woman's. They want to get to them."

Oh, how, at this, poor Mrs. Grose appeared to study them! "But for what?"

"For the love of all the evil that, in those dreadful days, the pair put into them. And to ply them with that evil still, to keep up the work of demons, is what brings the others back."

"Laws!" said my friend under her breath. The exclamation was homely, but it revealed a real acceptance of my further proof of what, in the bad time—for there had been a worse even than this!—must have occurred. There could have been no such justification for me as the plain assent of her experience to whatever depth of depravity I found credible in our brace of scoundrels. It was in obvious submission of memory that she brought out after a moment: "They *were* rascals! But what can they now do?" she pursued.

"Do?" I echoed so loud that Miles and Flora, as they passed at their distance, paused an instant in their walk and looked at us. "Don't they do enough?" I demanded in a lower tone, while the children, having smiled and nodded and kissed hands to us, resumed their exhibition. We were held by it a minute; then I answered: "They can destroy them!" At this my companion did turn, but the inquiry she launched was a silent one, the effect of which was to make me more explicit. "They don't know, as yet, quite how—but they're trying hard. They're seen only across, as it were, and beyond—in strange places and on high places, the top of towers, the roof of houses, the outside of windows, the further edge of pools; but there's a deep design, on either side, to shorten the distance and overcome the obstacle; and the success of the tempters is only a question of time. They've only to keep to their suggestions of danger."

"For the children to come?"

"And perish in the attempt!" Mrs. Grose slowly got up, and I scrupulously added: "Unless, of course, we can prevent!"

Standing there before me while I kept my seat, she visibly turned things over. "Their uncle must do the preventing. He must take them away."

"And who's to make him?"

She had been scanning the distance, but she now dropped on me a foolish face. "You, Miss."

"By writing to him that his house is poisoned and his little nephew and niece mad?"

"But if they *are*, Miss?"

"And if I am myself, you mean? That's charming news to be sent him by a governess whose prime undertaking was to give him no worry."

Mrs. Grose considered, following the children again. "Yes, he do hate worry. That was the great reason——"

"Why those fiends took him in so long? No doubt, though his indifference must have been awful. As I'm not a fiend, at any rate, I shouldn't take him in."

My companion, after an instant and for all answer, sat down again and grasped my arm. "Make him at any rate come to you."

I stared. "To *me*?" I had a sudden fear of what she might do. "'Him'?"

"He ought to *be* here—he ought to help."

I quickly rose, and I think I must have shown her a queerer face than ever yet. "You see me asking him for a visit?" No, with her eyes on my face she evidently couldn't. Instead of it even—as a woman reads another—she could see what I myself saw: his derision, his amusement, his contempt for the break-down of my resignation at being left alone and for the fine machinery I had set in motion to attract his attention to my slighted charms. She didn't know—no one knew—how proud I had been to serve him and to stick to our terms; yet she none the less took the measure, I think, of the warning I now gave her. "If you should so lose your head as to appeal to him for me——"

She was really frightened. "Yes, Miss?"

"I would leave, on the spot, both him and you."

XIII

It was all very well to join them, but speaking to them proved quite as much as ever an effort beyond my strength—offered, in close quarters, difficulties as insurmountable as before. This situation continued a month, and with new aggravations and particular notes, the note above all, sharper and sharper, of the small ironic consciousness on the part of my pupils. It was not, I am as sure today as I was sure then, my mere infernal imagination: it was absolutely traceable that they were aware of my predicament and that this strange relation made, in a manner, for a long time, the air in which we moved. I don't mean that they had their tongues in their cheeks or did anything vulgar, for that was not one of their dangers: I do mean, on the other hand, that the element of the unnamed and untouched became, between us, greater than any other, and that so much avoidance could not have been so successfully effected without a great deal of tacit arrangement. It was as if, at moments, we were perpetually coming into sight of subjects before which we must stop short, turning suddenly out of alleys that we perceived to be blind, closing with a little bang that made us look at each other—for, like all bangs, it was something louder than we had intended—the doors we had indiscreetly opened. All roads lead to Rome, and there were times when it might have struck us that almost every branch of study or subject of conversation skirted forbidden ground. Forbidden ground was the question of the return of the dead in general and of whatever, in especial, might survive, in memory, of the friends little children had lost. There were days when I could have sworn that one of them had, with a small invisible nudge, said to the other: "She thinks she'll do it this time—but she *won't!*" To "do it" would have been to indulge for instance—and for once in a way—in some direct reference to the lady who had prepared them for my discipline. They had a delightful endless appetite for passages in my own history, to which I had again and again treated them; they were in possession of everything that had ever happened to me, had had, with every circumstance the story of my smallest adventures and of those of my brothers and sisters and of the cat and the dog at home, as well as many particulars of the eccentric nature of my father, of the furniture and arrangement of our house, and of the conversation of the old women of our village. There were things enough, taking one with another, to chatter about, if one went very fast and knew by instinct when to go round. They pulled with an art of their own the strings of my invention and my memory; and nothing else perhaps, when I thought of such occasions afterwards, gave me so the suspicion of being watched from under cover. It was in any case over *my* life, *my* past, and *my* friends alone that we could take anything like our ease—a state of affairs that led them sometimes without the least pertinence to break out into sociable reminders. I was invited—with no visible connection—to repeat afresh Goody Gosling's celebrated *mot* or to confirm the details already supplied as to the cleverness of the vicarage pony.

It was partly at such junctures as these and partly at quite different ones that, with the turn my matters had now taken, my predicament, as I have called it, grew most sensible. The fact that the days passed for me without another encounter ought, it would have appeared, to have done something toward soothing my nerves. Since the light brush, that second night on the upper landing, of the presence of a woman at the foot of the stair, I had seen nothing, whether in or out of the house, that one had better not have seen. There was many a corner round which I expected to come upon Quint, and many a situation that, in a merely sinister way, would have favoured the appearance of Miss Jessel. The summer had turned, the summer had gone; the autumn had dropped upon Bly and had blown out half our lights. The place, with its grey sky and withered garlands, its bared spaces and scattered dead leaves, was like a theatre after the performance—all strewn with crumpled playbills. There were exactly states of the air, conditions of sound and of stillness, unspeakable impressions of the *kind* of ministering moment, that brought back to me, long enough to catch it, the feeling of the medium in which, that June evening out-of-doors, I had had my first sight of Quint, and in which, too, at those other instants, I had, after seeing him through the window, looked for him in vain in the circle of shrubbery. I recognised the signs, the portents—I recognised the moment, the spot. But they remained unaccompanied and empty, and I continued unmolested; if unmolested one could call a young woman whose sensibility had, in the most extraordinary fashion, not declined but deepened. I had said in my talk with Mrs. Grose on that horrid scene of Flora's by the lake—and had perplexed her by so saying—that it would from that moment distress me much more to lose my power than to keep it. I had then expressed what was vividly in my mind: the truth that, whether the children really saw or not—since, that is, it was not yet definitely proved—I greatly preferred, as a safeguard, the fulness of my own exposure. I was ready to know the very worst that was to be known. What I had then had an ugly glimpse of was that my eyes might be sealed just while theirs were most opened. Well, my eyes *were* sealed, it appeared, at present—a consummation for which it seemed blasphemous not to thank God. There was, alas, a difficulty about that: I would have thanked him with all my soul had I not had in a proportionate measure this conviction of the secret of my pupils.

How can I retrace today the strange steps of my obsession? There were times of our being together when I would have been ready to swear that, literally, in my presence, but with my direct sense of it closed, they had visitors who were known and were welcome. Then it was that, had I not been deterred by the very chance that such an injury might prove greater than the injury to be averted, my exultation would have broken out. "They're here, they're here, you little wretches," I would have cried, "and you can't deny it now!" The little wretches denied it with all the added volume of their sociability and their tenderness, in just the crystal depths of which—like the flash of a fish in a stream—the mockery of their advantage peeped up. The shock, in truth, had sunk into me still deeper than I knew on the night when, looking out to see either Quint or Miss Jessel under the stars, I had beheld the boy over whose rest I watched and who had immediately brought in with him—had straightway, there, turned it on me—the lovely upward look with which, from the battlements above me, the hideous apparition of Quint had played. If it was a question of a scare, my discovery on this occasion had scared me more than any other, and it was in the condition of nerves produced by it that I made my actual inductions. They harassed me so that sometimes, at odd moments, I shut myself up audibly to rehearse—it was at once a fantastic relief and a renewed despair—the manner in which I might come to the point. I approached it from one side and the other while, in my room, I flung myself about, but I always broke down in the monstrous utterance of names. As they died away on my lips, I said to myself that I should indeed help them to represent something infamous if, by pronouncing them, I should violate as rare a little case of instinctive delicacy as any schoolroom, probably, had ever known. When I said to myself: "*They* have the manners to be silent, and you, trusted as you are, the baseness to speak!" I felt myself crimson and I covered my face with my hands. After these secret scenes I chattered more than ever, going on volubly enough till one of our prodigious, palpable hushes occurred—I can call them nothing else—the strange, dizzy lift or swim (I try for terms!) into a stillness, a pause of all life, that had nothing to do with the more or less noise that at the moment we might be engaged in making and that I could hear through any deepened exhilaration or quickened recitation or louder strum of the piano. Then it was that the others, the outsiders, were there. Though they were not angels, they "passed," as the French, say, causing me, while they stayed, to tremble with the fear of their addressing to their younger victims some yet more infernal message or more vivid image than they had thought good enough for myself.

What it was most impossible to get rid of was the cruel idea that, whatever I had seen, Miles and Flora saw *more*—things terrible and unguessable and that sprang from dreadful passages of intercourse in the past. Such things naturally left on the surface, for the time, a chill which we vociferously denied that we felt; and we had, all three, with repetition, got into such splendid training that we went, each time, almost automatically, to mark the close of the incident, through the very same movements. It was striking of the children, at all events, to kiss me inveterately with a kind of wild irrelevance and never to fail—one or the other—of the precious question that had helped us through many a peril. "When do you think he *will* come? Don't you think we *ought* to write?"—there was nothing like that inquiry, we found by experience, for carrying off an awkwardness. "He" of course was their uncle in Harley Street; and we lived in much profusion of theory that he might at any moment arrive to mingle in our circle. It was impossible to have given less encouragement than he had done to such a doctrine, but if we had not had the doctrine to fall back upon we should have deprived each other of some of our finest exhibitions. He never wrote to them—that may have been selfish, but it was a part of the flattery of his trust of me; for the way in which a man pays his highest tribute to a woman is apt to be but by the more festal celebration of one of the sacred laws of his comfort; and I held that I carried out the spirit of the pledge given not to appeal to him when I let my charges understand that their own letters were but charming literary exercises. They were too beautiful to be posted; I kept them myself; I have them all to this hour. This was a rule indeed which only added to the satiric effect of my being plied with the supposition that he might at any moment be among us. It was exactly as if my charges knew how almost more awkward than anything else that might be for me. There appears to me, moreover, as I look back, no note in all this more extraordinary than the mere fact that, in spite of my tension and of their triumph, I never lost patience with them. Adorable they must in truth have been, I now reflect, that I didn't in these days hate them! Would exasperation, however, if relief had longer been postponed, finally have betrayed me? It little matters, for relief arrived. I call it relief, though it was only the relief that a snap brings to a strain or the burst of a thunderstorm to a day of suffocation. It was at least change, and it came with a rush.

XIV

WALKING to church a certain Sunday morning, I had little Miles at my side and his sister, in advance of us and at Mrs. Grose's, well in sight. It was a crisp, clear day, the first of its order for some time; the night had brought a touch of frost, and the autumn air, bright and sharp, made the church-bells almost gay. It was an odd accident of thought that I should have happened at such a moment to be particularly and very gratefully struck with the obedience of my little charges. Why did they never resent my inexorable, my perpetual society? Something or other had brought nearer home to me that I had all but pinned the boy to my shawl and that, in the way our companions were marshalled before me, I might have appeared to provide against some danger of rebellion. I was like a gaoler with an eye to possible surprises and escapes. But all this belonged—I mean their magnificent little surrender— just to the special array of the facts that were most abysmal. Turned out for Sunday by his uncle's tailor, who had had a free hand and a notion of pretty waistcoats and of his grand little air, Miles's whole title to independence, the rights of his sex and situation, were so stamped upon him that if he had suddenly struck for freedom I should have had nothing to say. I was by the strangest of chances wondering how I should meet him when the revolution unmistakeably occurred. I call it a revolution because I now see how, with the word he spoke, the curtain rose on the last act of my dreadful drama and the catastrophe was precipitated. "Look here, my dear, you know," he charmingly said, "when in the world, please, am I going back to school?"

Transcribed here the speech sounds harmless enough, particularly as uttered in the sweet, high, casual pipe with which, at all interlocutors, but above all at his eternal governess, he threw off intonations as if he were tossing roses. There was something in them that always made one "catch" and I caught, at any rate, now so effectually that I stopped as short as if one of the trees of the park had fallen across the road. There was something new, on the spot, between us, and he was perfectly aware that I recognised it, though, to enable me to do so, he had no need to look a whit less candid and charming than usual. I could feel in him how he already, from my at first finding nothing to reply, perceived the advantage he had gained. I was so slow to find anything that he had plenty of time, after a minute, to continue with his suggestive but inconclusive smile: "You know, my dear, that for a fellow to be with a lady *always*——!" His "my dear" was constantly on his lips for me, and nothing could have expressed more the exact shade of the sentiment with which I desired to inspire my pupils than its fond familiarity. It was so respectfully easy.

But, oh, how I felt that at present I must pick my own phrases! I remember that, to gain time, I tried to laugh, and I seemed to see in the beautiful face with which he watched me how ugly and queer I looked. "And always with the same lady?" I returned.

He neither blenched nor winked. The whole thing was virtually out between us. "Ah, of course, she's a jolly, 'perfect' lady; but, after all, I'm a fellow, don't you see? that's—well, getting on."

I lingered there with him an instant ever so kindly. "Yes, you're getting on." Oh, but I felt helpless!

I have kept to this day the heartbreaking little idea of how he seemed to know that and to play with it. "And you can't say I've not been awfully good, can you?"

I laid my hand on his shoulder, for, though I felt how much better it would have been to walk on, I was not yet quite able. "No, I can't say that, Miles."

"Except just that one night, you know——!"

"That one night?" I couldn't look as straight as he.

"Why, when I went down—went out of the house."

"Oh, yes. But I forget what you did it for."

"You forget?"—he spoke with the sweet extravagance of childish reproach. "Why, it was to show you I could!"

"Oh, yes, you could."

"And I can again."

I felt that I might, perhaps, after all, succeed in keeping my wits about me. "Certainly. But you won't."

"No, not *that* again. It was nothing."

"It was nothing," I said. "But we must go on."

He resumed our walk with me, passing his hand into my arm. "Then when *am* I going back?"

I wore, in turning it over, my most responsible air. "Were you very happy at school?"

He just considered. "Oh, I'm happy enough anywhere!"

"Well, then," I quavered, "if you're just as happy here——!"

"Ah, but that isn't everything! Of course *you* know a lot——"

"But you hint that you know almost as much?" I risked as he paused.

"Not half I want to!" Miles honestly professed. "But it isn't so much that."

"What is it, then?"

"Well—I want to see more life."

"I see; I see." We had arrived within sight of the church and of various persons, including several of the household of Bly, on their way to it and clustered about the door to see us go in. I quickened our step; I wanted to get there before the question between us opened up much further; I reflected hungrily that, for more than an hour, he would have to be silent; and I thought with envy of the comparative dusk of the pew and of the almost spiritual help of the hassock on which I might bend my knees. I seemed literally to be running a race with some confusion to which he was about to reduce me, but I felt that he had got in first when, before we had even entered the churchyard, he threw out—

"I want my own sort!"

It literally made me bound forward. "There are not many of your own sort, Miles!" I laughed. "Unless perhaps dear little Flora!"

"You really compare me to a baby girl?"

This found me singularly weak. "Don't you, then, *love* our sweet Flora?"

"If I didn't—and you too; if I didn't——!" he repeated as if retreating for a jump, yet leaving his thought so unfinished that, after we had come into the gate, another stop, which he imposed on me by the pressure of his arm, had become inevitable. Mrs. Grose and Flora had passed into the church, the other worshippers had followed, and we were, for the minute, alone among the old, thick graves. We had paused, on the path from the gate, by a low, oblong, tablelike tomb.

"Yes, if you didn't——?"

He looked, while I waited, about at the graves. "Well, you know what!" But he didn't move, and he presently produced something that made me drop straight down on the stone slab, as if suddenly to rest. "Does my uncle think what *you* think?"

I markedly rested. "How do you know what I think?"

"Ah, well, of course I don't; for it strikes me you never tell me. But I mean does *he* know?"

"Know what, Miles?"

"Why, the way I'm going on."

82

I perceived quickly enough that I could make, to this inquiry, no answer that would not involve something of a sacrifice of my employer. Yet it appeared to me that we were all, at Bly, sufficiently sacrificed to make that venial. "I don't think your uncle much cares."

Miles, on this, stood looking at me. "Then don't you think he can be made to?"

"In what way?"

"Why, by his coming down."

"But who'll get him to come down?"

"*I* will!" the boy said with extraordinary brightness and emphasis. He gave me another look charged with that expression and then marched off alone into church.

XV

THE business was practically settled from the moment I never followed him. It was a pitiful surrender to agitation, but my being aware of this had somehow no power to restore me. I only sat there on my tomb and read into what my little friend had said to me the fulness of its meaning; by the time I had grasped the whole of which I had also embraced, for absence, the pretext that I was ashamed to offer my pupils and the rest of the congregation such an example of delay. What I said to myself above all was that Miles had got something out of me and that the proof of it, for him, would be just this awkward collapse. He had got out of me that there was something I was much afraid of and that he should probably be able to make use of my fear to gain, for his own purpose, more freedom. My fear was of having to deal with the intolerable question of the grounds of his dismissal from school, for that was really but the question of the horrors gathered behind. That his uncle should arrive to treat with me of these things was a solution that, strictly speaking, I ought now to have desired to bring on; but I could so little face the ugliness and the pain of it that I simply procrastinated and lived from hand to mouth. The boy, to my deep discomposure, was immensely in the right, was in a position to say to me: "Either you clear up with my guardian the mystery of this interruption of my studies, or you cease to expect me to lead with you a life that's so unnatural for a boy." What was so unnatural for the particular boy I was concerned with was this sudden revelation of a consciousness and a plan.

That was what really overcame me, what prevented my going in. I walked round the church, hesitating, hovering; I reflected that I had already, with him, hurt myself beyond repair. Therefore I could patch up nothing, and it was too extreme an effort to squeeze beside him into the pew: he would be so much more sure than ever to pass his arm into mine and make me sit there for an hour in close, silent contact with his commentary on our talk. For the first minute since his arrival I wanted to get away from him. As I paused beneath the high east window and listened to the sounds of worship, I was taken with an impulse that might master me, I felt, completely should I give it the least encouragement. I might easily put an end to my predicament by getting away altogether. Here was my chance; there was no one to stop me; I could give the whole thing up—turn my back and retreat. It was only a question of hurrying again, for a few preparations, to the house which the attendance at church of so many of the servants would practically have left unoccupied. No one, in short, could blame me if I should just drive desperately off. What was it to get away if I got away only till dinner? That would be in a couple of hours, at the end of which—I had the acute prevision—my little pupils would play at innocent wonder about my non-appearance in their train.

"What *did* you do, you naughty, bad thing? Why in the world, to worry us so—and take our thoughts off too, don't you know?—did you desert us at the very door?" I couldn't meet such questions nor, as they asked them, their false little lovely eyes; yet it was all so exactly what I should have to meet that, as the prospect grew sharp to me, I at last let myself go.

I got, so far as the immediate moment was concerned, away; I came straight out of the churchyard and, thinking hard, retraced my steps through the park. It seemed to me that by the time I reached the house I had made up my mind I would fly. The Sunday stillness both of the approaches and of the interior, in which I met no one, fairly excited me with a sense of opportunity. Were I to get off quickly, this way, I should get off without a scene, without a word. My quickness would have to be remarkable, however, and the question of a conveyance was the great one to settle. Tormented, in the hall, with difficulties and obstacles, I remember sinking down at the foot of the staircase—suddenly collapsing there on the lowest step and then, with a revulsion, recalling that it was exactly where more than a month before, in the darkness of night and just so bowed with evil things, I had seen the spectre of the most horrible of women. At this I was able to straighten myself; I went the rest of the way up; I made, in my bewilderment, for the schoolroom, where there were objects belonging to me that I should have to take. But I opened the door to find again, in a flash, my eyes unsealed. In the presence of what I saw I reeled straight back upon my resistance.

Seated at my own table in clear noonday light I saw a person whom, without my previous experience, I should have taken at the first blush for some housemaid who might have stayed at home to look after the place and who, availing herself of rare relief from observation and of the schoolroom table and my pens, ink, and paper, had applied herself to the considerable effort of a letter to her sweetheart. There was an effort in the way that, while her arms rested on the table, her hands with evident weariness supported her head; but at the moment I took this in I had already become aware that, in spite of my entrance, her attitude strangely persisted. Then it was—with the very act of its announcing itself—that her identity flared up in a change of posture. She rose, not as if she had heard me, but with an indescribable grand melancholy of indifference and detachment, and, within a dozen feet of me, stood there as my vile predecessor. Dishonoured and tragic, she was all before me; but even as I fixed and, for memory, secured it, the awful image passed away. Dark as midnight in her black dress, her haggard beauty and her unutterable woe, she had looked at me long enough to appear to say that her right to sit at my table was as good as mine to sit at hers. While these instants lasted indeed I had the extraordinary chill of a feeling that it was I who was the intruder. It was as a wild protest against it that, actually addressing her—"You terrible, miserable woman!"—I heard myself break into a sound that, by the open door, rang through the long passage and the empty house. She looked at me as if she heard me, but I had recovered myself and cleared the air. There was nothing in the room the next minute but the sunshine and a sense that I must stay.

XVI

I HAD so perfectly expected that the return of my pupils would be marked by a demonstration that I was freshly upset at having to take into account that they were dumb about my absence. Instead of gaily denouncing and caressing me, they made no allusion to my having failed them, and I was left, for the time, on perceiving that she too said nothing, to study Mrs. Grose's odd face. I did this to such purpose that I made sure they had in some way bribed her to silence; a silence that, however, I would engage to break down on the first private opportunity. This opportunity came before tea: I secured five minutes with her in the housekeeper's room, where, in the twilight, amid a smell of lately-baked bread, but with the place all swept and garnished, I found her sitting in pained placidity before the fire. So I see her still, so I see her best: facing the flame from her straight chair in the dusky, shining room, a large clean image of the "put away"—of drawers closed and locked and rest without a remedy.

"Oh, yes, they asked me to say nothing; and to please them—so long as they were there—of course I promised. But what had happened to you?"

"I only went with you for the walk," I said. "I had then to come back to meet a friend."

She showed her surprise. "A friend—*you*?"

"Oh, yes, I have a couple!" I laughed. "But did the children give you a reason?"

"For not alluding to your leaving us? Yes; they said you would like it better. Do you like it better?"

My face had made her rueful. "No, I like it worse!" But after an instant I added: "Did they say why I should like it better?"

"No; Master Miles only said, 'We must do nothing but what she likes!'"

"I wish indeed he would! And what did Flora say?"

"Miss Flora was too sweet. She said, 'Oh, of course, of course!'—and I said the same."

I thought a moment. "You were too sweet too—I can hear you all. But none the less, between Miles and me, it's now all out."

"All out?" My companion stared. "But what, Miss?"

"Everything. It doesn't matter. I've made up my mind. I came home, my dear," I went on, "for a talk with Miss Jessel."

I had by this time formed the habit of having Mrs. Grose literally well in hand in advance of my sounding that note; so that even now, as she bravely blinked under the signal of my word, I could keep her comparatively firm. "A talk! Do you mean she spoke?"

"It came to that. I found her, on my return, in the schoolroom."

"And what did she say?" I can hear the good woman still, and the candour of her stupefaction.

"That she suffers the torments——!"

It was this, of a truth, that made her, as she filled out my picture, gape. "Do you mean," she faltered, "—of the lost?"

"Of the lost. Of the damned. And that's why, to share them——" I faltered myself with the horror of it.

But my companion, with less imagination, kept me up. "To share them——?"

"She wants Flora." Mrs. Grose might, as I gave it to her, fairly have fallen away from me had I not been prepared. I still held her there, to show I was. "As I've told you, however, it doesn't matter."

"Because you've made up your mind? But to what?"

"To everything."

"And what do you call 'everything'?"

"Why, sending for their uncle."

"Oh, Miss, in pity do," my friend broke out.

"Ah, but I will, I *will!* I see it's the only way. What's 'out,' as I told you, with Miles is that if he thinks I'm afraid to—and has ideas of what he gains by that—he shall see he's mistaken. Yes, yes; his uncle shall have it here from me on the spot (and before the boy himself if necessary) that if I'm to be reproached with having done nothing again about more school——"

"Yes, Miss——" my companion pressed me.

"Well, there's that awful reason."

There were now clearly so many of these for my poor colleague that she was excusable for being vague. "But—a—which?"

"Why, the letter from his old place."

"You'll show it to the master?"

"I ought to have done so on the instant."

"Oh, no!" said Mrs. Grose with decision.

"I'll put it before him," I went on inexorably, "that I can't undertake to work the question on behalf of a child who has been expelled——"

"For we've never in the least known what!" Mrs. Grose declared.

"For wickedness. For what else—when he's so clever and beautiful and perfect? Is he stupid? Is he untidy? Is he infirm? Is he ill-natured? He's exquisite—so it can be only *that*; and that would open up the whole thing. After all," I said, "it's their uncle's fault. If he left here such people——!"

"He didn't really in the least know them. The fault's mine." She had turned quite pale.

"Well, you shan't suffer," I answered.

"The children shan't!" she emphatically returned.

I was silent awhile; we looked at each other. "Then what am I to tell him?"

"You needn't tell him anything. *I'll* tell him."

I measured this. "Do you mean you'll write——?" Remembering she couldn't, I caught myself up. "How do you communicate?"

"I tell the bailiff. *He* writes."

"And should you like him to write our story?"

My question had a sarcastic force that I had not fully intended, and it made her, after a moment, inconsequently break down. The tears were again in her eyes. "Ah, Miss, *you* write!"

"Well—tonight," I at last answered; and on this we separated.

XVII

I went so far, in the evening, as to make a beginning. The weather had changed back, a great wind was abroad, and beneath the lamp, in my room, with Flora at peace beside me, I sat for a long time before a blank sheet of paper and listened to the lash of the rain and the batter of the gusts. Finally I went out, taking a candle; I crossed the passage and listened a minute at Miles's door. What, under my endless obsession, I had been impelled to listen for was some betrayal of his not being at rest, and I presently caught one, but not in the form I had expected. His voice tinkled out. "I say, you there— come in." It was a gaiety in the gloom!

I went in with my light and found him, in bed, very wide awake, but very much at his ease. "Well, what are *you* up to?" he asked with a grace of sociability in which it occurred to me that Mrs. Grose, had she been present, might have looked in vain for proof that anything was "out."

I stood over him with my candle. "How did you know I was there?"

"Why, of course I heard you. Did you fancy you made no noise? You're like a troop of cavalry!" he beautifully laughed.

"Then you weren't asleep?"

"Not much! I lie awake and think."

I had put my candle, designedly, a short way off, and then, as he held out his friendly old hand to me, had sat down on the edge of his bed. "What is it," I asked, "that you think of?"

"What in the world, my dear, but *you*?"

"Ah, the pride I take in your appreciation doesn't insist on that! I had so far rather you slept."

"Well, I think also, you know, of this queer business of ours."

I marked the coolness of his firm little hand. "Of what queer business, Miles?"

"Why, the way you bring me up. And all the rest!"

I fairly held my breath a minute, and even from my glimmering taper there was light enough to show how he smiled up at me from his pillow. "What do you mean by all the rest?"

"Oh, you know, you know!"

I could say nothing for a minute, though I felt, as I held his hand and our eyes continued to meet, that my silence had all the air of admitting his charge and that nothing in the whole world of reality was perhaps at that moment so fabulous as our actual relation. "Certainly you shall go back to school," I said, "if it be that that troubles you. But not to the old place—we must find another, a better. How could I know it did trouble you, this question, when you never told me so, never spoke of it at all?" His clear, listening face, framed in its smooth whiteness, made him for the minute as appealing as some wistful patient in a children's hospital; and I would have given, as the resemblance came to me, all I possessed on earth really to be the nurse or the sister of charity who might have helped to cure him. Well, even as it was, I perhaps might help! "Do you know you've never said a word to me about your school—I mean the old one; never mentioned it in any way?"

He seemed to wonder; he smiled with the same loveliness. But he clearly gained time; he waited, he called for guidance. "Haven't I?" It wasn't for *me* to help him—it was for the thing I had met!

Something in his tone and the expression of his face, as I got this from him, set my heart aching with such a pang as it had never yet known; so unutterably touching was it to see his little brain puzzled and his little resources taxed to play, under the spell laid on him, a part of innocence and consistency. "No, never—from the hour you came back. You've never mentioned to me one of your masters, one of your comrades, nor the least little thing that ever happened to you at school. Never, little Miles—no, never—have you given me an inkling of anything that *may* have happened there. Therefore you can fancy how much I'm in the dark. Until you came out, that way, this morning, you had, since the first hour I saw you, scarce even made a reference to anything in your previous life. You seemed so perfectly to accept the present." It was extraordinary how my absolute conviction of his secret precocity (or whatever I might call the poison of an influence that I dared but half to phrase) made him, in spite of the faint breath of his inward trouble, appear as accessible as an older person—imposed him almost as an intellectual equal. "I thought you wanted to go on as you are."

It struck me that at this he just faintly coloured. He gave, at any rate, like a convalescent slightly fatigued, a languid shake of his head. "I don't—I don't. I want to get away."

"You're tired of Bly?"

"Oh, no, I like Bly."

"Well, then——?"

"Oh, *you* know what a boy wants!"

I felt that I didn't know so well as Miles, and I took temporary refuge. "You want to go to your uncle?"

Again, at this, with his sweet ironic face, he made a movement on the pillow. "Ah, you can't get off with that!"

I was silent a little, and it was I, now, I think, who changed colour. "My dear, I don't want to get off!"

"You can't, even if you do. You can't, you can't!"—he lay beautifully staring. "My uncle must come down, and you must completely settle things."

"If we do," I returned with some spirit, "you may be sure it will be to take you quite away."

"Well, don't you understand that that's exactly what I'm working for? You'll have to tell him—about the way you've let it all drop: you'll have to tell him a tremendous lot!"

The exultation with which he uttered this helped me somehow, for the instant, to meet him rather more. "And how much will *you*, Miles, have to tell him? There are things he'll ask you!"

He turned it over. "Very likely. But what things?"

"The things you've never told me. To make up his mind what to do with you. He can't send you back——"

"Oh, I don't want to go back!" he broke in. "I want a new field."

He said it with admirable serenity, with positive unimpeachable gaiety; and doubtless it was that very note that most evoked for me the poignancy, the unnatural childish tragedy, of his probable reappearance at the end of three months with all this bravado and still more dishonour. It overwhelmed me now that I should never be able to bear that, and it made me let myself go. I threw myself upon him and in the tenderness of my pity I embraced him. "Dear little Miles, dear little Miles——!"

My face was close to his, and he let me kiss him, simply taking it with indulgent good-humour. "Well, old lady?"

"Is there nothing—nothing at all that you want to tell me?"

He turned off a little, facing round toward the wall and holding up his hand to look at as one had seen sick children look. "I've told you—I told you this morning."

Oh, I was sorry for him! "That you just want me not to worry you?"

He looked round at me now, as if in recognition of my understanding him; then ever so gently, "To let me alone," he replied.

There was even a singular little dignity in it, something that made me release him, yet, when I had slowly risen, linger beside him. God knows I never wished to harass him, but I felt that merely, at this, to turn my back on him was to abandon or, to put it more truly, to lose him. "I've just begun a letter to your uncle," I said.

"Well, then, finish it!"

I waited a minute. "What happened before?"

He gazed up at me again. "Before what?"

"Before you came back. And before you went away."

For some time he was silent, but he continued to meet my eyes. "What happened?"

It made me, the sound of the words, in which it seemed to me that I caught for the very first time a small faint quaver of consenting consciousness— it made me drop on my knees beside the bed and seize once more the chance of possessing him. "Dear little Miles, dear little Miles, if you *knew* how I want to help you! It's only that, it's nothing but that, and I'd rather die than give you a pain or do you a wrong—I'd rather die than hurt a hair of you. Dear little Miles"—oh, I brought it out now even if I *should* go too far—"I just want you to help me to save you!" But I knew in a moment after this that I had gone too far. The answer to my appeal was instantaneous, but it came in the form of an extraordinary blast and chill, a gust of frozen air and a shake of the room as great as if, in the wild wind, the casement had crashed in. The boy gave a loud, high shriek, which, lost in the rest of the shock of sound, might have seemed, indistinctly, though I was so close to him, a note either of jubilation or of terror. I jumped to my feet again and was conscious of darkness. So for a moment we remained, while I stared about me and saw that the drawn curtains were unstirred and the window tight. "Why, the candle's out!" I then cried.

"It was I who blew it, dear!" said Miles.

XVIII

THE next day, after lessons, Mrs. Grose found a moment to say to me quietly: "Have you written, Miss?"

"Yes—I've written." But I didn't add—for the hour—that my letter, sealed and directed, was still in my pocket. There would be time enough to send it before the messenger should go to the village. Meanwhile there had been, on the part of my pupils, no more brilliant, more exemplary morning. It was exactly as if they had both had at heart to gloss over any recent little friction. They performed the dizziest feats of arithmetic, soaring quite out of *my* feeble range, and perpetrated, in higher spirits than ever, geographical and historical jokes. It was conspicuous of course in Miles in particular that he appeared to wish to show how easily he could let me down. This child, to my memory, really lives in a setting of beauty and misery that no words can translate; there was a distinction all his own in every impulse he revealed; never was a small natural creature, to the uninitiated eye all frankness and freedom, a more ingenious, a more extraordinary little gentleman. I had perpetually to guard against the wonder of contemplation into which my initiated view betrayed me; to check the irrelevant gaze and discouraged sigh in which I constantly both attacked and renounced the enigma of what such a little gentleman could have done that deserved a penalty. Say that, by the dark prodigy I knew, the imagination of all evil *had* been opened up to him: all the justice within me ached for the proof that it could ever have flowered into an act.

He had never, at any rate, been such a little gentleman as when, after our early dinner on this dreadful day, he came round to me and asked if I shouldn't like him, for half an hour, to play to me. David playing to Saul could never have shown a finer sense of the occasion. It was literally a charming exhibition of tact, of magnanimity, and quite tantamount to his saying outright: "The true knights we love to read about never push an advantage too far. I know what you mean now: you mean that—to be let alone yourself and not followed up—you'll cease to worry and spy upon me, won't keep me so close to you, will let me go and come. Well, I 'come,' you see—but I don't go! There'll be plenty of time for that. I do really delight in your society, and I only want to show you that I contended for a principle." It may be imagined whether I resisted this appeal or failed to accompany him again, hand in hand, to the schoolroom. He sat down at the old piano and played as he had never played, and if there are those who think he had better have been kicking a football I can only say that I wholly agree with them. For at the end of a time that under his influence I had quite ceased to measure I started up with a strange sense of having literally slept at my post. It was after luncheon, and by the schoolroom fire, and yet I hadn't really, in the least, slept: I had only done something much worse—I had forgotten. Where, all this time, was Flora? When I put the question to Miles he played on a minute before answering, and then could only say: "Why, my dear, how do *I* know?"—breaking moreover into a happy laugh which, immediately after, as if it were a vocal accompaniment, he prolonged into incoherent, extravagant song.

I went straight to my room, but his sister was not there; then, before going downstairs, I looked into several others. As she was nowhere about she would surely be with Mrs. Grose, whom, in the comfort of that theory, I accordingly proceeded in quest of. I found her where I had found her the evening before, but she met my quick challenge with blank, scared ignorance. She had only supposed that, after the repast, I had carried off both the children; as to which she was quite in her right, for it was the very first time I had allowed the little girl out of my sight without some special provision. Of course now indeed she might be with the maids, so that the immediate thing was to look for her without an air of alarm. This we promptly arranged between us; but when, ten minutes later and in pursuance of our arrangement, we met in the hall, it was only to report on either side that after guarded inquiries we had altogether failed to trace her. For a minute there, apart from observation, we exchanged mute alarms, and I could feel with what high interest my friend returned me all those I had from the first given her.

"She'll be above," she presently said—"in one of the rooms you haven't searched."

"No; she's at a distance." I had made up my mind. "She has gone out."

Mrs. Grose stared. "Without a hat?"

I naturally also looked volumes. "Isn't that woman always without one?"

"She's with *her*?"

"She's with *her*!" I declared. "We must find them."

My hand was on my friend's arm, but she failed for the moment, confronted with such an account of the matter, to respond to my pressure. She communed, on the contrary, on the spot, with her uneasiness. "And where's Master Miles?"

"Oh, *he's* with Quint. They're in the schoolroom."

"Lord, Miss!" My view, I was myself aware—and therefore I suppose my tone—had never yet reached so calm an assurance.

"The trick's played," I went on; "they've successfully worked their plan. He found the most divine little way to keep me quiet while she went off."

"'Divine'?" Mrs. Grose bewilderedly echoed.

"Infernal, then!" I almost cheerfully rejoined. "He has provided for himself as well. But come!"

She had helplessly gloomed at the upper regions. "You leave him——?"

"So long with Quint? Yes—I don't mind that now."

She always ended, at these moments, by getting possession of my hand, and in this manner she could at present still stay me. But after gasping an instant at my sudden resignation, "Because of your letter?" she eagerly brought out.

I quickly, by way of answer, felt for my letter, drew it forth, held it up, and then, freeing myself, went and laid it on the great hall-table. "Luke will take it," I said as I came back. I reached the house-door and opened it; I was already on the steps.

My companion still demurred: the storm of the night and the early morning had dropped, but the afternoon was damp and grey. I came down to the drive while she stood in the doorway. "You go with nothing on?"

"What do I care when the child has nothing? I can't wait to dress," I cried, "and if you must do so, I leave you. Try meanwhile, yourself, upstairs."

"With *them*?" Oh, on this, the poor woman promptly joined me!

XIX

WE went straight to the lake, as it was called at Bly, and I dare say rightly called, though I reflect that it may in fact have been a sheet of water less remarkable than it appeared to my untravelled eyes. My acquaintance with sheets of water was small, and the pool of Bly, at all events on the few occasions of my consenting, under the protection of my pupils, to affront its surface in the old flat-bottomed boat moored there for our use, had impressed me both with its extent and its agitation. The usual place of embarkation was half a mile from the house, but I had an intimate conviction that, wherever

Flora might be, she was not near home. She had not given me the slip for any small adventure, and, since the day of the very great one that I had shared with her by the pond, I had been aware, in our walks, of the quarter to which she most inclined. This was why I had now given to Mrs. Grose's steps so marked a direction—a direction that made her, when she perceived it, oppose a resistance that showed me she was freshly mystified. "You're going to the water, Miss?—you think she's *in*——?"

"She may be, though the depth is, I believe, nowhere very great. But what I judge most likely is that she's on the spot from which, the other day, we saw together what I told you."

"When she pretended not to see——?"

"With that astounding self-possession! I've always been sure she wanted to go back alone. And now her brother has managed it for her."

Mrs. Grose still stood where she had stopped. "You suppose they really *talk* of them?"

I could meet this with a confidence! "They say things that, if we heard them, would simply appal us."

"And if she *is* there——?"

"Yes?"

"Then Miss Jessel is?"

"Beyond a doubt. You shall see."

"Oh, thank you!" my friend cried, planted so firm that, taking it in, I went straight on without her. By the time I reached the pool, however, she was close behind me, and I knew that, whatever, to her apprehension, might befall me, the exposure of my society struck her as her least danger. She exhaled a moan of relief as we at last came in sight of the greater part of the water without a sight of the child. There was no trace of Flora on that nearer side of the bank where my observation of her had been most startling, and none on the opposite edge, where, save for a margin of some twenty yards, a thick copse came down to the water. The pond, oblong in shape, had a width so scant compared to its length that, with its ends out of view, it might have been taken for a scant river. We looked at the empty expanse, and then I felt the suggestion of my friend's eyes. I knew what she meant and I replied with a negative headshake.

"No, no; wait! She has taken the boat."

My companion stared at the vacant mooring-place and then again across the lake. "Then where is it?"

"Our not seeing it is the strongest of proofs. She has used it to go over, and then has managed to hide it."

"All alone—that child?"

"She's not alone, and at such times she's not a child: she's an old, old woman." I scanned all the visible shore while Mrs. Grose took again, into the queer element I offered her, one of her plunges of submission; then I pointed out that the boat might perfectly be in a small refuge formed by one of the recesses of the pool, an indentation masked, for the hither side, by a projection of the bank and by a clump of trees growing close to the water.

"But if the boat's there, where on earth's *she*?" my colleague anxiously asked.

"That's exactly what we must learn." And I started to walk further.

"By going all the way round?"

"Certainly, far as it is. It will take us but ten minutes, but it's far enough to have made the child prefer not to walk. She went straight over."

"Laws!" cried my friend again; the chain of my logic was ever too much for her. It dragged her at my heels even now, and when we had got half-way round—a devious, tiresome process, on ground much broken and by a path choked with overgrowth—I paused to give her breath. I sustained her with a grateful arm, assuring her that she might hugely help me; and this started us afresh, so that in the course of but few minutes more we reached a point from which we found the boat to be where I had supposed it. It had been intentionally left as much as possible out of sight and was tied to one of the stakes of a fence that came, just there, down to the brink and that had been an assistance to disembarking. I recognised, as I looked at the pair of short, thick oars, quite safely drawn up, the prodigious character of the feat for a little girl; but I had lived, by this time, too long among wonders and had panted to too many livelier measures. There was a gate in the fence, through which we passed, and that brought us, after a trifling interval, more into the open. Then, "There she is!" we both exclaimed at once.

Flora, a short way off, stood before us on the grass and smiled as if her performance was now complete. The next thing she did, however, was to stoop straight down and pluck—quite as if it were all she was there for—a big, ugly spray of withered fern. I instantly became sure she had just come out of the copse. She waited for us, not herself taking a step, and I was conscious of the rare solemnity with which we presently approached her. She smiled and smiled, and we met; but it was all done in a silence by this time flagrantly ominous. Mrs. Grose was the first to break the spell: she threw herself on her knees and, drawing the child to her breast, clasped in a long embrace the little tender, yielding body. While this dumb convulsion lasted I could only watch it—which I did the more intently when I saw Flora's face peep at me over our companion's shoulder. It was serious now—the flicker had left it; but it strengthened the pang with which I at that moment envied Mrs. Grose the simplicity of *her* relation. Still, all this while, nothing more passed between us save that Flora had let her foolish fern again drop to the ground. What she and I had virtually said to each other was that pretexts were useless now. When Mrs. Grose finally got up she kept the child's hand, so that the two were still before me; and the singular reticence of our communion was even more marked in the frank look she launched me. "I'll be hanged," it said, "if *I'll* speak!"

It was Flora who, gazing all over me in candid wonder, was the first. She was struck with our bareheaded aspect. "Why, where are your things?"

"Where yours are, my dear!" I promptly returned.

100

She had already got back her gaiety, and appeared to take this as an answer quite sufficient. "And where's Miles?" she went on.

There was something in the small valour of it that quite finished me: these three words from her were, in a flash like the glitter of a drawn blade, the jostle of the cup that my hand, for weeks and weeks, had held high and full to the brim and that now, even before speaking, I felt overflow in a deluge. "I'll tell you if you'll tell *me*——" I heard myself say, then heard the tremor in which it broke.

"Well, what?"

Mrs. Grose's suspense blazed at me, but it was too late now, and I brought the thing out handsomely. "Where, my pet, is Miss Jessel?"

XX

JUST as in the churchyard with Miles, the whole thing was upon us. Much as I had made of the fact that this name had never once, between us, been sounded, the quick, smitten glare with which the child's face now received it fairly likened my breach of the silence to the smash of a pane of glass. It added to the interposing cry, as if to stay the blow, that Mrs. Grose, at the same instant, uttered over my violence—the shriek of a creature scared, or rather wounded, which, in turn, within a few seconds, was completed by a gasp of my own. I seized my colleague's arm. "She's there, she's there!"

Miss Jessel stood before us on the opposite bank exactly as she had stood the other time, and I remember, strangely, as the first feeling now produced in me, my thrill of joy at having brought on a proof. She was there, and I was justified; she was there, and I was neither cruel nor mad. She was there for poor scared Mrs. Grose, but she was there most for Flora; and no moment of my monstrous time was perhaps so extraordinary as that in which I consciously threw out to her—with the sense that, pale and ravenous demon as she was, she would catch and understand it—an inarticulate message of gratitude. She rose erect on the spot my friend and I had lately quitted, and there was not, in all the long reach of her desire, an inch of her evil that fell short. This first vividness of vision and emotion were things of a few seconds, during which Mrs. Grose's dazed blink across to where I pointed struck me as a sovereign sign that she too at last saw, just as it carried my own eyes precipitately to the child. The revelation then of the manner in which Flora was affected startled me, in truth, far more than it would have done to find her also merely agitated, for direct dismay was of course not what I had expected. Prepared and on her guard as our pursuit had actually made her, she would repress every betrayal; and I was therefore shaken, on the spot, by my first glimpse of the particular one for which I had not allowed. To see her, without a convulsion of her small pink face, not even feign to glance in the direction of the prodigy I announced, but only, instead of that, turn at *me* an expression of hard, still gravity, an expression absolutely new and unprecedented and that appeared to read and accuse and judge me—this was a stroke that somehow converted the little girl herself into the very presence that could make me quail. I quailed even though my certitude that she thoroughly saw was never greater than at that instant, and in the immediate need to defend myself I called it passionately to witness. "She's there, you little unhappy thing—there, there, *there*, and you see her as well as you see me!" I had said shortly before to Mrs. Grose that she was not at these times a child, but an old, old woman, and that description of her could not have been more strikingly confirmed than in the way in which, for all answer to this, she simply showed me, without a concession, an admission, of her eyes, a countenance of deeper and deeper, of indeed suddenly quite fixed, reprobation. I was by this time—if I can put the whole thing at all together—more appalled at what I may properly call her manner than at anything else, though it was simultaneously with this that I became aware of having Mrs. Grose also, and very formidably, to reckon with. My elder companion, the next moment, at any rate, blotted out everything but her own flushed face and her loud, shocked protest, a burst of high disapproval. "What a dreadful turn, to be sure, Miss! Where on earth do you see anything?"

I could only grasp her more quickly yet, for even while she spoke the hideous plain presence stood undimmed and undaunted. It had already lasted a minute, and it lasted while I continued, seizing my colleague, quite thrusting her at it and presenting her to it, to insist with my pointing hand. "You don't see her exactly as *we* see?—you mean to say you don't now—*now*? She's as big as a blazing fire! Only look, dearest woman, *look*——!" She looked, even as I did, and gave me, with her deep groan of negation, repulsion, compassion— the mixture with her pity of her relief at her exemption—a sense, touching to me even then, that she would have backed me up if she could. I might well have needed that, for with this hard blow of the proof that her eyes were hopelessly sealed I felt my own situation horribly crumble, I felt—I saw—my livid predecessor press, from her position, on my defeat, and I was conscious, more than all, of what I should have from this instant to deal with in the astounding little attitude of Flora. Into this attitude Mrs. Grose immediately and violently entered, breaking, even while there pierced through my sense of ruin a prodigious private triumph, into breathless reassurance.

"She isn't there, little lady, and nobody's there—and you never see nothing, my sweet! How can poor Miss Jessel—when poor Miss Jessel's dead and buried? *We* know, don't we, love?"—and she appealed, blundering in, to the child. "It's all a mere mistake and a worry and a joke—and we'll go home as fast as we can!"

Our companion, on this, had responded with a strange, quick primness of propriety, and they were again, with Mrs. Grose on her feet, united, as it were, in pained opposition to me. Flora continued to fix me with her small mask of reprobation, and even at that minute I prayed God to forgive me for seeming to see that, as she stood there holding tight to our friend's dress, her incomparable childish beauty had suddenly failed, had quite vanished. I've said it already—she was literally, she was hideously, hard; she had turned common and almost ugly. "I don't know what you mean. I see nobody. I see nothing. I never *have*. I think you're cruel. I don't like you!" Then, after this deliverance, which might have been that of a vulgarly pert little girl in the street, she hugged Mrs. Grose more closely and buried in her skirts the dreadful little face. In this position she produced an almost furious wail. "Take me away, take me away—oh, take me away from *her*!"

"From *me?*" I panted.

"From you—from you!" she cried.

Even Mrs. Grose looked across at me dismayed, while I had nothing to do but communicate again with the figure that, on the opposite bank, without a movement, as rigidly still as if catching, beyond the interval, our voices, was as vividly there for my disaster as it was not there for my service. The wretched child had spoken exactly as if she had got from some outside source each of her stabbing little words, and I could therefore, in the full despair of all I had to accept, but sadly shake my head at her. "If I had ever doubted, all my doubt would at present have gone. I've been living with the miserable truth, and now it has only too much closed round me. Of course I've lost you: I've interfered, and you've seen—under *her* dictation"—with which I faced, over the pool again, our infernal witness—"the easy and perfect way to meet it. I've done my best, but I've lost you. Good-bye." For Mrs. Grose I had an imperative, an almost frantic "Go, go!" before which, in infinite distress, but mutely possessed of the little girl and clearly convinced, in spite of her blindness, that something awful had occurred and some collapse engulfed us, she retreated, by the way we had come, as fast as she could move.

Of what first happened when I was left alone I had no subsequent memory. I only knew that at the end of, I suppose, a quarter of an hour, an odorous dampness and roughness, chilling and piercing my trouble, had made me understand that I must have thrown myself, on my face, on the ground and given way to a wildness of grief. I must have lain there long and cried and sobbed, for when I raised my head the day was almost done. I got up and looked a moment, through the twilight, at the grey pool and its blank, haunted edge, and then I took, back to the house, my dreary and difficult course. When I reached the gate in the fence the boat, to my surprise, was gone, so that I had a fresh reflection to make on Flora's extraordinary command of the situation. She passed that night, by the most tacit, and I should add, were not the word so grotesque a false note, the happiest of arrangements, with Mrs. Grose. I saw neither of them on my return, but, on the other hand, as by an ambiguous compensation, I saw a great deal of Miles. I saw—I can use no other phrase—so much of him that it was as if it were more than it had ever been. No evening I had passed at Bly had the portentous quality of this one; in spite of which—and in spite also of the deeper depths of consternation that had opened beneath my feet—there was literally, in the ebbing actual, an extraordinarily sweet sadness. On reaching the house I had never so much as looked for the boy; I had simply gone straight to my room to change what I was wearing and to take in, at a glance, much material testimony to Flora's rupture. Her little belongings had all been removed. When later, by the schoolroom fire, I was served with tea by the usual maid, I indulged, on the article of my other pupil, in no inquiry whatever. He had his freedom now—he might have it to the end! Well, he did have it; and it consisted—in part at least—of his coming in at about eight o'clock and sitting down with me in silence. On the removal of the tea-things I had blown out the candles and drawn my chair closer: I was conscious of a mortal coldness and felt as if I should never again be warm. So, when he appeared, I was sitting in the glow with my thoughts. He paused a moment by the door as if to look at me; then—as if to share them—came to the other side of the hearth and sank into a chair. We sat there in absolute stillness; yet he wanted, I felt, to be with me.

XXI

BEFORE a new day, in my room, had fully broken, my eyes opened to Mrs. Grose, who had come to my bedside with worse news. Flora was so markedly feverish that an illness was perhaps at hand; she had passed a night of extreme unrest, a night agitated above all by fears that had for their subject not in the least her former, but wholly her present, governess. It was not against the possible re-entrance of Miss Jessel on the scene that she protested—it was conspicuously and passionately against mine. I was promptly on my feet of course, and with an immense deal to ask; the more that my friend had discernibly now girded her loins to meet me once more. This I felt as soon as I had put to her the question of her sense of the child's sincerity as against my own. "She persists in denying to you that she saw, or has ever seen, anything?"

My visitor's trouble, truly, was great. "Ah, Miss, it isn't a matter on which I can push her! Yet it isn't either, I must say, as if I much needed to. It has made her, every inch of her, quite old."

"Oh, I see her perfectly from here. She resents, for all the world like some high little personage, the imputation on her truthfulness and, as it were, her respectability. 'Miss Jessel indeed—*she*!' Ah, she's 'respectable,' the chit! The impression she gave me there yesterday was, I assure you, the very strangest of all; it was quite beyond any of the others. I *did* put my foot in it! She'll never speak to me again."

Hideous and obscure as it all was, it held Mrs. Grose briefly silent; then she granted my point with a frankness which, I made sure, had more behind it. "I think indeed, Miss, she never will. She do have a grand manner about it!"

"And that manner"—I summed it up—"is practically what's the matter with her now!"

Oh, that manner, I could see in my visitor's face, and not a little else besides! "She asks me every three minutes if I think you're coming in."

"I see—I see." I too, on my side, had so much more than worked it out. "Has she said to you since yesterday—except to repudiate her familiarity with anything so dreadful—a single other word about Miss Jessel?"

"Not one, Miss. And of course you know," my friend added, "I took it from her, by the lake, that, just then and there at least, there *was* nobody."

"Rather! And, naturally, you take it from her still."

"I don't contradict her. What else can I do?"

"Nothing in the world! You've the cleverest little person to deal with. They've made them—their two friends, I mean—still cleverer even than nature did; for it was wondrous material to play on! Flora has now her grievance, and she'll work it to the end."

"Yes, Miss; but to *what* end?"

"Why, that of dealing with me to her uncle. She'll make me out to him the lowest creature——!"

I winced at the fair show of the scene in Mrs. Grose's face; she looked for a minute as if she sharply saw them together. "And him who thinks so well of you!"

"He has an odd way—it comes over me now," I laughed, "—of proving it! But that doesn't matter. What Flora wants, of course, is to get rid of me."

My companion bravely concurred. "Never again to so much as look at you."

"So that what you've come to me now for," I asked, "is to speed me on my way?" Before she had time to reply, however, I had her in check. "I've a better idea—the result of my reflections. My going *would* seem the right thing, and on Sunday I was terribly near it. Yet that won't do. It's *you* who must go. You must take Flora."

My visitor, at this, did speculate. "But where in the world——?"

"Away from here. Away from *them*. Away, even most of all, now, from me. Straight to her uncle."

"Only to tell on you——?"

"No, not 'only'! To leave me, in addition, with my remedy."

She was still vague. "And what *is* your remedy?"

"Your loyalty, to begin with. And then Miles's."

She looked at me hard. "Do you think he——?"

"Won't if he has the chance, turn on me? Yes, I venture still to think it. At all events, I want to try. Get off with his sister as soon as possible and leave me with him alone." I was amazed, myself, at the spirit I had still in reserve, and therefore perhaps a trifle the more disconcerted at the way in which, in spite of this fine example of it, she hesitated. "There's one thing, of course," I went on: "they mustn't, before she goes, see each other for three seconds."

Then it came over me that, in spite of Flora's presumable sequestration from the instant of her return from the pool, it might already be too late. "Do you mean," I anxiously asked, "that they *have* met?"

At this she quite flushed. "Ah, Miss, I'm not such a fool as that! If I've been obliged to leave her three or four times, it has been each time with one of the maids, and at present, though she's alone, she's locked in safe. And yet—and yet!" There were too many things.

"And yet what?"

"Well, are you so sure of the little gentleman?"

"I'm not sure of anything but *you*. But I have, since last evening, a new hope. I think he wants to give me an opening. I do believe that—poor little exquisite wretch!—he wants to speak. Last evening, in the firelight and the silence, he sat with me for two hours as if it were just coming."

Mrs. Grose looked hard, through the window, at the grey, gathering day. "And did it come?"

"No, though I waited and waited, I confess it didn't, and it was without a breach of the silence or so much as a faint allusion to his sister's condition and absence that we at last kissed for good-night. All the same," I continued, "I can't, if her uncle sees her, consent to his seeing her brother without my having given the boy—and most of all because things have got so bad—a little more time."

My friend appeared on this ground more reluctant than I could quite understand. "What do you mean by more time?"

"Well, a day or two—really to bring it out. He'll then be on *my* side—of which you see the importance. If nothing comes, I shall only fail, and you will, at the worst, have helped me by doing, on your arrival in town, whatever you may have found possible." So I put it before her, but she continued for a little so inscrutably embarrassed that I came again to her aid. "Unless, indeed," I wound up, "you really want *not* to go."

I could see it, in her face, at last clear itself; she put out her hand to me as a pledge. "I'll go—I'll go. I'll go this morning."

I wanted to be very just. "If you *should* wish still to wait, I would engage she shouldn't see me."

"No, no: it's the place itself. She must leave it." She held me a moment with heavy eyes, then brought out the rest. "Your idea's the right one. I myself, Miss——"

"Well?"

"I can't stay."

The look she gave me with it made me jump at possibilities. "You mean that, since yesterday, you *have* seen——?"

She shook her head with dignity. "I've *heard*——!"

"Heard?"

"From that child—horrors! There!" she sighed with tragic relief. "On my honour, Miss, she says things——!" But at this evocation she broke down; she dropped, with a sudden sob, upon my sofa and, as I had seen her do before, gave way to all the grief of it.

It was quite in another manner that I, for my part, let myself go. "Oh, thank God!"

She sprang up again at this, drying her eyes with a groan. "'Thank God'?"

"It so justifies me!"

"It does that, Miss!"

I couldn't have desired more emphasis, but I just hesitated. "She's so horrible?"

I saw my colleague scarce knew how to put it. "Really shocking."

"And about me?"

"About you, Miss—since you must have it. It's beyond everything, for a young lady; and I can't think wherever she must have picked up——"

"The appalling language she applied to me? I can, then!" I broke in with a laugh that was doubtless significant enough.

It only, in truth, left my friend still more grave. "Well, perhaps I ought to also—since I've heard some of it before! Yet I can't bear it," the poor woman went on while, with the same movement, she glanced, on my dressing-table, at the face of my watch. "But I must go back."

I kept her, however. "Ah, if you can't bear it——!"

"How can I stop with her, you mean? Why, just *for* that: to get her away. Far from this," she pursued, "far from *them*——"

"She may be different? she may be free?" I seized her almost with joy. "Then, in spite of yesterday, you *believe*——"

"In such doings?" Her simple description of them required, in the light of her expression, to be carried no further, and she gave me the whole thing as she had never done. "I believe."

Yes, it was a joy, and we were still shoulder to shoulder: if I might continue sure of that I should care but little what else happened. My support in the presence of disaster would be the same as it had been in my early need of confidence, and if my friend would answer for my honesty, I would answer for all the rest. On the point of taking leave of her, none the less, I was to some extent embarrassed. "There's one thing of course—it occurs to me—to remember. My letter, giving the alarm, will have reached town before you."

I now perceived still more how she had been beating about the bush and how weary at last it had made her. "Your letter won't have got there. Your letter never went."

"What then became of it?"

"Goodness knows! Master Miles——"

"Do you mean *he* took it?" I gasped.

She hung fire, but she overcame her reluctance. "I mean that I saw yesterday, when I came back with Miss Flora, that it wasn't where you had put it. Later in the evening I had the chance to question Luke, and he declared that he had neither noticed nor touched it." We could only exchange, on this, one of our deeper mutual soundings, and it was Mrs. Grose who first brought up the plumb with an almost elate "You see!"

"Yes, I see that if Miles took it instead he probably will have read it and destroyed it."

"And don't you see anything else?"

I faced her a moment with a sad smile. "It strikes me that by this time your eyes are open even wider than mine."

They proved to be so indeed, but she could still blush, almost, to show it. "I make out now what he must have done at school." And she gave, in her simple sharpness, an almost droll disillusioned nod. "He stole!"

I turned it over—I tried to be more judicial. "Well—perhaps."

She looked as if she found me unexpectedly calm. "He stole *letters!*"

She couldn't know my reasons for a calmness after all pretty shallow; so I showed them off as I might. "I hope then it was to more purpose than in this case! The note, at any rate, that I put on the table yesterday," I pursued, "will have given him so scant an advantage—for it contained only the bare demand for an interview—that he is already much ashamed of having gone so far for so little, and that what he had on his mind last evening was precisely the need of confession." I seemed to myself, for the instant, to have mastered it, to see it all. "Leave us, leave us"—I was already, at the door, hurrying her off. "I'll get it out of him. He'll meet me—he'll confess. If he confesses, he's saved. And if he's saved——"

"Then *you* are?" The dear woman kissed me on this, and I took her farewell. "I'll save you without him!" she cried as she went.

XXII

YET it was when she had got off—and I missed her on the spot—that the great pinch really came. If I had counted on what it would give me to find myself alone with Miles, I speedily perceived, at least, that it would give me a measure. No hour of my stay in fact was so assailed with apprehensions as that of my coming down to learn that the carriage containing Mrs. Grose and my younger pupil had already rolled out of the gates. Now I *was*, I said to myself, face to face with the elements, and for much of the rest of the day, while I fought my weakness, I could consider that I had been supremely rash. It was a tighter place still than I had yet turned round in; all the more that, for the first time, I could see in the aspect of others a confused reflection of the crisis. What had happened naturally caused them all to stare; there was too little of the explained, throw out whatever we might, in the suddenness of my colleague's act. The maids and the men looked blank; the effect of which on my nerves was an aggravation until I saw the necessity of making it a positive aid. It was precisely, in short, by just clutching the helm that I avoided total wreck; and I dare say that, to bear up at all, I became, that morning, very grand and very dry. I welcomed the consciousness that I was charged with much to do, and I caused it to be known as well that, left thus to myself, I was quite remarkably firm. I wandered with that manner, for the next hour or two, all over the place and looked, I have no doubt, as if I were ready for any onset. So, for the benefit of whom it might concern, I paraded with a sick heart.

The person it appeared least to concern proved to be, till dinner, little Miles himself. My perambulations had given me, meanwhile, no glimpse of him, but they had tended to make more public the change taking place in our relation as a consequence of his having at the piano, the day before, kept me, in Flora's interest, so beguiled and befooled. The stamp of publicity had of course been fully given by her confinement and departure, and the change itself was now ushered in by our non-observance of the regular custom of the schoolroom. He had already disappeared when, on my way down, I pushed open his door, and I learned below that he had breakfasted—in the presence of a couple of the maids—with Mrs. Grose and his sister. He had then gone out, as he said, for a stroll; than which nothing, I reflected, could better have expressed his frank view of the abrupt transformation of my office. What he would now permit this office to consist of was yet to be settled: there was a queer relief, at all events—I mean for myself in especial—in the renouncement of one pretension. If so much had sprung to the surface, I scarce put it too strongly in saying that what had perhaps sprung highest was the absurdity of our prolonging the fiction that I had anything more to teach him. It sufficiently stuck out that, by tacit little tricks in which even more than myself he carried out the care for my dignity, I had had to appeal to him to let me off straining to meet him on the ground of his true capacity. He had at any rate his freedom now; I was never to touch it again; as I had amply shown, moreover, when, on his joining me in the schoolroom the previous night, I had uttered, on the subject of the interval just concluded, neither challenge nor hint. I had too much, from this moment, my other ideas. Yet when he at last arrived the difficulty of applying them, the accumulations of my problem, were brought straight home to me by the beautiful little presence on which what had occurred had as yet, for the eye, dropped neither stain nor shadow.

To mark, for the house, the high state I cultivated I decreed that my meals with the boy should be served, as we called it, downstairs; so that I had been awaiting him in the ponderous pomp of the room outside of the window of which I had had from Mrs. Grose, that first scared Sunday, my flash of something it would scarce have done to call light. Here at present I felt afresh—for I had felt it again and again—how my equilibrium depended on the success of my rigid will, the will to shut my eyes as tight as possible to the truth that what I had to deal with was, revoltingly, against nature. I could only get on at all by taking "nature" into my confidence and my account, by treating my monstrous ordeal as a push in a direction unusual, of course, and unpleasant, but demanding, after all, for a fair front, only another turn of the screw of ordinary human virtue. No attempt, none the less, could well require more tact than just this attempt to supply, one's self, *all* the nature. How could I put even a little of that article into a suppression of reference to what had occurred? How, on the other hand, could I make a reference without a new plunge into the hideous obscure? Well, a sort of answer, after a time, had come to me, and it was so far confirmed as that I was met, incontestably, by the quickened vision of what was rare in my little companion. It was indeed as if he had found even now—as he had so often found at lessons—still some other delicate way to ease me off. Wasn't there light in the fact which, as we shared our solitude, broke out with a specious glitter it had never yet quite worn?—the fact that (opportunity aiding, precious opportunity which had now come) it would be preposterous, with a child so endowed, to forgo the help one might wrest from absolute intelligence? What had his intelligence been given him for but to save him? Mightn't one, to reach his mind, risk the stretch of an angular arm over his character? It was as if, when we were face to face in the dining-room, he had literally shown me the way. The roast mutton was on the table, and I had dispensed with attendance. Miles, before he sat down, stood a moment with his hands in his pockets and looked at the joint, on which he seemed on the point of passing some humorous judgment. But what he presently produced was: "I say, my dear, is she really very awfully ill?"

"Little Flora? Not so bad but that she'll presently be better. London will set her up. Bly had ceased to agree with her. Come here and take your mutton."

He alertly obeyed me, carried the plate carefully to his seat, and, when he was established, went on. "Did Bly disagree with her so terribly suddenly?"

"Not so suddenly as you might think. One had seen it coming on."

"Then why didn't you get her off before?"

"Before what?"

"Before she became too ill to travel."

I found myself prompt. "She's *not* too ill to travel: she only might have become so if she had stayed. This was just the moment to seize. The journey will dissipate the influence"—oh, I was grand!—"and carry it off."

114

"I see, I see"—Miles, for that matter, was grand too. He settled to his repast with the charming little "table manner" that, from the day of his arrival, had relieved me of all grossness of admonition. Whatever he had been driven from school for, it was not for ugly feeding. He was irreproachable, as always, today; but he was unmistakeably more conscious. He was discernibly trying to take for granted more things than he found, without assistance, quite easy; and he dropped into peaceful silence while he felt his situation. Our meal was of the briefest—mine a vain pretence, and I had the things immediately removed. While this was done Miles stood again with his hands in his little pockets and his back to me—stood and looked out of the wide window through which, that other day, I had seen what pulled me up. We continued silent while the maid was with us—as silent, it whimsically occurred to me, as some young couple who, on their wedding-journey, at the inn, feel shy in the presence of the waiter. He turned round only when the waiter had left us. "Well—so we're alone!"

XXIII

"Oh, more or less." I fancy my smile was pale. "Not absolutely. We shouldn't like that!" I went on.

"No—I suppose we shouldn't. Of course we have the others."

"We have the others—we have indeed the others," I concurred.

"Yet even though we have them," he returned, still with his hands in his pockets and planted there in front of me, "they don't much count, do they?"

I made the best of it, but I felt wan. "It depends on what you call 'much'!"

"Yes"—with all accommodation—"everything depends!" On this, however, he faced to the window again and presently reached it with his vague, restless, cogitating step. He remained there awhile, with his forehead against the glass, in contemplation of the stupid shrubs I knew and the dull things of November. I had always my hypocrisy of "work," behind which, now, I gained the sofa. Steadying myself with it there as I had repeatedly done at those moments of torment that I have described as the moments of my knowing the children to be given to something from which I was barred, I sufficiently obeyed my habit of being prepared for the worst. But an extraordinary impression dropped on me as I extracted a meaning from the boy's embarrassed back—none other than the impression that I was not barred now. This inference grew in a few minutes to sharp intensity and seemed bound up with the direct perception that it was positively *he* who was. The frames and squares of the great window were a kind of image, for him, of a kind of failure. I felt that I saw him, at any rate, shut in or shut out. He was admirable, but not comfortable: I took it in with a throb of hope. Wasn't he looking, through the haunted pane, for something he couldn't see?—and wasn't it the first time in the whole business that he had known such a lapse? The first, the very first: I found it a splendid portent. It made him anxious, though he watched himself; he had been anxious all day and, even while in his usual sweet little manner he sat at table, had needed all his small strange genius to give it a gloss. When he at last turned round to meet me, it was almost as if this genius had succumbed. "Well, I think I'm glad Bly agrees with *me*!"

"You would certainly seem to have seen, these twenty-four hours, a good deal more of it than for some time before. I hope," I went on bravely, "that you've been enjoying yourself."

"Oh, yes, I've been ever so far; all round about—miles and miles away. I've never been so free."

He had really a manner of his own, and I could only try to keep up with him. "Well, do you like it?"

He stood there smiling; then at last he put into two words—"Do *you*?"—more discrimination than I had ever heard two words contain. Before I had time to deal with that, however, he continued as if with the sense that this was an impertinence to be softened. "Nothing could be more charming than the way you take it, for of course if we're alone together now it's you that are alone most. But I hope," he threw in, "you don't particularly mind!"

"Having to do with you?" I asked. "My dear child, how can I help minding? Though I've renounced all claim to your company,—you're so beyond me,—I at least greatly enjoy it. What else should I stay on for?"

He looked at me more directly, and the expression of his face, graver now, struck me as the most beautiful I had ever found in it. "You stay on just for *that*?"

"Certainly. I stay on as your friend and from the tremendous interest I take in you till something can be done for you that may be more worth your while. That needn't surprise you." My voice trembled so that I felt it impossible to suppress the shake. "Don't you remember how I told you, when I came and sat on your bed the night of the storm, that there was nothing in the world I wouldn't do for you?"

"Yes, yes!" He, on his side, more and more visibly nervous, had a tone to master; but he was so much more successful than I that, laughing out through his gravity, he could pretend we were pleasantly jesting. "Only that, I think, was to get me to do something for *you*!"

"It was partly to get you to do something," I conceded. "But, you know, you didn't do it."

"Oh, yes," he said with the brightest superficial eagerness, "you wanted me to tell you something."

"That's it. Out, straight out. What you have on your mind, you know."

"Ah, then, is *that* what you've stayed over for?"

He spoke with a gaiety through which I could still catch the finest little quiver of resentful passion; but I can't begin to express the effect upon me of an implication of surrender even so faint. It was as if what I had yearned for had come at last only to astonish me. "Well, yes—I may as well make a clean breast of it. It was precisely for that."

He waited so long that I supposed it for the purpose of repudiating the assumption on which my action had been founded; but what he finally said was: "Do you mean now—here?"

"There couldn't be a better place or time." He looked round him uneasily, and I had the rare—oh, the queer!—impression of the very first symptom I had seen in him of the approach of immediate fear. It was as if he were suddenly afraid of me—which struck me indeed as perhaps the best thing to make him. Yet in the very pang of the effort I felt it vain to try sternness, and I heard myself the next instant so gentle as to be almost grotesque. "You want so to go out again?"

"Awfully!" He smiled at me heroically, and the touching little bravery of it was enhanced by his actually flushing with pain. He had picked up his hat, which he had brought in, and stood twirling it in a way that gave me, even as I was just nearly reaching port, a perverse horror of what I was doing. To do it in *any* way was an act of violence, for what did it consist of but the obtrusion of the idea of grossness and guilt on a small helpless creature who had been for me a revelation of the possibilities of beautiful intercourse? Wasn't it base to create for a being so exquisite a mere alien awkwardness? I suppose I now read into our situation a clearness it couldn't have had at the time, for I seem to see our poor eyes already lighted with some spark of a prevision of the anguish that was to come. So we circled about, with terrors and scruples, like fighters not daring to close. But it was for each other we feared! That kept us a little longer suspended and unbruised. "I'll tell you everything," Miles said—"I mean I'll tell you anything you like. You'll stay on with me, and we shall both be all right and I *will* tell you—I *will*. But not now."

"Why not now?"

My insistence turned him from me and kept him once more at his window in a silence during which, between us, you might have heard a pin drop. Then he was before me again with the air of a person for whom, outside, someone who had frankly to be reckoned with was waiting. "I have to see Luke."

I had not yet reduced him to quite so vulgar a lie, and I felt proportionately ashamed. But, horrible as it was, his lies made up my truth. I achieved thoughtfully a few loops of my knitting. "Well, then, go to Luke, and I'll wait for what you promise. Only, in return for that, satisfy, before you leave me, one very much smaller request."

He looked as if he felt he had succeeded enough to be able still a little to bargain. "Very much smaller——?"

"Yes, a mere fraction of the whole. Tell me"—oh, my work preoccupied me, and I was off-hand!—"if, yesterday afternoon, from the table in the hall, you took, you know, my letter."

XXIV

My sense of how he received this suffered for a minute from something that I can describe only as a fierce split of my attention—a stroke that at first, as I sprang straight up, reduced me to the mere blind movement of getting hold of him, drawing him close, and, while I just fell for support against the nearest piece of furniture, instinctively keeping him with his back to the window. The appearance was full upon us that I had already had to deal with here: Peter Quint had come into view like a sentinel before a prison. The next thing I saw was that, from outside, he had reached the window, and then I knew that, close to the glass and glaring in through it, he offered once more to the room his white face of damnation. It represents but grossly what took place within me at the sight to say that on the second my decision was made; yet I believe that no woman so overwhelmed ever in so short a time recovered her grasp of the *act*. It came to me in the very horror of the immediate presence that the act would be, seeing and facing what I saw and faced, to keep the boy himself unaware. The inspiration—I can call it by no other name—was that I felt how voluntarily, how transcendently, I *might*. It was like fighting with a demon for a human soul, and when I had fairly so appraised it I saw how the human soul—held out, in the tremor of my hands, at arm's length—had a perfect dew of sweat on a lovely childish forehead. The face that was close to mine was as white as the face against the glass, and out of it presently came a sound, not low nor weak, but as if from much further away, that I drank like a waft of fragrance.

"Yes—I took it."

At this, with a moan of joy, I enfolded, I drew him close; and while I held him to my breast, where I could feel in the sudden fever of his little body the tremendous pulse of his little heart, I kept my eyes on the thing at the window and saw it move and shift its posture. I have likened it to a sentinel, but its slow wheel, for a moment, was rather the prowl of a baffled beast. My present quickened courage, however, was such that, not too much to let it through, I had to shade, as it were, my flame. Meanwhile the glare of the face was again at the window, the scoundrel fixed as if to watch and wait. It was the very confidence that I might now defy him, as well as the positive certitude, by this time, of the child's unconsciousness, that made me go on. "What did you take it for?"

"To see what you said about me."

"You opened the letter?"

"I opened it."

My eyes were now, as I held him off a little again, on Miles's own face, in which the collapse of mockery showed me how complete was the ravage of uneasiness. What was prodigious was that at last, by my success, his sense was sealed and his communication stopped: he knew that he was in presence, but knew not of what, and knew still less that I also was and that I did know. And what did this strain of trouble matter when my eyes went back to the window only to see that the air was clear again and—by my personal triumph—the influence quenched? There was nothing there. I felt that the cause was mine and that I should surely get *all*. "And you found nothing!"—I let my elation out.

He gave the most mournful, thoughtful little headshake. "Nothing."

"Nothing, nothing!" I almost shouted in my joy.

"Nothing, nothing," he sadly repeated.

I kissed his forehead; it was drenched. "So what have you done with it?"

"I've burnt it."

"Burnt it?" It was now or never. "Is that what you did at school?"

Oh, what this brought up! "At school?"

"Did you take letters?—or other things?"

"Other things?" He appeared now to be thinking of something far off and that reached him only through the pressure of his anxiety. Yet it did reach him. "Did I *steal*?"

I felt myself redden to the roots of my hair as well as wonder if it were more strange to put to a gentleman such a question or to see him take it with allowances that gave the very distance of his fall in the world. "Was it for that you mightn't go back?"

The only thing he felt was rather a dreary little surprise. "Did you know I mightn't go back?"

"I know everything."

He gave me at this the longest and strangest look. "Everything?"

"Everything. Therefore *did* you——?" But I couldn't say it again.

Miles could, very simply. "No. I didn't steal."

My face must have shown him I believed him utterly; yet my hands—but it was for pure tenderness—shook him as if to ask him why, if it was all for nothing, he had condemned me to months of torment. "What then did you do?"

He looked in vague pain all round the top of the room and drew his breath, two or three times over, as if with difficulty. He might have been standing at the bottom of the sea and raising his eyes to some faint green twilight. "Well—I said things."

"Only that?"

"They thought it was enough!"

"To turn you out for?"

121

Never, truly, had a person "turned out" shown so little to explain it as this little person! He appeared to weigh my question, but in a manner quite detached and almost helpless. "Well, I suppose I oughtn't."

"But to whom did you say them?"

He evidently tried to remember, but it dropped—he had lost it. "I don't know!"

He almost smiled at me in the desolation of his surrender, which was indeed practically, by this time, so complete that I ought to have left it there. But I was infatuated—I was blind with victory, though even then the very effect that was to have brought him so much nearer was already that of added separation. "Was it to everyone?" I asked.

"No; it was only to——" But he gave a sick little headshake. "I don't remember their names."

"Were they then so many?"

"No—only a few. Those I liked."

Those he liked? I seemed to float not into clearness, but into a darker obscure, and within a minute there had come to me out of my very pity the appalling alarm of his being perhaps innocent. It was for the instant confounding and bottomless, for if he *were* innocent, what then on earth was *I*? Paralysed, while it lasted, by the mere brush of the question, I let him go a little, so that, with a deep-drawn sigh, he turned away from me again; which, as he faced toward the clear window, I suffered, feeling that I had nothing now there to keep him from. "And did they repeat what you said?" I went on after a moment.

He was soon at some distance from me, still breathing hard and again with the air, though now without anger for it, of being confined against his will. Once more, as he had done before, he looked up at the dim day as if, of what had hitherto sustained him, nothing was left but an unspeakable anxiety. "Oh, yes," he nevertheless replied—"they must have repeated them. To those *they* liked," he added.

There was, somehow, less of it than I had expected; but I turned it over. "And these things came round———?"

"To the masters? Oh, yes!" he answered very simply. "But I didn't know they'd tell."

"The masters? They didn't—they've never told. That's why I ask you."

He turned to me again his little beautiful fevered face. "Yes, it was too bad."

"Too bad?"

"What I suppose I sometimes said. To write home."

I can't name the exquisite pathos of the contradiction given to such a speech by such a speaker; I only know that the next instant I heard myself throw off with homely force: "Stuff and nonsense!" But the next after that I must have sounded stern enough. "What *were* these things?"

My sternness was all for his judge, his executioner; yet it made him avert himself again, and that movement made *me*, with a single bound and an irrepressible cry, spring straight upon him. For there again, against the glass, as if to blight his confession and stay his answer, was the hideous author of our woe—the white face of damnation. I felt a sick swim at the drop of my victory and all the return of my battle, so that the wildness of my veritable leap only served as a great betrayal. I saw him, from the midst of my act, meet it with a divination, and on the perception that even now he only guessed, and that the window was still to his own eyes free, I let the impulse flame up to convert the climax of his dismay into the very proof of his liberation. "No more, no more, no more!" I shrieked, as I tried to press him against me, to my visitant.

"Is she *here*?" Miles panted as he caught with his sealed eyes the direction of my words. Then as his strange "she" staggered me and, with a gasp, I echoed it, "Miss Jessel, Miss Jessel!" he with a sudden fury gave me back.

I seized, stupefied, his supposition—some sequel to what we had done to Flora, but this made me only want to show him that it was better still than that. "It's not Miss Jessel! But it's at the window—straight before us. It's *there*—the coward horror, there for the last time!"

At this, after a second in which his head made the movement of a baffled dog's on a scent and then gave a frantic little shake for air and light, he was at me in a white rage, bewildered, glaring vainly over the place and missing wholly, though it now, to my sense, filled the room like the taste of poison, the wide, overwhelming presence. "It's *he?*"

I was so determined to have all my proof that I flashed into ice to challenge him. "Whom do you mean by 'he'?"

"Peter Quint—you devil!" His face gave again, round the room, its convulsed supplication. "*Where?*"

They are in my ears still, his supreme surrender of the name and his tribute to my devotion. "What does he matter now, my own?—what will he *ever* matter? *I* have you," I launched at the beast, "but he has lost you for ever!" Then, for the demonstration of my work, "There, *there!*" I said to Miles.

But he had already jerked straight round, stared, glared again, and seen but the quiet day. With the stroke of the loss I was so proud of he uttered the cry of a creature hurled over an abyss, and the grasp with which I recovered him might have been that of catching him in his fall. I caught him, yes, I held him—it may be imagined with what a passion; but at the end of a minute I began to feel what it truly was that I held. We were alone with the quiet day, and his little heart, dispossessed, had stopped.

COVERING END

I

AT the foot of the staircase he waited and listened, thinking he had heard her call to him from the gallery, high aloft but out of view, to which he had allowed her independent access and whence indeed, on her first going up, the sound of her appreciation had reached him in rapid movements, evident rushes and dashes, and in droll, charming cries that echoed through the place. He had afterwards, expectant and restless, been, for another look, to the house-door, and then had fidgeted back into the hall, where her voice again caught him. It was many a day since such a voice had sounded in those empty chambers, and never perhaps, in all the years, for poor Chivers, had any voice at all launched a note so friendly and so free.

"Oh, no, mum, there ain't no one whatever come yet. It's quite all right, mum,—you can please yourself!" If he left her to range, all his pensive little economy seemed to say, wasn't it just his poor pickings? He quitted the stairs, but stopped again, with his hand to his ear, as he heard her once more appeal to him. "Lots of lovely——? Lovely *what*, mum? Little ups and downs?" he quavered aloft. "Oh, as you say, mum: as many as in a poor man's life!" She was clearly disposed, as she roamed in delight from point to point, to continue to talk, and, with his better ear and his scooped hand, he continued to listen hard. "'Dear little crooked steps'? Yes, mum; please mind 'em, mum: they be cruel in the dark corners!" She appeared to take another of her light scampers, the sign of a fresh discovery and a fresh response; at which he felt his heart warm with the success of a trust of her that might after all have been rash. Once more her voice reached him and once more he gossiped back. "Coming up too? Not if you'll kindly indulge me, mum—I must be where I can watch the bell. It takes watching as well as hearing!"—he dropped, as he resumed his round, to a murmur of great patience. This was taken up the next moment by the husky plaint of the signal itself, which seemed to confess equally to short wind and creaking joints. It moved, however, distinguishably, and its motion made him start much more as if he had been guilty of sleeping at his post than as if he had waited half the day. "Mercy, if I *didn't* watch——!" He shuffled across the wide stone-paved hall and, losing himself beneath the great arch of the short passage to the entrance-front, hastened to admit his new visitor. He gives us thereby the use of his momentary absence for a look at the place he has left.

This is the central hall, high and square, brown and grey, flagged beneath and timbered above, of an old English country-house; an apartment in which a single survey is a perception of long and lucky continuities. It would have been difficult to find elsewhere anything at once so old and so actual, anything that had plainly come so far, far down without, at any moment of the endless journey, losing its way. To stand there and look round was to wonder a good deal—yet without arriving at an answer—whether it had been most neglected or most cherished; there was such resignation in its long survival and yet such bravery in its high polish. If it had never been spoiled, this was partly, no doubt, because it had been, for a century, given up; but what it had been given up to was, after all, homely and familiar use. It had in it at the present moment indeed much of the chill of fallen fortunes; but there was no concession in its humility and no hypocrisy in its welcome. It was magnificent and shabby, and the eyes of the dozen dark old portraits seemed, in their eternal attention, to count the cracks in the pavement, the rents in the seats of the chairs, and the missing tones in the Flemish tapestry. Above the tapestry, which, in its turn, was above the high oak wainscot, most of these stiff images—on the side on which it principally reigned—were placed; and they held up their heads to assure all comers that a tone or two was all that *was* missing, and that they had never waked up in winter dawns to any glimmer of bereavement, in the long night, of any relic or any feature. Such as it was, the company was all there; every inch of old oak, every yard of old arras, every object of ornament or of use to which these surfaces formed so rare a background. If the watchers on the walls had ever found a gap in their own rank, the ancient roof, of a certainty, would have been shaken by their collective gasp. As a matter of fact it was rich and firm—it had almost the dignity of the vault of a church. On this Saturday afternoon in August, a hot, still day, such of the casements as freely worked in the discoloured glass of the windows stood open in one quarter to a terrace that overlooked a park and in another to a wonderful old empty court that communicated with a wonderful old empty garden. The staircase, wide and straight, mounted, full in sight, to a landing that was half-way up; and on the right, as you faced this staircase, a door opened out of the brown panelling into a glimpse of a little morning-room, where, in a slanted, gilded light, there was brownness too, mixed with notes of old yellow. On the left, toward court and garden, another door stood open to the warm air. Still as you faced the staircase you had at your right, between that monument and the morning-room, the arch through which Chivers had disappeared.

His reappearance interrupts and yet in a manner, after all, quickens our intense impression; Chivers on the spot, and in this severe but spacious setting, was so perfect an image of immemorial domesticity. It would have been impossible perhaps, however, either to tell his age or to name his use: he was of the age of all the history that lurked in all the corners and of any use whatever you might be so good as still to find for him. Considerably shrunken and completely silvered, he had perpetual agreement in the droop of his kind white head and perpetual inquiry in the jerk of the idle old hands now almost covered by the sleeves of the black dress-coat which, twenty years before, must have been by a century or two the newest thing in the house and into which his years appeared to have declined very much as a shrunken family moves into a part of its habitation. This attire was completed by a white necktie that, in honour of the day, he himself had this morning done up. The humility he betrayed and the oddity he concealed were alike brought out by his juxtaposition with the gentleman he had admitted.

To admit Mr. Prodmore was anywhere and at any time, as you would immediately have recognised, an immense admission. He was a personage of great presence and weight, with a large smooth face in which a small sharp meaning was planted like a single pin in the tight red toilet-cushion of a guest-chamber. He wore a blue frock-coat and a stiff white waistcoat and a high white hat that he kept on his head with a kind of protesting cock, while in his buttonhole nestled a bold prize plant on which he occasionally lowered a proprietary eye that seemed to remind it of its being born to a public career. Mr. Prodmore's appearance had evidently been thought out, but it might have struck you that the old portraits took it in with a sterner stare, with a fixedness indeed in which a visitor more sensitive would have read a consciousness of his remaining, in their presence, so jauntily, so vulgarly covered. He had never a glance for them, and it would have been easy after a minute to see that this was an old story between them. Their manner, as it were, sensibly increased the coolness. This coolness became a high rigour as Mr. Prodmore encountered, from the very threshold, a disappointment.

"No one here?" he indignantly demanded.

"I'm sorry to say no one has come, sir," Chivers replied; "but I've had a telegram from Captain Yule."

Mr. Prodmore's apprehension flared out. "Not to say he ain't coming?"

"He was to take the 2.20 from Paddington; he certainly *should* be here!" The old man spoke as if his non-arrival were the most unaccountable thing in the world, especially for a poor person ever respectful of the mystery of causes.

"He should have been here this hour or more. And so should my fly-away daughter!"

Chivers surrounded this description of Miss Prodmore with the deep discretion of silence, and then, after a moment, evidently reflected that silence, in a world bestrewn with traps to irreverence, might be as rash as speech. "Were they coming—a—together, sir?"

He had scarcely mended the matter, for his visitor gave an inconsequent stare. "Together?—for what do you take Miss Prodmore?" This young lady's parent glared about him again as if to alight on something else that was out of place; but the good intentions expressed in the attitude of every object might presently have been presumed to soothe his irritation. It had at any rate the effect of bridging, for poor Chivers, some of his gaps. "It *is* in a sense true that their 'coming together,' as you call it, is exactly what I've made my plans for today: my calculation was that we should all punctually converge on this spot. Attended by her trusty maid, Miss Prodmore, who happens to be on a week's visit to her grandmother at Bellborough, was to take the 1.40 from that place. I was to drive over—ten miles—from the most convenient of my seats. Captain Yule"—the speaker wound up his statement as with the mention of the last touch in a masterpiece of his own sketching—"was finally to shake off for a few hours the peculiar occupations that engage him."

The old man listened with his head askance to favour his good ear, but his visible attention all on a sad spot in one of the half-dozen worn rugs. "They *must* be peculiar, sir, when a gentleman comes into a property like this and goes three months without so much as a nat'ral curiosity——! I don't speak of anything but what *is* nat'ral, sir; but there have *been* people here——"

"There have repeatedly been people here!" Mr. Prodmore complacently interrupted.

"As you say, sir—to be shown over. With the master himself never shown!" Chivers dismally commented.

"He *shall* be, so that nobody can miss him!" Mr. Prodmore, for his own reassurance as well, hastened to retort.

His companion risked a tiny explanation. "It will be a mercy indeed to look on him; but I meant that he has not been taken round."

"That's what I meant too. *I'll* take him—round and round: it's exactly what I've come for!" Mr. Prodmore rang out; and his eyes made the lower circuit again, looking as pleased as such a pair of eyes could look with nobody as yet quite good enough either to terrify or to tickle. "He can't fail to be affected, though he *has* been up to his neck in such a different class of thing."

Chivers clearly wondered awhile what class of thing it could be. Then he expressed a timid hope. "In nothing, I dare say, but what's right, sir——?"

"In everything," Mr. Prodmore distinctly informed him, "that's wrong! But here he is!" that gentleman added with elation as the doorbell again sounded. Chivers, under the double agitation of the appeal and the disclosure, proceeded to the front as fast as circumstances allowed; while Mr. Prodmore, left alone, would have been observed—had not his solitude been so bleak—to recover a degree of cheerfulness. Cheerfulness in solitude at Covering End was certainly not irresistible, but particular feelings and reasons had pitched, for their campaign, the starched, if now somewhat ruffled, tent of his large white waistcoat. If they had issued audibly from that pavilion, they would have represented to us his consciousness of the reinforcement he might bring up for attack should Captain Yule really resist the house. The sound he next heard from the front caused him none the less, for that matter, to articulate a certain drop. "Only Cora?—Well," he added in a tone somewhat at variance with his "only," "he shan't, at any rate, resist *her*!" This announcement would have quickened a spectator's interest in the young lady whom Chivers now introduced and followed, a young lady who straightway found herself the subject of traditionary discipline. "I've waited. What do you mean?"

Cora Prodmore, who had a great deal of colour in her cheeks and a great deal more—a bold variety of kinds—in the extremely high pitch of her new, smart clothes, meant, on the whole, it was easy to see, very little, and met this challenge with still less show of support either from the sources I have mentioned or from any others. A dull, fresh, honest, overdressed damsel of two-and-twenty, she was too much out of breath, too much flurried and frightened, to do more than stammer: "Waited, papa? Oh, I'm sorry!"

Her regret appeared to strike her father still more as an impertinence than as a vanity. "Would you then, if I had not had patience for you, have wished not to find me? Why the dickens are you so late?"

Agitated, embarrassed, the girl was at a loss. "I'll tell you, papa!" But she followed up her pledge with an air of vacuity and then, dropping into the nearest seat, simply closed her eyes to her danger. If she desired relief, she had caught at the one way to get it. "I feel rather faint. Could I have some tea?"

Mr. Prodmore considered both the idea and his daughter's substantial form. "Well, as I shall expect you to put forth *all* your powers—yes!" He turned to Chivers. "Some tea."

The old man's eyes had attached themselves to Miss Prodmore's symptoms with more solicitude than those of her parent. "I did think it might be required!" Then as he gained the door of the morning-room: "I'll lay it out here."

The young lady, on his withdrawal, recovered herself sufficiently to rise again. "It was my train, papa—so very awfully behind. I walked up, you know, also, from the station—there's such a lovely footpath across the park."

"You've been roaming the country then alone?" Mr. Prodmore inquired.

The girl protested with instant eagerness against any such picture. "Oh, dear no, not *alone*!" She spoke, absurdly, as if she had had a train of attendants; but it was an instant before she could complete the assurance. "There were ever so many people about."

"Nothing is more possible than that there should be *too* many!" said her father, speaking as for his personal convenience, but presenting that as enough. "But where, among them all," he demanded, "is your trusty maid?"

Cora's reply made up in promptitude what it lacked in felicity. "I didn't bring her." She looked at the old portraits as if to appeal to them to help her to remember why. Apparently indeed they gave a sign, for she presently went on: "She was so extremely unwell."

Mr. Prodmore met this with reprobation. "Wasn't she to understand from the first that we don't permit——"

"Anything of that sort?"—the girl recalled it at least as a familiar law. "Oh, yes, papa—I *thought* she did."

"But she doesn't?"—Mr. Prodmore pressed the point. Poor Cora, at a loss again, appeared to wonder if the point had better be a failure of brain or of propriety, but her companion continued to press. "What on earth's the matter with her?"

She again communed with their silent witnesses. "I really don't quite know, but I think that at Granny's she eats too much."

"I'll soon put an end to *that*!" Mr. Prodmore returned with decision. "You expect then to pursue your adventures quite into the night—to return to Bellborough as you came?"

The girl had by this time begun a little to find her feet. "Exactly as I came, papa dear,—under the protection of a new friend I've just made, a lady whom I met in the train and who is also going back by the 6.19. She was, like myself, on her way to this place, and I expected to find her here."

Mr. Prodmore chilled on the spot any such expectations. "What does she want at this place?"

Cora was clearly stronger for her new friend than for herself. "She wants to see it."

Mr. Prodmore reflected on this complication. "Today?" It was practically presumptuous. "Today won't do."

"So I suggested," the girl declared. "But do you know what she said?"

"How should I know," he coldly demanded, "what a nobody says?"

But on this, as if with the returning taste of a new strength, his daughter could categorically meet him. "She's not a nobody. She's an American."

Mr. Prodmore, for a moment, was struck: he embraced the place, instinctively, in a flash of calculation. "An American?"

"Yes, and she's wild——"

He knew all about that. "Americans mostly *are*!"

"I mean," said Cora, "to see this place. 'Wild' was what she herself called it—and I think she also said she was 'mad.'"

"She gave"—Mr. Prodmore reviewed the affair—"a fine account of herself! But she won't do."

The effect of her new acquaintance on his companion had been such that she could, after an instant, react against this sentence. "Well, when I told her that this particular day perhaps wouldn't, she said it would just *have* to."

"Have to do?" Mr. Prodmore showed again, through a chink, his speculative eye. "For *what*, then, with such grand airs?"

"Why, I suppose, for what Americans want."

He measured the quantity. "They want everything."

"Then I wonder," said Cora, "that she hasn't arrived."

"When she does arrive," he answered, "I'll tackle her; and I shall thank you, in future, not to take up, in trains, with indelicate women of whom you know nothing."

"Oh, I did know something," his daughter pleaded; "for I saw her yesterday at Bellborough."

Mr. Prodmore contested even this freedom. "And what was she doing at Bellborough?"

"Staying at the Blue Dragon, to see the old abbey. She says she just loves old abbeys. It seems to be the same feeling," the girl went on, "that brought her over, today, to see this old house."

"She 'just loves' old houses? Then why the deuce didn't she accompany you properly, since she is so pushing, to the door?"

"Because she went off in a fly," Cora explained, "to see, first, the old hospital. She just loves old hospitals. She asked me if this isn't a show-house. I told her"—the girl was anxious to disclaim responsibility—"that I hadn't the least idea."

"It *is*!" Mr. Prodmore cried almost with ferocity. "I wonder, on such a speech, what she thought of *you*!"

Miss Prodmore meditated with distinct humbleness. "I know. She told me."

He had looked her up and down. "That you're really a hopeless frump?"

Cora, oddly enough, seemed almost to court this description. "That I'm not, as she rather funnily called it, a show-girl."

"Think of your having to be reminded—by the very strangers you pick up," Mr. Prodmore groaned, "of what my daughter should pre-eminently be! Your friend, all the same," he bethought himself, "is evidently loud."

"Well, when she comes," the girl again so far agreed as to reply, "you'll certainly hear her. But don't judge her, papa, till you do. She's tremendously clever," she risked—"there seems to be nothing she doesn't know."

"And there seems to be nothing you do! You're *not* tremendously clever," Mr. Prodmore pursued; "so you'll permit me to demand of you a slight effort of intelligence." Then, as for the benefit of the listening walls themselves, he struck the high note. "I'm expecting Captain Yule."

Cora's consciousness blinked. "The owner of this property?"

Her father's tone showed his reserves. "That's what it depends on you to make him!"

"On me?" the girl gasped.

"He came into it three months ago by the death of his great-uncle, who had lived to ninety-three, but who, having quarrelled mortally with his father, had always refused to receive either sire or son."

Our young lady bent her eyes on this page of family history, then raised them but dimly lighted. "But now, at least, doesn't he live here?"

"So little," her companion replied, "that he comes here today for the very first time. I've some business to discuss with him that can best be discussed on this spot; and it's a vital part of that business that you too should take pains to make him welcome."

Miss Prodmore failed to ignite. "In his own house?"

"That it's *not* his own house is just the point I seek to make! The way I look at it is that it's *my* house! The way I look at it even, my dear"—in his demonstration of his ways of looking Mr. Prodmore literally expanded—"is that it's *our* house. The whole thing is mortgaged, as it stands, for every penny of its value; and I'm in the pleasant position—do you follow me?" he trumpeted.

Cora jumped. "Of holding the mortgages?"

He caught her with a smile of approval and indeed of surprise. "You keep up with me better than I hoped. I hold every scrap of paper, and it's a precious collection."

She smothered, perceptibly, a vague female sigh, glancing over the place more attentively than she had yet done. "Do you mean that you can come down on him?"

"I don't need to 'come,' my dear—I *am* 'down.' *This* is down!"—and the iron point of Mr. Prodmore's stick fairly struck, as he rapped it, a spark from the cold pavement. "I came many weeks ago—commercially speaking—and haven't since budged from the place."

The girl moved a little about the hall, then turned with a spasm of courage. "Are you going to be very hard?"

If she read the eyes with which he met her she found in them, in spite of a certain accompanying show of pleasantry, her answer. "Hard with *you*?"

"No—that doesn't matter. Hard with the Captain."

Mr. Prodmore thought an instant. "'Hard' is a stupid, shuffling term. What do you mean by it?"

"Well, I don't understand business," Cora said; "but I think I understand *you*, papa, enough to gather that you've got, as usual, a striking advantage."

"As usual, I *have* scored; but my advantage won't be striking perhaps till I have sent the blow home. What I appeal to you, as a father, at present to do"—he continued broadly to demonstrate—"is to nerve my arm. I look to you to see me through."

"Through what, then?"

"Through this most important transaction. Through the speculation of which you've been the barely dissimulated subject. I've brought you here to receive an impression, and I've brought you, even more, to make one."

The girl turned honestly flat. "But on whom?"

"On me, to begin with—by not being a fool. And then, Miss, on *him*."

Erect, but as if paralysed, she had the air of facing the worst. "On Captain Yule?"

"By bringing him to the point."

"But, father," she asked in evident anguish—"to *what* point?"

"The point where a gentleman *has* to."

Miss Prodmore faltered. "Go down on his knees?"

Her father considered. "No—they don't do that now."

"What *do* they do?"

Mr. Prodmore carried his eyes with a certain sustained majesty to a remote point. "He will know himself."

"Oh, no, indeed, he won't," the girl cried; "they don't *ever*!"

"Then the sooner they learn—whoever teaches 'em!—the better: the better I mean in particular," Mr. Prodmore added with an intention discernibly vicious, "for the master of this house. I'll guarantee that he shall understand that," he concluded, "for I shall do my part."

She looked at him as if his part were really to be hated. "But how on earth, sir, can I ever do mine? To begin with, you know, I've never even seen him."

Mr. Prodmore took out his watch; then, having consulted it, put it back with a gesture that seemed to dispose at the same time and in the same manner of the objection. "You'll see him *now*—from one moment to the other. He's remarkably handsome, remarkably young, remarkably ambitious, and remarkably clever. He has one of the best and oldest names in this part of the country—a name that, far and wide here, one could do so much with that I'm simply indignant to see him do so little. I propose, my dear, to do with it all he hasn't, and I further propose, to that end, first to get hold of it. It's you, Miss Prodmore, who shall take it out of the fire."

"The fire?"—he had terrible figures.

"Out of the mud, if you prefer. You must pick it up, do you see? My plan is, in short," Mr. Prodmore pursued, "that when we've brushed it off and rubbed it down a bit, blown away the dust and touched up the rust, my daughter shall gracefully bear it."

She could only oppose, now, a stiff, thick transparency that yielded a view of the course in her own veins, after all, however, mingled with a feebler fluid, of the passionate blood of the Prodmores. "And pray is it also Captain Yule's plan?"

Her father's face warned her off the ground of irony, but he replied without violence. "His plans have not yet quite matured. But nothing is more natural," he added with an ominous smile, "than that they shall do so on the sunny south wall of Miss Prodmore's best manner."

Miss Prodmore's spirit was visibly rising, and a note that might have meant warning for warning sounded in the laugh produced by this sally. "You speak of them, papa, as if they were sour little plums! You exaggerate, I think, the warmth of Miss Prodmore's nature. It has always been thought remarkably cold."

"Then you'll be so good, my dear, as to confound—it mightn't be amiss even a little to scandalise—that opinion. I've spent twenty years in giving you what your poor mother used to call advantages, and they've cost me hundreds and hundreds of pounds. It's now time that, both as a parent and as a man of business, I should get my money back. I couldn't help your temper," Mr. Prodmore conceded, "nor your taste, nor even your unfortunate resemblance to the estimable, but far from ornamental, woman who brought you forth; but I paid out a small fortune that you should have, damn you, don't you know? a good manner. You never show it to me, certainly; but do you mean to tell me that, at this time of day—for other persons—you *haven't* got one?"

This pulled our young lady perceptibly up; there was a directness in the argument that was like the ache of old pinches. "If you mean by 'other persons' persons who are particularly civil—well, Captain Yule may not see his way to be one of them. He may not *think*—don't you see?—that I've a good manner."

"Do your duty, Miss, and never mind what he thinks!" Her father's conception of her duty momentarily sharpened. "Don't look at him like a sick turkey, and he'll be sure to think right."

The colour that sprang into Cora's face at this rude comparison was such, unfortunately, as perhaps a little to justify it. Yet she retained, in spite of her emotion, some remnant of presence of mind. "I remember your saying once, some time ago, that that was just what he would be sure *not* to do: I mean when he began to go in for his dreadful ideas——"

Mr. Prodmore took her boldly up. "About the 'radical programme,' the 'social revolution,' the spoliation of everyone, and the destruction of everything? Why, you stupid thing, I've worked round to a complete agreement with him. The taking from those who have by those who haven't——"

"Well?" said the girl, with some impatience, as he sought the right way of expressing his notion.

"What is it but to receive, from consenting hands, the principal treasure of the rich? If I'm rich, my daughter is my largest property, and I freely make her over. I shall, in other words, forgive my young friend his low opinions if he renounces them for *you*."

Cora, at this, started as with a glimpse of delight. "He won't renounce them! He *shan't!*"

Her father appeared still to enjoy the ingenious way he had put it, so that he had good humour to spare. "If you suggest that you're in political sympathy with him, you mean then that you'll take him as he *is?*"

"I won't take him at all!" she protested with her head very high; but she had no sooner uttered the words than the sound of the approach of wheels caused her dignity to drop. "A fly?—it must be *he!*" She turned right and left, for a retreat or an escape, but her father had already caught her by the wrist. "Surely," she pitifully panted, "you don't want me to bounce on him *thus?*"

138

Mr. Prodmore, as he held her, estimated the effect. "Your frock won't do—with what it cost me?"

"It's not my frock, papa,—it's his thinking I've come here for him to see me!"

He let her go and, as she moved away, had another look for the social value of the view of her stout back. It appeared to determine him, for, with a touch of mercy, he passed his word. "He doesn't think it, and he shan't know it."

The girl had made for the door of the morning-room, before reaching which she flirted breathlessly round. "But he knows you want me to hook him!"

Mr. Prodmore was already in the parliamentary attitude the occasion had suggested to him for the reception of his visitor. "The way to 'hook' him will be not to be hopelessly vulgar. He doesn't know that you know anything." The house-bell clinked, and he waved his companion away. "Await us there with tea, and mind you toe the mark!"

Chivers, at this moment, summoned by the bell, reappeared in the morning-room doorway, and Cora's dismay brushed him as he sidled past her and off into the passage to the front. Then, from the threshold of her refuge, she launched a last appeal. "Don't *kill* me, father: give me time!" With which she dashed into the room, closing the door with a bang.

II

MR. PRODMORE, in Chivers's absence, remained staring as if at a sudden image of something rather fine. His child had left with him the sense of a quick irradiation, and he failed to see why, at the worst, such lightnings as she was thus able to dart shouldn't strike somewhere. If he had spoken to her of her best manner perhaps *that* was her best manner. He heard steps and voices, however, and immediately invited to his aid his own, which was simply magnificent. Chivers, returning, announced solemnly "Captain Yule!" and ushered in a tall young man in a darkish tweed suit and a red necktie, attached in a sailor's knot, who, as he entered, removed a soft brown hat. Mr. Prodmore, at this, immediately saluted him by uncovering. "Delighted at last to see you here!"

It was the young man who first, in his comparative simplicity, put out a hand. "If I've not come before, Mr. Prodmore, it was—very frankly speaking—from the dread of seeing *you*!" His speech contradicted, to some extent, his gesture, but Clement Yule's was an aspect in which contradictions were rather remarkably at home. Erect and slender, but as strong as he was straight, he was set up, as the phrase is, like a soldier, and yet finished, in certain details—matters of expression and suggestion only indeed—like a man in whom sensibility had been recklessly cultivated. He was hard and fine, just as he was sharp and gentle, just as he was frank and shy, just as he was serious and young, just as he looked, though you could never have imitated it, distinctly "kept up" and yet considerably reduced. His features were thoroughly regular, but his complete shaving might have been designed to show that they were, after all, not absurd. The face Mr. Prodmore offered him fairly glowed, on this new showing, with instant pride of possession, and there was that in Captain Yule's whole air which justified such a sentiment without consciously rewarding it.

"Ah, surely," said the elder man, "my presence is not without a motive!"

"It's just the motive," Captain Yule returned, "that makes me wince at it! Certainly I've no illusions," he added, "about the ground of our meeting. Your thorough knowledge of what you're about has placed me at your mercy—you hold me in the hollow of your hand."

It was vivid in every inch that Mr. Prodmore's was a nature to expand in the warmth, or even in the chill, of any tribute to his financial subtlety. "Well, I won't, on my side, deny that when, in general, I go in deep I don't go in for nothing. I make it pay double!" he smiled.

"You make it pay so well—'double' surely doesn't do you justice!—that, if I've understood you, you can do quite as you like with this preposterous place. Haven't you brought me down exactly that I may *see* you do it?"

"I've certainly brought you down that you may open your eyes!" This, apparently, however, was not what Mr. Prodmore himself had arrived to do with his own. These fine points of expression literally contracted with intensity. "Of course, you know, you can always clear the property. You can pay off the mortgages."

Captain Yule, by this time, had, as he had not done at first, looked up and down, round about and well over the scene, taking in, though at a mere glance, it might have seemed, more particularly, the row, high up, of strenuous ancestors. But Mr. Prodmore's last words rang none the less on his ear, and he met them with mild amusement. "Pay off——? What can I pay off with?"

"You can always raise money."

"What can I raise it on?"

Mr. Prodmore looked massively gay. "On your great political future."

"Oh, I've not taken—for the short run at least—the lucrative line," the young man said, "and I know what you think of *that*."

Mr. Prodmore's blandness confessed, by its instant increase, to this impeachment. There was always the glory of intimacy in Yule's knowing what he thought. "I hold that you keep, in public, very dangerous company; but I also hold that you're extravagant mainly because you've nothing at stake. A man has the right opinions," he developed with pleasant confidence, "as soon as he has something to lose by having the wrong. Haven't I already hinted to you how to set your political house in order? You drop into the lower regions because you keep the best rooms empty. You're a firebrand, in other words my dear Captain, simply because you're a bachelor. That's one of the early complaints we all pass through, but it's soon over, and the treatment for it quite simple. I have your remedy."

141

The young man's eyes, wandering again about the house, might have been those of an auditor of the fiddling before the rise of the curtain. "A remedy worse than the disease?"

"There's nothing worse, that I've ever heard of," Mr. Prodmore sharply replied, "than your particular fix. Least of all a heap of gold———"

"A heap of gold?" His visitor idly settled, as if the curtain were going up.

Mr. Prodmore raised it bravely. "In the lap of a fine fresh lass! Give pledges to fortune, as somebody says—*then* we'll talk. You want money—that's what you want. Well, marry it!"

Clement Yule, for a little, never stirred, save that his eyes yet again strayed vaguely. At last they stopped with a smile. "Of course I could do that in a moment!"

"It's even just my own danger from you," his companion returned. "I perfectly recognise that any woman would now jump———"

"I don't like jumping women," Captain Yule threw in; "but that perhaps is a detail. It's more to the point that I've yet to see the woman whom, by an advance of my own———"

"You'd care to keep in the really attractive position———?"

"Which can never, of course, be anything"—Yule took his friend up again—"but that of waiting quietly."

"Never, never anything!" Mr. Prodmore, most assentingly, banished all other thought. "But I haven't asked you, you know, to make an advance."

"You've only asked me to receive one?"

Mr. Prodmore waited a little. "Well, I've asked you—I asked you a month ago—to think it all over."

"I *have* thought it all over," Clement Yule said; "and the strange sequel seems to be that my eyes have got accustomed to my darkness. I seem to make out, in the gloom of my meditations, that, at the worst, I can let the whole thing slide."

"The property?"—Mr. Prodmore jerked back as if it were about to start.

"Isn't it the property," his visitor inquired, "that positively throws me up? If I can afford neither to live on it nor to disencumber it, I can at least let it save its own bacon and pay its own debts. I can say to you simply: 'Take it, my dear sir, and the devil take *you!*'"

Mr. Prodmore gave a quick, strained smile. "You wouldn't be so shockingly rude!"

"Why not—if I'm a firebrand and a keeper of low company and a general nuisance? Sacrifice for sacrifice, that might very well be the least!"

This was put with such emphasis that Mr. Prodmore was for a moment arrested. He could stop very short, however, and yet talk as still going. "How do you know, if you haven't compared them? It's just to make the comparison—in all the proper circumstances—that you're here at this hour." He took, with a large, though vague, exhibitory gesture, a few turns about. "Now that you stretch yourself—for an hour's relaxation and rocked, as it were, by my friendly hand—in the ancient cradle of your race, can you seriously entertain the idea of parting with such a venerable family relic?"

It was evident that, as he decorously embraced the scene, the young man, in spite of this dissuasive tone, was entertaining ideas. It might have appeared at the moment to a spectator in whom fancy was at all alert that the place, becoming in a manner conscious of the question, felt itself on its honour, and that its honour could make no compromise. It met Clement Yule with no grimace of invitation, with no attenuation of its rich old sadness. It was as if the two hard spirits, the grim *genius loci* and the quick modern conscience, stood an instant confronted. "The cradle of my race bears, for me, Mr. Prodmore, a striking resemblance to its tomb." The sigh that dropped from him, however, was not quite void of tenderness. It might, for that matter, have been a long, sad creak, portending collapse, of some immemorial support of the Yules. "Heavens, how melancholy——!"

Mr. Prodmore, somewhat ambiguously, took up the sound. "Melancholy?"—he just balanced. That well might be, even a little *should* be—yet agreement might depreciate.

143

"Musty, mouldy;" then with a poke of his stick at a gap in the stuff with which an old chair was covered, "mangy!" Captain Yule responded. "Is this the character throughout?"

Mr. Prodmore fixed a minute the tell-tale tatter. "You must judge for yourself—you must go over the house." He hesitated again; then his indecision vanished—the right line was clear. "It does look a bit run down, but I'll tell you what I'll do. I'll do it up for you—neatly: I'll throw *that* in!"

His young friend turned on him an eye that, though markedly enlivened by his offer, was somehow only the more inscrutable. "Will you put in the electric light?"

Mr. Prodmore's own twinkle—at this touch of a spring he had not expected to work—was, on the other hand, temporarily veiled. "Well, if you'll meet me half-way! We're dealing here"—he backed up his gravity—"with fancy-values. Don't you feel," he appealed, "as you take it all in, a kind of a something-or-other down your back?"

Clement Yule gazed awhile at one of the pompous quarterings in the faded old glass that, in tones as of late autumn, crowned with armorial figures the top of the great hall-window; then with abruptness he turned away. "Perhaps I *don't* take it all in; but what I do feel is—since you mention it—a sort of stiffening of the spine! The whole thing is too queer—too cold—too cruel."

"Cruel?"—Mr. Prodmore's demur was virtuous.

"Like the face of some stuck-up distant relation who won't speak first. I see in the stare of the old dragon, I taste in his very breath, all the helpless mortality he has tucked away!"

"Lord, sir—you *have* fancies!" Mr. Prodmore was almost scandalised.

But the young man's fancies only multiplied as he moved, not at all critical, but altogether nervous, from object to object. "I don't know what's the matter—but there *is* more here than meets the eye." He tried as for his amusement or his relief to figure it out. "I miss the old presences. I feel the old absences. I hear the old voices. I see the old ghosts."

144

This last was a profession that offered some common ground. "The old ghosts, Captain Yule," his companion promptly replied, "are worth so much a dozen, and with no reduction, I must remind you—with the price indeed rather raised—for the quantity taken!" Feeling then apparently that he had cleared the air a little by this sally, Mr. Prodmore proceeded to pat his interlocutor on a back that he by no means wished to cause to be put to the wall. "Look about you, at any rate, a little more." He crossed with his toes well out the line that divides encouragement from patronage. "Do make yourself at home."

"Thank you very much, Mr. Prodmore. May I light a cigarette?" his visitor asked.

"In your own house, Captain?"

"That's just the question: it seems so much less my own house than before I had come into it!" The Captain offered Mr. Prodmore a cigarette which that gentleman, also taking a light from him, accepted; then he lit his own and began to smoke. "As I understand you," he went on, "you *lump* your two conditions? I mean I must accept both or neither?"

Mr. Prodmore threw back his shoulders with a high recognition of the long stride represented by this question. "You *will* accept both, for, by doing so, you'll clear the property at a stroke. The way I put it is—see?—that if you'll stand for Gossage, you'll get returned for Gossage."

"And if I get returned for Gossage, I shall marry your daughter. Accordingly," the young man pursued, "if I marry your daughter——"

"I'll burn up, before your eyes," said this young lady's proprietor, "every scratch of your pen. It will be a bonfire of signatures. There won't be a penny to pay—there'll only be a position to take. You'll take it with peculiar grace."

"Peculiar, Mr. Prodmore—very!"

The young man had assented more than he desired, but he was not deterred by it from completing the picture. "You'll settle down here in comfort and honour."

Clement Yule took several steps; the effect of his host was the reverse of soothing; yet the latter watched his irritation as if it were the working of a charm. "Are you very sure of the 'honour' if I turn my political coat?"

"You'll only be turning it back again to the way it was always worn. Gossage will receive you with open arms and press you to a heaving Tory bosom. That bosom"—Mr. Prodmore followed himself up—"has never heaved but to sound Conservative principles. The cradle, as I've called it,— or at least the rich, warm coverlet,—of your race, Gossage was the political property, so to speak, of generations of your family. Stand therefore in the good old interest and you'll stand like a lion."

"I'm afraid you mean," Captain Yule laughed, "that I must first roar like one."

"Oh, *I'll* do the roaring!"—and Mr. Prodmore shook his mane. "Leave that to me."

"Then why the deuce don't you stand yourself?"

Mr. Prodmore knew so familiarly why! "Because I'm not a remarkably handsome young man with the grand old home and the right old name. Because I'm a different sort of matter altogether. But if I haven't these advantages," he went on, "you'll do justice to my natural desire that my daughter at least shall have them."

Clement Yule watched himself smoke a minute. "Doing justice to natural desires is just what, of late, I've tried to make a study of. But I confess I don't quite grasp the deep attraction you appear to discover in so large a surrender of your interests."

"My surrenders are my own affair," Mr. Prodmore rang out, "and as for my interests, as I never, on principle, give anything for nothing, I dare say I may be trusted to know them when I see them. You come high—I don't for a moment deny it; but when I look at you, in this pleasant, intimate way, my dear boy—if you'll allow me so to describe things—I recognise one of those cases, unmistakeable when really met, in which one must put down

146

one's money. There's not an article in the whole shop, if you don't mind the comparison, that strikes me as better value. I intend you shall be, Captain," Mr. Prodmore wound up in a frank, bold burst, "the true comfort of my life!"

The young man was as hushed for a little as if an organ-tone were still in the air. "May I inquire," he at last returned, "if Miss Prodmore's ideas of comfort are as well defined—and in her case, I may add, as touchingly modest—as her father's? Is she a responsible party of this ingenious arrangement?"

Mr. Prodmore rendered homage—his appreciation was marked—to the elevated character of his young friend's scruple. "Miss Prodmore, Captain Yule, may be perhaps best described as a large smooth sheet of blank, though gilt-edged, paper. No image of any tie but the true and perfect filial has yet, I can answer for it, formed itself on the considerable expanse. But for that image to be projected——"

"I've only, in person, to appear?" Yule asked with an embarrassment that he tried to laugh off.

"And, naturally, in person," Mr. Prodmore intelligently assented, "do yourself, as well as the young lady, justice. Do you remember what you said when I first, in London, laid the matter before you?"

Clement Yule did remember, but his amusement increased. "I think I said it struck me I should first take a look at—what do you call it?—the *corpus delicti.*"

"You should first see for yourself what you had really come into? I was not only eager for that," said Mr. Prodmore, "but I'm willing to go further: I'm quite ready to hear you say that you think you should also first see the young lady."

Captain Yule continued to laugh. "There is something in that then, since you mention it!"

"I think you'll find that there's everything." Mr. Prodmore again looked at his watch. "Which will you take first?"

"First?"

"The young lady or the house?"

His companion, at this, unmistakeably started. "Do you mean your daughter's *here*?"

Mr. Prodmore glowed with consciousness. "In the morning-room."

"Waiting for me?"

The tone showed a consternation that Mr. Prodmore's was alert to soothe. "Ah, as long, you know, as you like!"

Yule's alarm, however, was not assuaged; it appeared to grow as he stared, much discomposed, yet sharply thinking, at the door to which his friend had pointed. "Oh, longer than *this*, please!" Then as he turned away: "Do you mean she knows——?"

"That she's here on view?" Mr. Prodmore hung fire a moment, but was equal to the occasion. "She knows nothing whatever. She's as unconscious as the rose on its stem!"

His companion was visibly relieved. "That's right—let her remain so! I'll first take the house," said Clement Yule.

"Shall I go round *with* you?" Mr. Prodmore asked.

The young man's reflection was brief. "Thank you. I'd rather, on the whole, go round alone."

The old servant who had admitted the gentlemen came back at this crisis from the morning-room, looking from under a bent brow and with much limpid earnestness from one of them to the other. The one he first addressed had evidently, though quite unaware of it, inspired him with a sympathy from which he now took a hint. "There's tea on, sir!" he persuasively jerked as he passed the younger man.

The elder answered. "Then I'll join my daughter." He gained the morning-room door, whence he repeated with an appropriate gesture—that of offering proudly, with light, firm fingers, a flower of his own celebrated raising—his happy formula of Miss Prodmore's state. "The rose on its stem!" Scattering petals, diffusing fragrance, he thus passed out.

Chivers, meanwhile, had rather pointlessly settled once more in its place some small object that had not strayed; to whom Clement Yule, absently watching him, abruptly broke out. "I say, my friend, what colour is the rose?"

The old man looked up with a dimness that presently glimmered. "The rose, sir?" He turned to the open door and the shining day. "Rather a brilliant——"

"A brilliant——?" Yule was interested.

"Kind of old-fashioned red." Chivers smiled with the pride of being thus able to testify, but the next instant his smile went out. "It's the only one left—on the old west wall."

His visitor's mirth, at this, quickly enough revived. "My dear fellow, I'm not alluding to the sole ornament of the garden, but to the young lady at present in the morning-room. Do you happen to have noticed if she's pretty?"

Chivers stood queerly rueful. "Laws, sir—it's a matter I mostly notice; but isn't it, at the same time, sir, a matter—like—of taste?"

"Pre-eminently. That's just why I appeal with such confidence to yours."

The old man acknowledged with a flush of real embarrassment a responsibility he had so little invited. "Well, sir,—mine was always a sort of fancy for something more merry-like."

"She isn't merry-like then, poor Miss Prodmore?" Captain Yule's attention, however, dropped before the answer came, and he turned off the subject with an "Ah, if you come to that, neither am I! But it doesn't signify," he went on. "What are *you*?" he more sociably demanded.

Chivers clearly had to think a bit. "Well, sir, I'm not quite *that*. Whatever has there been to make me, sir?" he asked in dim extenuation.

"How in the world do *I* know? I mean to whom do you belong?"

Chivers seemed to scan impartially the whole field. "If you could just only *tell* me, sir! I quite seem to waste away—for someone to take an order of."

Clement Yule, by this time, had become aware he was amusing. "Who pays your wages?"

"No one at all, sir," said the old man very simply.

His friend, fumbling an instant in a waistcoat pocket, produced something that his hand, in obedience to a little peremptory gesture and by a trick of which he had unlearned, through scant custom, the neatness, though the propriety was instinctive, placed itself in a shy practical relation to. "Then there's a sovereign. And I haven't many!" the young man, turning away resignedly, threw after it.

Chivers, for an instant, intensely studied him. "Ah, then, shouldn't it stay in the family?"

Clement Yule wheeled round, first struck, then, at the sight of the figure made by his companion in this offer, visibly touched. "I think it does, old boy."

Chivers kept his eyes on him now. "I've served your house, sir."

"How long?"

"All my life."

So, for a time, they faced each other, and something in Chivers made Yule at last speak. "Then I won't give *you* up!"

"Indeed, sir, I hope you won't give up anything."

The Captain took up his hat. "It remains to be seen." He looked over the place again; his eyes wandered to the open door. "Is that the garden?"

"It *was!*"—and the old man's sigh was like the creak of the wheel of time. "Shall I show you how it used to be?"

"It's just as it *is*, alas, that I happen to require it!" Captain Yule reached the door and stood looking beyond. "Don't come," he then said; "I want to think." With which he walked out.

Chivers, left alone, appeared to wonder at it, and his wonder, like that of most old people, lay near his lips. "What does he want, poor dear, to think about?" This speculation, however, was immediately checked by a high, clear voice that preceded the appearance on the stairs, before she had reached the middlemost landing, of the wonderful figure of a lady, a lady who, with the almost trumpeted cheer of her peremptory but friendly call—"Housekeeper, Butler, old Family Servant!"—fairly waked the sleeping echoes. Chivers gazed up at her in quick remembrance, half dismayed, half dazzled, of a duty neglected. She appeared now; she shone at him out of the upper dusk; reaching the middle, she had begun to descend, with beautiful laughter and rustling garments; and though she was alone she gave him the sense of coming in a crowd and with music. "Oh, I should have told him of *her!*"

III

SHE was indeed an apparition, a presence requiring announcement and explanation just in the degree in which it seemed to show itself in a relation quite of its own to all social preliminaries. It evidently either assumed them to be already over or wished to forestall them altogether; what was clear at any rate was that it allowed them scant existence. She was young, tall, radiant, lovely, and dressed in a manner determined at once, obviously, by the fact and by the humour of her journey—it might have proclaimed her so a pilgrim or so set her up as a priestess. Most journeys, for this lady, at all events, were clearly a brush of Paris. "Did you think I had got snapped down in an old box like that poor girl—what's her name? the one who was poking round too—in the celebrated poem? You dear, delightful man, why didn't you tell me?"

"Tell you, mum——?"

151

"Well, that you're so perfectly—perfect! You're ever so much better than anyone has ever said. Why, in the name of common sense, has nobody ever said *anything*? You're everything in the world you ought to be, and not the shade of a shade of anything you oughtn't!"

It was a higher character to be turned out with than poor Chivers had ever dreamed. "Well, mum, I try!" he gaped.

"Oh, no, you don't—that's just your charm! *I* try," cried his friend, "but you do nothing: here you simply *are*—you can't help it!"

He stood overwhelmed. "Me, mum?"

She took him in at the eyes—she could take everything at once. "Yes, you too, you positive old picture! I've seen the old masters—but you're the old master!"

"The master—I?" He fairly fell back.

"'The good and faithful servant'—Rembrandt van Rhyn: with three stars. *That's* what you are!" Nothing would have been more droll to a spectator than her manner of meeting his humbleness, or more charming indeed than the practical sweetness of her want of imagination of it. "The house is a vision of beauty, and you're simply worthy of the house. I can't say more for you!"

"I find it a bit of a strain, mum," Chivers candidly replied, "to keep up—fairly to call it—with what you *do* say."

"That's just what everyone finds it!"—she broke into the happiest laugh. "Yet I haven't come here to suffer in silence, you know—to suffer, I mean, from envy and despair." She was in constant movement, from side to side, observing, comparing, returning, taking notes while she gossiped and gossiping, too, for remembrance. The intention of remembrance even had in it, however, some prevision of failure or some alloy of irritation. "You're so fatally right and so deadly complete, all the same, that I can really scarcely bear it: with every fascinating feature that I had already heard of and thought I was prepared for, and ever so many others that, strange to say, I hadn't and wasn't, and that you just spring right *at* me like a series of things going off. What do you call it," she asked—"a royal salute, a hundred guns?"

152

Her enthusiasm had a bewildering form, but it had by this time warmed the air, and the old man rubbed his hands as over a fire to which the bellows had been applied. "I saw as soon as you arrived, mum, that you were looking for more things than ever *I* heard tell of!"

"Oh, I had got you by heart," she returned, "from books and drawings and photos; I had you in my pocket when I came: so, you see, as soon as you were so good as to give me my head and let me loose, I knew my way about. It's all here, every inch of it," she competently continued, "and now at last I can do what I want!"

A light of consternation, at this, just glimmered in Chivers's face. "And pray, mum, what might that be?"

"Why, take you right back with me—to Missoura Top."

This answer seemed to fix his bewilderment, but he was there for the general convenience.

"Do I understand you, mum, that you require to take *me*?"

Her particular convenience, on the spot, embraced him, so new and delightful a sense had he suddenly read into her words. "Do you mean to say you'd come—as the old Family Servant? Then *do*, you nice real thing: it's just what I'm dying for—an old Family Servant! You're somebody's else, yes—but everything, over here, is somebody's else, and I want, too, a first-rate second-hand one, all ready made, as you are, but not too much done up. You're the best I've seen yet, and I wish I could have you packed—put up in paper and bran—as I shall have my old pot there." She whisked about, remembering, recovering, eager: "Don't let me *forget* my precious pot!" Excited, with quick transitions, she quite sociably appealed to her companion, who shuffled sympathetically to where, out of harm, the object had been placed on a table. "Don't you just love old crockery? That's awfully sweet old Chelsea."

He took up the piece with tenderness, though, in his general agitation, not perhaps with all the caution with which, for daily service, he handled ancient frailties. He at any rate turned on this fresh subject an interested,

153

puzzled eye. "Where is it I've known this very bit—though not to say, as *you* do, by name?" Suddenly it came to him. "In the pew-opener's front parlour!"

"No," his interlocutress cried, "in the pew-opener's best bedroom: on the old chest of drawers, you know—with those ducks of brass handles. I've got the handles too—I mean the whole thing; and the brass fender and fire-irons, and the chair her grandmother died in. Not in the fly," she added—"it was such a bore that they have to be sent."

Chivers, with the pot still in his hands, fairly rocked in the high wind of so much confidence and such great transactions. He had nothing for these, however, but approval. "You did right to take this out, mum, when the fly went to the stables. Them flymen do be cruel rash with anything that's delicate." Of the delicacy of the vessel it now rested with him to deposit safely again he was by this time so appreciatively aware that in returning with it to its safe niche he stumbled into some obscure trap literally laid for him by his nervousness. It was the matter of a few seconds, of a false movement, a knock of the elbow, a gasp, a shriek, a complete little crash. There was the pot on the pavement, in several pieces, and the clumsy cup-bearer blue with fear. "Mercy *on* us, mum,—I've brought shame on my old grey hairs!"

The little shriek of his companion had smothered itself in the utterance, and the next minute, with the ruin between them, they were contrastedly face to face. The charming woman, who had already found more voices in the air than anyone had found before, could, in the happy play of this power, find a poetry in her accident. "Oh, but the way you *take* it!" she laughed—"you're too quaint to live!" She looked at him as if he alone had suffered—as if his suffering indeed positively added to his charm. "The way you said that now—it's just the very 'type'! That's all I want of you now—to *be* the very type. It's what you are, you poor dear thing—for you *can't* help it; and it's what everything and everyone else is, over here; so that you had just better all make up your minds to it and not try to shirk it. There was a type in the train with me—the 'awfully nice girl' of all the English novels, the 'simple maiden in her flower' of—who is it?—your great poet. *She* couldn't help it either—in fact I

154

wouldn't have *let* her!" With this, while Chivers picked up his fragments, his lady had a happy recall. His face, as he stood there with the shapeless elements of his humiliation fairly rattling again in his hands, was a reflection of her extraordinary manner of enlarging the subject, or rather, more beneficently perhaps, the space that contained it. "By the way, the girl was coming right here. Has she come?"

Chivers crept solemnly away, as if to bury his dead, which he consigned, with dumb rites, to a situation of honourable publicity; then, as he came back, he replied without elation: "Miss Prodmore is here, mum. She's having her tea."

This, for his friend, was a confirmatory touch to be fitted with eagerness into the picture. "Yes, that's exactly it—they're always having their tea!"

"With Mr. Prodmore—in the morning-room," the old man supplemented. "Captain Yule's in the garden."

"Captain Yule?"

"The new master. He's also just arrived."

The wonderful lady gave an immediate "Oh!" to the effect of which her silence for another moment seemed to add. "She didn't tell me about *him*."

"Well, mum," said Chivers, "it do be a strange thing to tell. He had never—like, mum—so much as seen the place."

"Before today—his very own?" This too, for the visitor, was an impression among impressions, and, like most of her others, it ended after an instant as a laugh. "Well, I hope he likes it!"

"I haven't seen many, mum," Chivers boldly declared, "that like it as much as *you*."

She made with her handsome head a motion that appeared to signify still deeper things than he had caught. Her beautiful wondering eyes played high and low, like the flight of an imprisoned swallow, then, as she sank upon a seat, dropped at last as if the creature were bruised with its limits. "I should like it still better if it were *my* very own!"

"Well, mum," Chivers sighed, "if it wasn't against my duty I could wish indeed it were! But the Captain, mum," he conscientiously added, "is the lawful heir."

It was a wonder what she found in whatever he said; he touched with every word the spring of her friendly joy. "That's another of your lovely old things—I adore your lawful heirs!" She appeared to have, about everything that came up, a general lucid vision that almost glorified the particular case. "He has come to take possession?"

Chivers accepted, for the credit of the house, this sustaining suggestion. "He's a-taking of it now."

This evoked, for his companion, an instantaneous show. "What does he do and how does he do it? Can't I *see*?" She was all impatience, but she dropped to disappointment as her guide looked blank. "There's no grand fuss——?"

"I scarce think him, mum," Chivers with propriety hastened to respond, "the gentleman to make any about anything."

She had to resign herself, but she smiled as she thought. "Well, perhaps I like them better when they don't!" She had clearly a great range of taste, and it all came out in the wistfulness with which, before the notice apparently served on her, she prepared to make way. "I also"—she lingered and sighed— "have taken possession!"

Poor Chivers really rose to her. "It was you, mum," he smiled, "took it first!"

She sadly shook her head. "Ah, but for a poor little hour! *He's* for life."

The old man gave up, after a little, with equal depression, the pretence of dealing with such realities. "For mine, mum, I do at least hope."

She made again the circuit of the great place, picking up without interest the jacket she had on her previous entrance laid down. "I shall think of you, you know, here together." She vaguely looked about her as for anything else to take; then abruptly, with her eyes again on Chivers: "Do you suppose he'll be kind to you?"

His hand, in his trousers-pocket, seemed to turn the matter over. "He has already been, mum."

"Then be sure to be so to *him*!" she replied with some emphasis. The house-bell sounded as she spoke, giving her quickly another thought. "Is that his bell?"

Chivers was hardly less struck. "I must see whose!"—and hurrying, on this, to the front, he presently again vanished.

His companion, left alone, stood a minute with an air in which happy possession was oddly and charmingly mingled with desperate surrender; so much as to have left you in doubt if the next of her lively motions were curiosity or disgust. Impressed, in her divided state, with a small framed plaque of enamel, she impulsively detached it from the wall and examined it with hungry tenderness. Her hovering thought was so vivid that you might almost have traced it in sound. "Why, bless me if it isn't Limoges! I wish awfully I were a *bad* woman: then, I do devoutly hope, I'd just quietly take it!" It testified to the force of this temptation that on hearing a sound behind her she started like a guilty thing; recovering herself, however, and—just, of course, not to appear at fault—keeping the object familiarly in her hand as she jumped to a recognition of the gentleman who, coming in from the garden, had stopped in the open doorway. She gathered indeed from his being there a positive advantage, the full confidence of which was already in her charming tone. "Oh, Captain Yule, I'm delighted to meet you! It's such a comfort to ask you if I *may*!"

His surprise kept him an instant dumb, but the effort not too closely to betray it appeared in his persuasive inflection. "If you 'may,' madam——?"

"Why, just *be* here, don't you know? and poke round!" She presented such a course as almost vulgarly natural. "Don't tell me I can't now, because I already *have*: I've been upstairs and downstairs and in my lady's chamber—I won't answer for it even perhaps that I've not been in my lord's! I got round your lovely servant—if you don't look out I'll grab him. If you don't look out, you know, I'll grab everything." She gave fair notice and went on with amazing serenity; she gathered positive gaiety from his frank stupefaction. "That's what I came over for—just to lay your country waste. Your house is a wild old dream; and besides"—she dropped, oddly and quaintly, into real responsible judgment—"you've got some quite good things. Oh, yes, you *have*—several: don't coyly pretend you haven't!" Her familiarity took these flying leaps, and she alighted, as her victim must have phrased it to himself, without turning a hair. "Don't you *know* you have? Just look at that!" She thrust her enamel before him, but he took it and held it so blankly, with an attention so absorbed in the mere woman, that at the sight of his manner her zeal for his interest and her pity for his detachment again flashed out. "Don't you know *anything*? Why, it's Limoges!"

Clement Yule simply broke into a laugh—though his laugh indeed was comprehensive. "It seems absurd, but I'm not in the least acquainted with my house. I've never happened to see it."

She seized his arm. "Then do let me show it to you!"

"I shall be delighted." His laughter had redoubled in a way that spoke of his previous tension; yet his tone, as he saw Chivers return breathless from the front, showed that he had responded sincerely enough to desire a clear field. "Who in the world's there?"

The old man was full of it. "A party!"

"A party?"

Chivers confessed to the worst. "Over from Gossage—to see the house."

The worst, however, clearly, was quite good enough for their companion, who embraced the incident with sudden enthusiasm. "Oh, let *me* show it!" But before either of the men could reply she had, addressing herself to Chivers, one of those droll drops that betrayed the quickness of her wit and the freedom of her fancy. "Dear me, I forgot—*you* get the tips! But, you dear old creature," she went on, "I'll get them, too, and I'll simply make them over to you." She again pressed Yule—pressed him into this service. "Perhaps they'll be bigger—for me!"

He continued to be highly amused. "I should think they'd be enormous—for you! But I *should* like," he added with more concentration—"I should like extremely, you know, to go over with you alone."

She was held a moment. "Just you and me?"

"Just you and me—as you kindly proposed."

She stood reminded; but, throwing it off, she had her first inconsequence. "That must be for after——!"

"Ah, but not too late." He looked at his watch. "I go back tonight."

"Laws, sir!" Chivers irrepressibly groaned.

"You want to keep him?" the stranger asked. Captain Yule turned away at the question, but her look went after him, and she found herself, somehow, instantly answered. "Then I'll help you," she said to Chivers; "and the oftener we go over the better."

Something further, on this, quite immaterial, but quite adequate, passed, while the young man's back was turned, between the two others; in consequence of which Chivers again appealed to his master. "Shall I show them straight in, sir?"

His master, still detached, replied without looking at him. "By all means—if there's money in it!" This was jocose, but there would have been, for an observer, an increase of hope in the old man's departing step. The lady had exerted an influence.

She continued, for that matter, with a start of genial remembrance, to exert one in his absence. "Oh, and I promised to show it to Miss Prodmore!" Her conscience, with a kind smile for the young person she named, put the question to Clement Yule. "Won't you call her?"

The coldness of his quick response made it practically none. "'Call' her? Dear lady, I don't *know* her!"

"You must, then—she's wonderful." The face with which he met this drew from the dear lady a sharper look; but, for the aid of her good-nature, Cora Prodmore, at the moment she spoke, presented herself in the doorway of the morning-room. "See? She's charming!" The girl, with a glare of recognition, dashed across the open as if under heavy fire; but heavy fire, alas—the extremity of exposure—was promptly embodied in her friend's public embrace. "Miss Prodmore," said this terrible friend, "let me present Captain Yule." Never had so great a gulf been bridged in so free a span. "Captain Yule, Miss Prodmore. Miss Prodmore, Captain Yule."

There was stiffness, the cold mask of terror, in such notice as either party took of this demonstration, the convenience of which was not enhanced for the divided pair by the perception that Mr. Prodmore had now followed his daughter. Cora threw herself confusedly into it indeed, as with a vain rebound into the open. "Papa, let me 'present' you to Mrs. Gracedew. Mrs. Gracedew, Mr. Prodmore. Mr. Prodmore, Mrs. Gracedew."

Mrs. Gracedew, with a free salute and a distinct repetition, took in Mr. Prodmore as she had taken everything else. "Mr. Prodmore"—oh, she pronounced him, spared him nothing of himself. "So happy to meet your daughter's father. Your daughter's so perfect a specimen."

Mr. Prodmore, for the first moment, had simply looked large and at sea; then, like a practical man and without more question, had quickly seized the long perch held out to him in this statement. "So perfect a specimen, yes!" he seemed to pass it on to his young friend.

Mrs. Gracedew, if she observed his emphasis, drew from it no deterrence; she only continued to cover Cora with a gaze that kept her well in the middle. "So fresh, so quaint, so droll!"

It was apparently a result of what had passed in the morning-room that Mr. Prodmore had grasped afresh the need for effective action, which he clearly felt he did something to meet in clutching precipitately the helping hand popped so suddenly out of space, yet so beautifully gloved and so pressingly and gracefully brandished. "So fresh, so quaint, so droll!"—he again gave Captain Yule the advantage of the stranger's impression.

To what further appreciation this might have prompted the lady herself was not, however, just then manifest; for the return of Chivers had been almost simultaneous with the advance of the Prodmores, and it had taken place with forms that made it something of a circumstance. There was positive pomp in the way he preceded several persons of both sexes, not tourists at large, but simple sightseers of the half-holiday order, plain provincial folk already, on the spot, rather awestruck. The old man, with suppressed pulls and prayers, had drawn them up in a broken line, and the habit of more peopled years, the dull drone of the dead lesson, sounded out in his prompt beginning. The party stood close, in this manner, on one side of the apartment, while the master of the house and his little circle were grouped on the other. But as Chivers, guiding his squad, reached the centre of the space, Mrs. Gracedew, markedly moved, quite unreservedly engaged, came slowly forward to meet him. "This, ladies and gentlemen," he mechanically quavered, "is perhaps the most important feature—the grand old feudal, baronial 'all. Being, from all accounts, the most ancient portion of the edifice, it was erected in the very earliest ages." He paused a moment, to mark his effect, then gave a little cough which had become, obviously, in these great reaches of time, an essential part of the trick. "Some do say," he dispassionately remarked, "in the course of the fifteenth century."

Mrs. Gracedew, who had visibly thrown herself into the working of the charm, following him with vivid sympathy and hanging on his lips, took the liberty, at this, of quite affectionately pouncing on him. "*I* say in the fourteenth, my dear—you're robbing us of a hundred years!"

Her victim yielded without a struggle. "I do seem, in them dark old centuries, sometimes to trip a little." Yet the interruption of his ancient order distinctly discomposed him, all the more that his audience, gaping with a sense of the importance of the fine point, moved in its mass a little nearer. Thus put upon his honour, he endeavoured to address the group with a dignity

161

undiminished. "The Gothic roof is much admired, but the west gallery is a modern addition."

His discriminations had the note of culture, but his candour, all too promptly, struck Mrs. Gracedew as excessive. "What in the name of Methuselah do you call 'modern'? It was here at the visit of James the First, in 1611, and is supposed to have served, in the charming detail of its ornament, as a model for several that were constructed in his reign. The great fireplace," she handsomely conceded, "*is* Jacobean."

She had taken him up with such wondrous benignant authority—as if, for her life, if they *were* to have it, she couldn't help taking care that they had it out; she had interposed with an assurance that so converted her—as by the wave of a great wand, the motion of one of her own free arms—from mere passive alien to domesticated dragon, that poor Chivers could only assent with grateful obeisances. She so plunged into the old book that he had quite lost his place. The two gentlemen and the young lady, moreover, were held there by the magic of her manner. His own, as he turned again to his cluster of sightseers, took refuge in its last refinement. "The tapestry on the left Italian—the elegant wood-work Flemish."

Mrs. Gracedew was upon him again. "Excuse me if I just deprecate a misconception. The elegant wood-work Italian—the tapestry on the left Flemish." Suddenly she put it to him before them all, pleading as familiarly and gaily as she had done when alone with him, and looking now at the others, all round, gentry and poor folk alike, for sympathy and support. She had an idea that made her dance. "Do you really mind if *I* just do it? Oh, I know how: I can do quite beautifully the housekeeper last week at Castle Gaunt." She fraternised with the company as if it were a game they must play with her, though this first stage sufficiently hushed them. "How do you do? Ain't it thrilling?" Then with a laugh as free as if, for a disguise, she had thrown her handkerchief over her head or made an apron of her tucked-up skirt, she passed to the grand manner. "Keep well together, please—we're not doing puss-in-the-corner. I've my duty to all parties—I can't be partial to one!"

The contingent from Gossage had, after all, like most contingents, its spokesman—a very erect little personage in a very new suit and a very green necktie, with a very long face and upstanding hair. It was on an evident sense of having been practically selected for encouragement that he, in turn, made choice of a question which drew all eyes. "How many parties, now, can you manage?"

Mrs. Gracedew was superbly definite. "Two. The party up and the party down." Chivers gasped at the way she dealt with this liberty, and his impression was conspicuously deepened as she pointed to one of the escutcheons in the high hall-window. "Observe in the centre compartment the family arms." She did take his breath away, for before he knew it she had crossed with the lightest but surest of gestures to the black old portrait, on the opposite wall, of a long-limbed gentleman in white trunk-hose. "And observe the family legs!" Her method was wholly her own, irregular and broad; she flew, familiarly, from the pavement to the roof and then dropped from the roof to the pavement as if the whole air of the place were an element in which she floated. "Observe the suit of armour worn at Tewkesbury—observe the tattered banner carried at Blenheim." They bobbed their heads wherever she pointed, but it would have come home to any spectator that they saw her alone. This was the case quite as much with the opposite trio—the case especially with Clement Yule, who indeed made no pretence of keeping up with her signs. It was the signs themselves he looked at—not at the subjects indicated. But he never took his eyes from her, and it was as if, at last, she had been peculiarly affected by a glimpse of his attention. All her own, for a moment, frankly went back to him and was immediately determined by it. "Observe, above all, that you're in one of the most interesting old houses, of its type, in England; for which the ages have been tender and the generations wise: letting it change so slowly that there's always more left than taken—living their lives in it, but letting it shape their lives!"

Though this pretty speech had been unmistakeably addressed to the younger of the temporary occupants of Covering End, it was the elder who, on the spot, took it up. "A most striking and appropriate tribute to a real historical monument!" Mr. Prodmore had a natural ease that could deal

163

handsomely with compliments, and he manifestly, moreover, like a clever man, saw even more in such an explosion of them than fully met the ear. "You do, madam, bring the whole thing out!"

The visitor who had already with such impunity ventured had, on this, a loud renewal of boldness, but for the benefit of a near neighbour. "Doesn't she indeed, Jane, bring it out?"

Mrs. Gracedew, with a friendly laugh, caught the words in their passage. "But who in the world wants to keep it *in*? It isn't a secret—it isn't a strange cat or a political party!" The housekeeper, as she talked, had already dropped from her; her sense of the place was too fresh for control, though instead of half an hour it might have taken six months to become so fond. She soared again, at random, to the noble spring of the roof. "Just look at those lovely lines!" They all looked, all but Clement Yule, and several of the larger company, subdued, overwhelmed, nudged each other with strange sounds. Wherever she turned Mrs. Gracedew appeared to find a pretext for breaking out. "Just look at the tone of that glass, and the gilding of that leather, and the cutting of that oak, and the dear old flags of the very floor." It came back, came back easily, her impulse to appeal to the lawful heir, and she seemed, with her smile of universal intelligence, just to demand the charity of another moment for it. "To look, in this place, is to love!"

A voice from the party she had in hand took it up with an artless guffaw that resounded more than had doubtless been meant and that, at any rate, was evidently the accompaniment of some private pinch applied to one of the ladies. "I *say*—to love!"

It was one of the ladies who very properly replied. "It depends on who you look at!"

Mr. Prodmore, in the geniality of the hour, made his profit of the simple joke. "Do you hear *that*, Captain? You must look at the right person!"

Mrs. Gracedew certainly had not been looking at the wrong one. "I don't think Captain Yule cares. He doesn't do justice——!"

Though her face was still gay, she had faltered, which seemed to strike the young man even more than if she had gone on. "To what, madam?"

Well, on the chance she let him have it. "To the value of your house."

He took it beautifully. "I like to hear *you* express it!"

"I *can't* express it!" She once more looked all round, and so much more gravely than she had yet done that she might have appeared in trouble. She tried but, with a sigh, broke down. "It's too inexpressible!"

This was a view of the case to which Mr. Prodmore, for his own reasons, was not prepared to assent. Expression and formulation were what he naturally most desired, and he had just encountered a fountain of these things that he couldn't prematurely suffer to fail him. "Do what you can for it, madam. It would bring it quite home."

Thus excited, she gave with sudden sombre clearness another try. "Well—the value's a fancy value!"

Mr. Prodmore, receiving it as more than he could have hoped, turned triumphant to his young friend. "Exactly what I told you!"

Mrs. Gracedew explained indeed as if Mr. Prodmore's triumph was not perhaps exactly what she had argued for. Still, the truth was too great. "When a thing's unique, it's unique!"

That was every bit Mr. Prodmore required. "It's unique!"

This met, moreover, the perception of the gentleman in the green necktie. "It's unique!" They all, in fact, demonstratively—almost vociferously now—caught the point.

Mrs. Gracedew, finding herself so sustained, and still with her eyes on the lawful heirs, put it yet more strongly. "It's worth anything you like."

What was this but precisely what Mr. Prodmore had always striven to prove? "Anything you like!" he richly reverberated.

The pleasant discussion and the general interest seemed to bring them all together. "Twenty thousand now?" one of the gentlemen from Gossage archly inquired—a very young gentleman with an almost coaxing voice, who blushed immensely as soon as he had spoken.

He blushed still more at the way Mrs. Gracedew faced him. "I wouldn't *look* at twenty thousand!"

Mr. Prodmore, on the other hand, was proportionately uplifted. "She wouldn't look at twenty thousand!" he announced with intensity to the Captain.

The visitor who had been the first to speak gave a shrewder guess. "Thirty, then, as it stands?"

Mrs. Gracedew looked more and more responsible; she communed afresh with the place; but she too evidently had her conscience. "It would be giving it away!"

Mr. Prodmore, at this, could scarcely contain himself. "It would be giving it away!"

The second speaker had meanwhile conceived the design of showing that, though still crimson, he was not ashamed. "You'd hold out for forty——?"

Mrs. Gracedew required a minute to answer—a very marked minute during which the whole place, pale old portraits and lurking old echoes and all, might have made you feel how much depended on her; to the degree that the consciousness in her face became finally a reason for her not turning it to Gossage. "Fifty thousand, Captain Yule, is what I think I should propose."

If the place had seemed to listen it might have been the place that, in admiring accents from the gentleman with the green tie, took up the prodigious figure. "Fifty thousand pound!"

It was echoed in a high note from the lady he had previously addressed. "Fifty thousand!"

Yet it was Mr. Prodmore who caught it up loudest and appeared to make it go furthest. "Fifty thousand—fifty thousand!" Mrs. Gracedew had put him in such spirits that he found on the spot, indicating to her his young friend, both the proper humour and the proper rigour for any question of what anyone might "propose." "He'll never part with the dear old home!"

Mrs. Gracedew could match at least the confidence. "Then I'll go over it again while I have the chance." Her own humour enjoined that she should drop into the housekeeper, in the perfect tone of which character she addressed herself once more to the party. "We now pass to the grand staircase." She gathered her band with a brave gesture, but before she had fairly impelled them to the ascent she heard herself rather sharply challenged by Captain Yule, who, during the previous scene, had uttered no sound, yet had remained as attentive as he was impenetrable. "Please let them pass without you!"

She was taken by surprise. "And stay here with *you*?"

"If you'll be so good. I want to speak to you." Turning then to Chivers and frowning on the party, he delivered himself for the first time as a person in a position. "For God's sake, remove them!"

The old man, at this blast of impatience, instantly fluttered forward. "We now pass to the grand staircase."

They all passed, Chivers covering their scattered ascent as a shepherd scales a hillside with his flock; but it became evident during the manœuvre that Cora Prodmore was quite out of tune. She had been standing beyond and rather behind Captain Yule; but she now moved quickly round and reached her new friend's right. "Mrs. Gracedew, may *I* speak to you?"

Her father, before the reply could come, had taken up the place. "*After* Captain Yule, my dear." He was in a state of positively polished lucidity. "You must make the most—don't you see?—of the opportunity of the others!"

He waved her to the staircase as one who knew what he was about, but, while the young man, turning his back, moved consciously and nervously away, the girl renewed her effort to provoke Mrs. Gracedew to detain her. It happened, to her sorrow, that this lady appeared for the moment, to the detriment of any free attention, to be absorbed in Captain Yule's manner; so that Cora could scarce disengage her without some air of invidious reference to it. Recognising as much, she could only for two seconds, but with great yearning, parry her own antagonist. "She'll *help* me, I think, papa!"

"That's exactly what strikes me, love!" he cheerfully replied. "But *I'll* help you too!" He gave her, toward the stairs, a push proportioned both to his authority and to her weight; and while she reluctantly climbed in the wake of the visitors, he laid on Mrs. Gracedew's arm, with a portentous glance at Captain Yule, a hand of commanding significance. "Just pile it on!"

Her attention came back—she seemed to see. "He doesn't like it?"

"Not half enough. Bring him round."

Her eyes rested again on their companion, who had fidgeted further away and who now, with his hands in his pockets and unaware of this private passage, stood again in the open doorway and gazed into the grey court. Something in the sight determined her. "I'll bring him round."

But at this moment Cora, pausing half-way up, sent down another entreaty. "Mrs. Gracedew, will you see *me*?"

The charming woman looked at her watch. "In ten minutes," she smiled back.

Mr. Prodmore, bland and assured, looked at his own. "You could put him through in five—but I'll allow you twenty. There!" he decisively cried to his daughter, whom he quickly rejoined and hustled on her course. Mrs. Gracedew kissed after her a hand of vague comfort.

IV

THE silence that reigned between the pair might have been registered as embarrassing had it lasted a trifle longer. Yule had continued to turn his back, but he faced about, though he was distinctly grave, in time to avert an awkwardness. "How do you come to know so much about my house?"

She was as distinctly not grave. "How do *you* come to know so little?"

"It's not my fault," he said very gently. "A particular combination of misfortunes has forbidden me, till this hour, to come within a mile of it."

These words evidently struck her as so exactly the right ones to proceed from the lawful heir that such a felicity of misery could only quicken her interest. He was plainly as good in his way as the old butler—the particular combination of misfortunes corresponded to the lifelong service. Her interest, none the less, in its turn, could only quicken her pity, and all her emotions, we have already seen, found prompt enough expression. What could any expression do indeed now but mark the romantic reality? "Why, you poor thing!"—she came toward him on the weary road. "Now that you've got here I hope at least you'll stay." Their intercourse must pitch itself—so far as she was concerned—in some key that would make up for things. "Do make yourself comfortable. Don't mind me."

Yule looked a shade less serious. "That's exactly what I wanted to say to *you*!"

She was struck with the way it came in. "Well, if you *had* been haughty, I shouldn't have been quite crushed, should I?"

The young man's gravity, at this, completely yielded. "I'm never haughty—oh, no!"

She seemed even more amused. "Fortunately then, as *I'm* never crushed. I don't think," she added, "that I'm really as crushable as you."

The smile with which he received this failed to conceal completely that it was something of a home thrust. "Aren't we really *all* crushable—by the right thing?"

She considered a little. "Don't you mean rather by the wrong?"

He had got, clearly, a trifle more accustomed to her being extraordinary. "Are you sure we always know them apart?"

169

She weighed the responsibility. "I always do. Don't you?"

"Not quite every time!"

"Oh," she replied, "I don't think, thank goodness, we have positively 'every time' to distinguish."

"Yet we must always act," he objected.

She turned this over; then with her wonderful living look, "I'm glad to hear it," she exclaimed, "because, I fear, I always *do*! You'll certainly think," she added with more gravity, "that I've taken a line today!"

"Do you mean that of mistress of the house? Yes—you do seem in possession!"

"*You* don't!" she honestly answered; after which, as to attenuate a little the rigour of the charge: "You don't comfortably look it, I mean. You don't look"—she was very serious—"as I want you to."

It was when she was most serious that she was funniest. "How do you 'want' me to look?"

She endeavoured, while he watched her, to make up her mind, but seemed only, after an instant, to recognise a difficulty. "When you look at *me*, you're all right!" she sighed. It was an obstacle to her lesson, and she cast her eyes about. "Look at that chimneypiece."

"Well——?" he inquired as his eyes came back from it.

"You mean to say it isn't lovely?"

He returned to it without passion—gave a vivid sign of mere disability. "I'm sure I don't know. I don't mean to say anything. I'm a rank outsider."

It had an instant effect on her—she almost pounced upon him. "Then you must let me put you up!"

"Up to what?"

170

"Up to everything!"—his levity added to her earnestness. "You were smoking when you came in," she said as she glanced about. "Where's your cigarette?"

The young man appreciatively produced another. "I thought perhaps I mightn't—here."

"You may everywhere."

He bent his head to the information. "Everywhere."

She laughed at his docility, yet could only wish to presume upon it. "It's a rule of the house!"

He took in the place with greater pleasure. "What delightful rules!"

"How could such a house have any others?"—she was already launched again in her brave relation to it. "I *may* go up just once more—mayn't I—to the long gallery?"

How could he tell? "The long gallery?"

With an added glow she remembered. "I forgot you've never seen it. Why, it's the leading thing about you!" She was full, on the spot, of the pride of showing it. "Come right up!"

Clement Yule, half seated on a table from which his long left leg nervously swung, only looked at her and smiled and smoked. "There's a party up."

She remembered afresh. "So *we* must be the party down? Well, you must give me a chance. That long gallery's the principal thing I came over for."

She was strangest of all when she explained. "Where in heaven's name did you come over from?"

"Missoura Top, where I'm building—just in this style. I came for plans and ideas," Mrs. Gracedew serenely pursued. "I felt I must look right *at* you."

"But what did you know about us?"

She kept it a moment as if it were too good to give him all at once. "Everything!"

He seemed indeed almost afraid to touch it. "At 'Missoura Top'?"

"Why not? It's a growing place—forty thousand the last census." She hesitated; then as if her warrant should be slightly more personal: "My husband left it to me."

The young man presently changed his posture. "You're a widow?"

Nothing was wanting to the simplicity of her quiet assent. "A very lone woman." Her face, for a moment, had the vision of a long distance. "My loneliness is great enough to want something big to hold it—and my taste good enough to want something beautiful. You see, I had your picture."

Yule's innocence made a movement. "Mine?"

Her smile reassured him; she nodded toward the main entrance. "A water colour I chanced on in Boston."

"In Boston?"

She stared. "Haven't you heard of Boston either?"

"Yes—but what has Boston heard of *me*?"

"It wasn't 'you,' unfortunately—it was your divine south front. The drawing struck me so that I got you up—in the books."

He appeared, however, rather comically, but half to make it out, or to gather at any rate that there was even more of it than he feared. "Are we in the books?"

"Did you never discover it?" Before his blankness, the dim apprehension in his fine amused and troubled face of how much there was of it, her frank, gay concern for him sprang again to the front. "Where in heaven's name, Captain Yule, have *you* come over from?"

He looked at her very kindly, but as if scarce expecting her to follow. "The East End of London."

172

She had followed perfectly, he saw the next instant, but she had by no means equally accepted. "What were you doing there?"

He could only put it, though a little over-consciously, very simply. "Working, you see. When I left the army—it was much too slow, unless one was personally a whirlwind of war—I began to make out that, for a fighting man——"

"There's always," she took him up, "somebody or other to go for?"

He considered her, while he smoked, with more confidence; as if she might after all understand. "The enemy, yes—everywhere in force. I went for *him*: misery and ignorance and vice—injustice and privilege and wrong. Such as you see me——"

"You're a rabid reformer?"—she understood beautifully. "I wish we had you at Missoura Top!"

He literally, for a moment, in the light of her beauty and familiarity, appeared to measure his possible use there; then, looking round him again, announced with a sigh that, predicament for predicament, his own would do. "I fear my work is nearer home. I hope," he continued, "since you're so good as to seem to care, to perform a part of that work in the next House of Commons. My electors have wanted me——"

"And you've wanted *them*," she lucidly put in, "and that has been why you couldn't come down."

"Yes, for all this last time. And before that, from my childhood up, there was another reason." He took a few steps away and brought it out as rather a shabby one. "A family feud."

She proved to be quite delighted with it. "Oh, I'm so glad—I *hoped* I'd strike a 'feud'! That rounds it off, and spices it up, and, for the heartbreak with which I take leave of you, just neatly completes the fracture!" Her reference to her going seemed suddenly, on this, to bring her back to a sense of proportion and propriety, and she glanced about once more for some wrap or reticule. This, in turn, however, was another recall. "Must I really wait—to go up?"

He had watched her movement, had changed colour, had shifted his place, had tossed away, plainly unwitting, a cigarette but half smoked; and now he stood in her path to the staircase as if, still unsatisfied, he abruptly sought a way to turn the tables. "Only till you tell me this: if you absolutely meant, awhile ago, that this old thing is so precious."

She met his doubt with amazement and his density with compassion. "Do you literally need I should *say* it? Can you stand here and not feel it?" If he had the misfortune of bandaged eyes, she could at least rejoice in her own vision, which grew intenser with her having to speak for it. She spoke as with a new rush of her impression. "It's a place to love——" Yet to say the whole thing was not easy.

"To love——?" he impatiently insisted.

"Well, as you'd love a person!" If that was saying the whole thing, saying the whole thing could only be to go. A sound from the "party up" came down at that moment, and she took it so clearly as a call that, for a sign of separation, she passed straight to the stairs. "Good-bye!"

The young man let her reach the foot, but then, though the greatest width of the hall now divided them, spoke, anxiously and nervously, as if the point she had just made brought them still more together. "I think I 'feel' it, you know; but it's simply you—your presence, as I may say, and the remarkable way you put it—that make me. I'm afraid that in your absence——" He struck a match to smoke again.

It gave her time apparently to make out something to pause for. "In my absence?"

He lit his cigarette. "I may come back——"

"Come back?" she took him almost sharply up. "I should like to see you *not*!"

He smoked a moment. "I mean to my old idea——"

She had quite turned round on him now. "Your old idea——?"

He faced her over the width still between them. "Well—that one *could* give it up."

Her stare, at this, fairly filled the space. "Give up Covering? How in the world—or why?"

"Because I can't afford to keep it."

It brought her straight back, but only half-way: she pulled up short as at a flash. "Can't you let it?"

Again he smoked before answering. "Let it to *you?*"

She gave a laugh, and her laugh brought her nearer. "I'd take it in a minute!"

Clement Yule remained grave. "I shouldn't have the face to charge you a rent that would make it worth one's while, and I think even you, dear lady"—his voice just trembled as he risked that address—"wouldn't have the face to offer me one." He paused, but something in his aspect and manner checked in her now any impulse to read his meaning too soon. "My lovely inheritance is Dead Sea fruit. It's mortgaged for all it's worth and I haven't the means to pay the interest. If by a miracle I could scrape the money together, it would leave me without a penny to live on." He puffed his cigarette profusely. "So if I find the old home at last—I lose it by the same luck!"

Mrs. Gracedew had hung upon his words, and she seemed still to wait, in visible horror, for something that would improve on them. But when she had to take them for his last, "I never heard of anything so awful!" she broke out. "Do you mean to say you can't arrange——?"

"Oh, yes," he promptly replied, "an arrangement—if that be the name to give it—has been definitely proposed to me."

"What's the matter, then?"—she had dropped into relief. "For heaven's sake, you poor thing, definitely accept it!"

He laughed, though with little joy, at her sweet simplifications. "I've made up my mind in the last quarter of an hour that I can't. It's such a peculiar case."

Mrs. Gracedew frankly wondered; her bias was clearly sceptical. "*How* peculiar——?"

He found the measure difficult to give. "Well—more peculiar than most cases."

Still she was not satisfied. "More peculiar than mine?"

"Than yours?"—Clement Yule knew nothing about that.

Something, at this, in his tone, his face—it might have been his "British" density—seemed to pull her up. "I forgot—you don't know mine. No matter. What *is* yours?"

He took a few steps in thought. "Well, the fact that I'm asked to change."

"To change what?"

He wondered how he could put it; then at last, on his own side, simplified. "My attitude."

"Is that all?"—she was relieved again. "Well, you're not a statue."

"No, I'm not a statue; but on the other hand, don't you see? I'm not a windmill." There was good-humour, none the less, in his rigour. "The mortgages I speak of have all found their way, like gregarious silly sheep, into the hands of one person—a devouring wolf, a very rich, a very sharp man of money. He holds me in this manner at his mercy. He consents to make things comfortable for me, but he requires that, in return, I shall do something for him that—don't you know?—rather sticks in my crop."

It appeared on this light showing to stick for a moment even in Mrs. Gracedew's. "Do you mean something wrong?"

He had not a moment's hesitation. "Exceedingly so!"

She turned it over as if pricing a Greek Aldus. "Anything immoral?"

"Yes—I may literally call it immoral."

She courted, however, frankly enough, the strict truth. "Too bad to tell?"

He indulged in another pensive fidget, then left her to judge. "He wants me to give up——" Yet again he faltered.

"To give up what?" What could it be, she appeared to ask, that was barely nameable?

He quite blushed to her indeed as he came to the point. "My fundamental views."

She was disappointed—she had waited for more. "Nothing but *them*?"

He met her with astonishment. "Surely they're quite enough, when one has unfortunately"—he rather ruefully smiled—"so very many!"

She laughed aloud; this was frankly so odd a plea. "Well, *I've* a neat collection too, but I'd 'swap,' as they say in the West, the whole set——!" She looked about the hall for something of equivalent price; after which she pointed, as it caught her eye, to the great cave of the fireplace. "I'd take *that* set!"

The young man scarcely followed. "The fire-irons?"

"For the whole fundamental lot!" She gazed with real yearning at the antique group. "*They're* three hundred years old. Do you mean to tell me your wretched 'views'——?"

"Have anything like that age? No, thank God," Clement Yule laughed, "my views—wretched as you please!—are quite in their prime! They're a hungry little family that has got to be fed. They keep me awake at night."

"Then you must make up your sleep!" Her impatience grew with her interest. "Listen to *me*!"

"That would scarce be the way!" he returned. But he added more sincerely: "You must surely see a fellow can't chuck his politics."

"'Chuck' them——?"

"Well—sacrifice them."

"I'd sacrifice mine," she cried, "for that old fire-back with your arms!" He glanced at the object in question, but with such a want of intelligence that she visibly resented it. "See how it has stood!"

"See how *I've* stood!" he answered with spirit. "I've glowed with a hotter fire than anything in any chimney, and the warmth and light I diffuse have attracted no little attention. How can I consent to reduce them to the state of that desolate hearth?"

His companion, freshly struck with the fine details of the desolation, had walked over to the chimney-corner, where, lost in her deeper impression, she lingered and observed. At last she turned away with her impatience controlled. "It's magnificent!"

"The fire-back?"

"Everything—everywhere. I don't understand your haggling."

He hesitated. "That's because you're ignorant." Then seeing in the light of her eye that he had applied to her the word in the language she least liked, he hastened to attenuate. "I mean of what's behind my reserves."

She was silent in a way that made their talk more of a discussion than if she had spoken. "What *is* behind them?" she presently asked.

"Why, my whole political history. Everything I've said, everything I've done. My scorching addresses and letters, reproduced in all the papers. I needn't go into details, but I'm a pure, passionate, pledged Radical."

Mrs. Gracedew looked him full in the face. "Well, what if you *are?*"

He broke into mirth at her tone. "Simply this—that I can't therefore, from one day to the other, pop up at Gossage in the purple pomp of the opposite camp. There's a want of transition. It may be timid of me—it may be abject. But I can't."

If she was not yet prepared to contest she was still less prepared to surrender it, and she confined herself for the instant to smoothing down with her foot the corner of an old rug. "Have you thought very much about it?"

He was vague. "About what?"

"About what Mr. Prodmore wants you to do."

He flushed up. "Oh, then, you know it's *he*?"

"I'm not," she said, still gravely enough, "of an intelligence absolutely infantile."

"You're the cleverest Tory I've ever met!" he laughed. "I didn't mean to mention my friend's name, but since *you've* done so——!" He gave up with a shrug his scruple.

Oh, she had already cleared the ground of it! "It's he who's the devouring wolf? It's he who holds your mortgages?"

The very lucidity of her interest just checked his assent. "He holds plenty of others, and he treats me very handsomely."

She showed of a sudden an inconsequent face. "Do you call *that* handsome—such a condition?"

He shed surprise. "Why, I thought it was just the condition you could meet."

She measured her inconsistency, but was not abashed. "We're not talking of what *I* can meet." Yet she found also a relief in dropping the point. "Why doesn't he stand himself?"

"Well, like other devouring wolves, he's not personally adored."

"Not even," she asked, "when he offers such liberal terms?"

Clement Yule had to explain. "I dare say he doesn't offer them to everyone."

"Only to you?"—at this she quite sprang. "You *are* personally adored; you will be still more if you stand; and that, you poor lamb, is why he wants you!"

The young man, obviously pleased to find her after all more at one with him, accepted gracefully enough the burden her sympathy imposed. "I'm the bearer of my name, I'm the representative of my family; and to my family and my name—since you've led me to it—this countryside has been for generations indulgently attached."

She listened to him with a sentiment in her face that showed how now, at last, she felt herself deal with the lawful heir. She seemed to perceive it with a kind of passion. "You do of course what you will with the countryside!"

"Yes"—he went with her—"if we do it as genuine Yules. I'm obliged of course to grant you that your genuine Yule's a Tory of Tories. It's Mr. Prodmore's belief that I should carry Gossage in that character, but in that character only. They won't look at me in any other."

It might have taxed a spectator to say in what character Mrs. Gracedew, on this, for a little, considered him. "Don't be too sure of people's not looking at you!"

He blushed again, but he laughed. "We must leave out my personal beauty."

"We can't!" she replied with decision. "Don't we take in Mr. Prodmore's?"

Captain Yule was not prepared. "You call him beautiful?"

"Hideous." She settled it; then pursued her investigation. "What's the extraordinary interest that he attaches——?"

"To the return of a Tory?" Here the young man *was* prepared. "Oh, his desire is born of his fear—his terror on behalf of Property, which he sees, somehow, with an intensely Personal, with a quite colossal 'P.' He has a great deal of that article, and very little of anything else."

Mrs. Gracedew, accepting provisionally his demonstration, had one of her friendly recalls. "Do you call that nice daughter 'very little'?"

The young man looked quite at a loss. "Is she very big? I really didn't notice her—and moreover she's just a part of the Property. He thinks things are going too far."

180

She sat straight down on a stiff chair; on which, with high distinctness: "Well, they *are*!"

He stood before her in the discomposure of her again thus appearing to fail him. "Aren't you then a lover of justice?"

"A passionate one!" She sat there as upright as if she held the scales. "Where's the justice of your losing this house?" Generous as well as strenuous, all her fairness thrown out by her dark old high-backed seat, she put it to him as from the judicial bench. "To keep Covering, you must carry Gossage!"

The odd face he made at it might have betrayed a man dazzled. "As a renegade?"

"As a genuine Yule. What business have you to be anything else?" She had already arranged it all. "You must close with Mr. Prodmore—you must stand in the Tory interest." She hung fire a moment; then as she got up: "If you will, I'll conduct your canvass!"

He stared at the distracting picture. "That puts the temptation high!"

But she brushed the mere picture away. "Ah, don't look at me as if *I* were the temptation! Look at this sweet old human home, and feel all its gathered memories. Do you want to know what they do to me?" She took the survey herself again, as if to be really sure. "They speak to me for Mr. Prodmore."

He followed with a systematic docility the direction of her eyes, but as if with the result only of its again coming home to him that there was no accounting for what things might do. "Well, there are others than these, you know," he good-naturedly pleaded—"things for which I've spoken, repeatedly and loudly, to others than you." The very manner of his speaking on such occasions appeared, for that matter, now to come back to him. "One's 'human home' is all very well, but the rest of one's humanity is better!" She gave, at this, a droll soft wail; she turned impatiently away. "I see you're disgusted with me, and I'm sorry; but one must take one's self as circumstances and experience have made one, and it's not my fault, don't you know? if they've made me a very modern man. I see something else in the world than the beauty of old show-houses and the glory of old show-families. There are thousands of people in England who can show no houses at all, and I don't feel it utterly shameful to share their poor fate!"

She had moved away with impatience, and it was the advantage of this for her that the back she turned prevented him from seeing how intently she listened. She seemed to continue to listen even after he had stopped; but if that gave him a sense of success, he might have been checked by the way she at last turned round with a sad and beautiful headshake. "We share the poor fate of humanity whatever we do, and we do something to help and console when we've something precious to show. What on earth is more precious than what the ages have slowly wrought? They've trusted us, in such a case, to keep it—to do something, in our turn, for *them*." She shone out at him as if her contention had the evidence of the noonday sun, and yet in her generosity she superabounded and explained. "It's such a virtue, in anything, to have lasted; it's such an honour, for anything, to have been spared. To all strugglers from the wreck of time hold out a pitying hand!"

Yule, on this argument,—of a strain which even a good experience of debate could scarce have prepared him to meet,—had not a congruous rejoinder absolutely pat, and his hesitation unfortunately gave him time to see how soon his companion made out that what had touched him most in it was her particular air in presenting it. She would manifestly have preferred he should have been floored by her mere moral reach; yet he was aware that his own made no great show as he took refuge in general pleasantry. "What a plea for looking backward, dear lady, to come from Missoura Top!"

"We're making a Past at Missoura Top as fast as ever we can, and I should like to see you lay your hand on an hour of the one we've made! It's a tight fit, as yet, I grant," she said, "and that's just why I like, in yours, to find room, don't you see? to turn round. You're *in* it, over here, and you can't get out; so just make the best of that and treat the thing as part of the fun!"

"The whole of the fun, to me," the young man replied, "is in hearing you defend it! It's like your defending hereditary gout or chronic rheumatism and sore throat—the things I feel aching in every old bone of these walls and groaning in every old draught that, I'm sure, has for centuries blown through them."

Mrs. Gracedew looked as if no woman could be shaken who was so prepared to be just all round. "If there be aches—there may be—you're here to soothe them, and if there be draughts—there *must* be!—you're here to stop them up. And do you know what *I'm* here for? If I've come so far and so straight, I've almost wondered myself. I've felt with a kind of passion—but now I see *why* I've felt." She moved about the hall with the excitement of this perception, and, separated from him at last by a distance across which he followed her discovery with a visible suspense, she brought out the news. "I'm here for an act of salvation—I'm here to avert a sacrifice!"

So they stood a little, with more, for the minute, passing between them than either really could say. She might have flung down a glove that he decided on the whole, passing his hand over his head as the seat of some confusion, not to pick up. Again, but flushed as well as smiling, he sought the easiest cover. "You're here, I think, madam, to be a memory for all my future!"

Well, she was willing, she showed as she came nearer, to take it, at the worst, for that. "You'll be one for mine, if I can see you by that hearth. Why do you make such a fuss about changing your politics? If you'd come to Missoura Top, you'd change them quick enough!" Then, as she saw further and struck harder, her eyes grew deep, her face even seemed to pale, and she paused, splendid and serious, with the force of her plea. "What do politics amount to, compared with religions? Parties and programmes come and go, but a duty like this abides. There's nothing you can break with"—she pressed him closer, ringing out—"that would be like breaking *here*. The very words are violent and ugly—as much a sacrilege as if you had been trusted with the key of the temple. This *is* the temple—don't profane it! Keep up the old altar kindly—you can't set up a new one as good. You *must* have beauty in your life, don't you see?—that's the only way to make sure of it for the lives of others. Keep leaving it to *them*, to all the poor others," she went on with her bright irony, "and heaven only knows what will become of it! Does it take one of *us* to feel that?—to preach you the truth? Then it's good, Captain Yule, we come right over—just to see, you know, what you may happen to be about. We know," she went on while her sense of proportion seemed to play into her sense of humour, "what we haven't got, worse luck; so that if you've happily got it you've got it also for *us*. You've got it in trust, you see, and oh! we have an eye on you. You've had it so for me, all these dear days that I've been drinking it in, that, to be grateful, I've wanted regularly to *do* something." With which, as if in the rich confidence of having convinced him, she came so near as almost to touch him. "Tell me now I shall have done it—I shall have kept you at your post!"

If he moved, on this, immediately further, it was with the oddest air of seeking rather to study her remarks at his ease than to express an independence of them. He kept, to this end, his face averted—he was so completely now in intelligent possession of her own. The sacrifice in question carried him even to the door of the court, where he once more stood so long engaged that the persistent presentation of his back might at last have suggested either a confession or a request.

Mrs. Gracedew, meanwhile, a little spent with her sincerity, seated herself again in the great chair, and if she sought, visibly enough, to read a meaning into his movement, she had as little triumph for one possible view of it as she had resentment for the other. The possibility that he yielded left her after all as vague in respect to a next step as the possibility that he merely wished to get rid of her. The moments elapsed without her abdicating; and indeed when he finally turned round his expression was an equal check to any power to feel she might have won. "You have," he queerly smiled at her, "a standpoint quite your own and a style of eloquence that the few scraps of parliamentary training I've picked up don't seem at all to fit me to deal with. Of course I don't pretend, you know, that I don't *care* for Covering."

That, at all events, she could be glad to hear, if only perhaps for the tone in it that was so almost comically ingenuous. But her relief was reasonable and her exultation temperate. "You haven't even seen it yet." She risked, however, a laugh. "Aren't you a bit afraid?"

He took a minute to reply, then replied—as if to make it up—with a grand collapse. "Yes; awfully. But if I am," he hastened in decency to add, "it isn't only Covering that makes me."

This left his friend apparently at a loss. "What else is it?"

"Everything. But it doesn't in the least matter," he loosely pursued. "You may be quite correct. When we talk of the house your voice comes to me somehow as the wind in its old chimneys."

Her amusement distinctly revived. "I hope you don't mean I roar!"

He blushed again; there was no doubt he was confused. "No—nor yet perhaps that you whistle! I don't believe the wind does either, here. It only whispers," he sought gracefully to explain; "and it sighs——"

"And I hope," she broke in, "that it sometimes laughs!"

The sound she gave only made him, as he looked at her, more serious. "Whatever it does, it's all right."

"All right?"—they were sufficiently together again for her to lay her hand straight on his arm. "Then you promise?"

"Promise what?"

He had turned as pale as if she hurt him, and she took her hand away. "To meet Mr. Prodmore."

"Oh, dear, no; not yet!"—he quite recovered himself. "I must wait—I must think."

She looked disappointed, and there was a momentary silence. "When have you to answer him?"

"Oh, he gives me time!" Clement Yule spoke very much as he might have said, "Oh, in two minutes!"

"*I* wouldn't give you time," Mrs. Gracedew cried with force—"I'd give you a shaking! For God's sake, at any rate"—and she really tried to push him off—"go upstairs!"

"And literally *find* the dreadful man?" This was so little his personal idea that, distinctly dodging her pressure, he had already reached the safe quarter.

But it befell that at the same moment she saw Cora reappear on the upper landing—a circumstance that promised her a still better conclusion. "He's coming down!"

Cora, in spite of this announcement, came down boldly enough without him and made directly for Mrs. Gracedew, to whom her eyes had attached themselves with an undeviating glare. Her plain purpose of treating this lady as an isolated presence allowed their companion perfect freedom to consider her arrival with sharp alarm. His disconcerted stare seemed for a moment to balance; it wandered, gave a wild glance at the open door, then searched the ascent of the staircase, in which, apparently, it now found a coercion. "I'll go up!" he gasped; and he took three steps at a time.

V

THE girl threw herself, in her flushed eagerness, straight upon the wonderful lady. "I've come back to you—I want to speak to you!" The need had been a rapid growth, but it was clearly immense. "May I confide in you?"

Her instant overflow left Mrs. Gracedew both astonished and amused. "You too?" she laughed. "Why it *is* good we come over!"

"It is, indeed!" Cora gratefully echoed. "You were so very kind to me and seemed to think me so curious."

The mirth of her friend redoubled. "Well, I loved you for it, and it was nothing moreover to what you thought *me!*"

Miss Prodmore found, for this, no denial—she only presented her frank high colour. "I loved *you*. But I'm the worst!" she generously added. "And I'm solitary."

186

"Ah, so am I!" Mrs. Gracedew declared with gaiety, but with emphasis. "A *very* queer thing always *is* solitary! But, since we have that link, by all means confide."

"Well, I was met here by tremendous news." Cora produced it with a purple glow. "He wants me to marry him!"

Mrs. Gracedew looked amiably receptive, but as if she failed as yet to follow. "'He' wants you?"

"Papa, of course. He has settled it!"

Mrs. Gracedew was still vague. "Settled what?"

"Why, the whole question. That I must take him."

Mrs. Gracedew seemed to frown at her own scattered wits. "But, my dear, take *whom?*"

The girl looked surprised at this lapse of her powers. "Why, Captain Yule, who just went up."

"Oh!" said Mrs. Gracedew with a full stare. "Oh!" she repeated, looking straight away.

"I thought you would know," Cora gently explained.

Her friend's eyes, with a kinder light now, came back to her. "I didn't know." Mrs. Gracedew looked, in truth, as if that had been sufficiently odd, and seemed also to wonder at two or three things more. It all, however, broke quickly into a question. "Has Captain Yule asked you?"

"No, but he *will*"—Cora was clear as a bell. "He'll do it to keep the house. It's mortgaged to papa, and Captain Yule buys it back."

Her friend had an illumination that was rapid for the way it spread. "By marrying you?" she quavered.

Cora, under further parental instruction, had plainly mastered the subject. "By giving me his name and his position. They're awfully great, and they're the price, don't you see?" she modestly mentioned. "*My* price. Papa's price. Papa wants them."

Mrs. Gracedew had caught hold; yet there were places where her grasp was weak, and she had, strikingly, begun again to reflect. "But his name and his position, great as they may be, are his dreadful politics!"

Cora threw herself with energy into this advance. "You *know* about his dreadful politics? He's to change them," she recited, "to get *me*. And if he gets me——"

"He keeps the house?"—Mrs. Gracedew snatched it up.

Cora continued to show her schooling. "I go *with* it—he's to have us both. But only," she admonishingly added, "if he changes. The question is—*will* he change?"

Mrs. Gracedew appeared profoundly to entertain it. "I see. *Will* he change?"

Cora's consideration of it went even further. "*Has* he changed?"

It went—and the effect was odd—a little too far for her companion, in whom, just discernibly, it had touched the spring of impatience. "My dear child, how in the world should *I* know?"

But Cora knew exactly how anyone would know. "He hasn't seemed to care enough for the house. *Does* he care?"

Mrs. Gracedew moved away, passed over to the fireplace, and stood a moment looking at the old armorial fire-back she had praised to its master—yet not, it must be added, as if she particularly saw it. Then as she faced about: "You had better ask him!"

They stood thus confronted, with the fine old interval between them, and the girl's air was for a moment that of considering such a course. "If he does care," she said at last, "he'll propose."

Mrs. Gracedew, from where she stood in relation to the stairs, saw at this point the subject of their colloquy restored to view: Captain Yule was just upon them—he had turned the upper landing. The sight of him forced from her in a flash an ejaculation that she tried, however, to keep private—"He does care!" She passed swiftly, before he reached them, back to the girl and, in a quick whisper, but with full conviction, let her have it: "He'll propose!"

Her movement had made her friend aware, and the young man, hurrying down, was now in the hall. Cora, at his hurry, looked dismay—"Then I fly!" With which, casting about for a direction, she reached the door to the court.

Captain Yule, however, at this result of his return, expressed instant regret. "I drive Miss Prodmore away!"

Mrs. Gracedew, more quickly still, eased off the situation. "It's all right!" She had embraced both parties with a smile, but it was most liberal now for Cora. "Do you mind, one moment?"—it conveyed, unmistakeably, a full intelligence and a fine explanation. "I've something to say to Captain Yule."

Cora stood in the doorway, robust against the garden-light, and looking from one to the other. "Yes—but I've also something more to say to *you*."

"Do you mean now?" the young man asked.

It was the first time he had spoken to her, and her hesitation might have signified a maidenly flutter. "No—but before she goes."

Mrs. Gracedew took it amiably up. "Come back, then; I'm not going." And there was both dismissal and encouragement in the way that, as on the occasion of the girl's former retreat, she blew her a familiar kiss. Cora, still with her face to them, waited just enough to show that she took it without a response; then, with a quick turn, dashed out, while Mrs. Gracedew looked at their visitor in vague surprise. "What's the matter with her?"

She had turned away as soon as she spoke, moving as far from him as she had moved a few moments before from Cora. The silence that, as he watched her, followed her question would have been seen by a spectator to be a hard one for either to break. "I don't know what's the matter with her," he said at

189

last; "I'm afraid I only know what's the matter with *me*. It will doubtless give you pleasure to learn," he added, "that I've closed with Mr. Prodmore."

It was a speech that, strangely enough, seemed but half to dissipate the hush. Mrs. Gracedew reached the great chimney again; again she stood there with her face averted; and when she finally replied it was in other words than he might have supposed himself naturally to inspire. "I thought you said he gave you time."

"Yes; but you produced just now so deep an effect on me that I thought best not to take any." He appeared to listen to a sound from above, and, for a moment, under this impulse, his eyes travelled about almost as if he were alone. Then he completed, with deliberation, his statement. "I came upon him right there, and I burnt my ships."

Mrs. Gracedew continued not to meet his face. "You do what he requires?"

The young man was markedly, consciously caught. "I do what he requires. I felt the tremendous force of all you said to me."

She turned round on him now, as if perhaps with a slight sharpness, the face of responsibility—even, it might be, of reproach. "So did I—or I shouldn't have said it!"

It was doubtless this element of justification in her tone that drew from him a laugh a tiny trifle dry. "You're perhaps not aware that you wield an influence of which it's not too much to say——"

But he paused at the important point so long that she took him up. "To say what?"

"Well, that it's practically irresistible!"

It sounded a little as if it had not been what he first meant; but it made her, none the less, still graver and just faintly ironical. "You've given me the most flattering proof of my influence that I've ever enjoyed in my life!"

190

He fixed her very hard, now distinctly so mystified that he could only wonder what different recall of her previous attitude she would have looked for. "This was inevitable, dear madam, from the moment you had converted me—and in about three minutes too!—into the absolute echo of your raptures."

Nothing was, indeed, more extraordinary than her air of having suddenly forgotten them. "My 'raptures'?"

He was amazed. "Why, about my home."

He might look her through and through, but she had no eyes for himself, though she had now quitted the fireplace and finally recognised this allusion. "Oh, yes—your home!" From where had she come back to it? "It's a nice tattered, battered old thing." This account of it was the more shrunken that her observation, even as she spoke, freshly went the rounds. "It has defects of course"—with this renewed attention they appeared suddenly to strike her. They had popped out, conspicuous, and for a little it might have been a matter of conscience. However, her conscience dropped. "But it's no use mentioning them now!"

They had half an hour earlier been vividly present to himself, but to see her thus oddly pulled up by them was to forget on the spot the ground he had taken. "I'm particularly sorry," he returned with some spirit, "that you didn't mention them before!"

At this imputation of inconsequence, of a levity not, after all, without its excuse, Mrs. Gracedew was reduced, in keeping her resentment down, to an effort not quite successfully disguised. It was in a tone, nevertheless, all the more mild in intention that she reminded him of where he had equally failed. "If you had really gone over the house, as I almost went on my knees to you to do, you might have discovered some of them yourself!"

"How can you say that," the young man asked with heat, "when I was precisely in the very act of it? It was just *because* I was that the first person I met above was Mr. Prodmore; on which, feeling that I must come to it sooner or later, I simply gave in to him on the spot—yielded him, to have it well over, the whole of his point."

She listened to this account of the matter as she might have gazed, from afar, at some queer object that was scarce distinguishable. It left her a moment in the deepest thought, but she presently recovered her tone. "Let me then congratulate you on at last knowing what you want!"

But there were, after all, he instantly showed, no such great reasons for that. "I only know it so far as *you* know it! I struck while the iron was hot—or at any rate while the hammer was."

"Of course I recognise"—she adopted his image with her restored gaiety—"that it can rarely have been exposed to such a fire. I blazed up, and I know that when I burn——"

She had pulled up with the foolish sense of this. "When you burn?"

"Well, I do it as Chicago does."

He also could laugh out now. "Isn't that usually down to the ground?"

Meeting his laugh, she threw up her light arms. "As high as the sky!" Then she came back, as with a scruple, to the real question. "I suppose you've still formalities to go through."

"With Mr. Prodmore?" Well, he would suppose it too if she liked. "Oh, endless, tiresome ones, no doubt!"

This sketch of them made her wonder. "You mean they'll take so very, very long?"

He seemed after all to know perfectly what he meant. "Every hour, every month, that I can possibly make them last!"

She was with him here, however, but to a certain point. "You mustn't drag them out *too* much—must you? Won't he think in that case you may want to retract?"

Yule apparently tried to focus Mr. Prodmore under this delusion, and with a success that had a quick, odd result. "I shouldn't be so terribly upset by his mistake, you know, even if he did!"

His manner, with its slight bravado, left her proportionately shocked. "Oh, it would never do to give him any colour whatever for supposing you to have any doubt that, as one may say, you've pledged your honour."

He devoted to this proposition more thought than its simplicity would have seemed to demand; but after a minute, at all events, his intelligence triumphed. "Of course not—not when I *haven't* any doubt!"

Though his intelligence had triumphed, she still wished to show she was there to support it. "How can you *possibly* have any—any more than you can possibly have that one's honour is everything in life?" And her charming eyes expressed to him her need to feel that he was quite at one with her on *that* point.

He could give her every assurance. "Oh, yes—everything in life!"

It did her much good, brought back the rest of her brightness. "Wasn't it just of the question of the honour of things that we talked awhile ago—and of the difficulty of sometimes keeping our sense of it clear? There's no more to be said therefore," she went on with the faintest soft sigh about it, "except that I leave you to your ancient glory as I leave you to your strict duty." She had these things there before her; they might have been a well-spread board from which she turned away fasting. "I hope you'll do justice to dear old Covering in spite of its weak points, and I hope above all you'll not be incommoded——"

As she hesitated here he was too intent. "Incommoded——?"

She saw it better than she could express it. "Well, by such a rage——!"

He challenged this description with a strange gleam. "You suppose it will be a rage?"

She laughed out at his look. "Are you afraid of the love that kills?"

He grew singularly grave. "*Will* it kill——?"

"Great passions *have*!"—she was highly amused.

But he could only stare. "Is it a great passion?"

"Surely—when so many feel it!"

He was fairly bewildered. "But how many——?"

She reckoned them up. "Let's see. If you count them all——"

"'All'?" Clement Yule gasped.

She looked at him, in turn, slightly mystified. "I see. You knock off some. About half?"

It was too obscure—he broke down. "Whom on earth are you talking about?"

"Why, the electors——"

"Of Gossage?"—he leaped at it. "Oh!"

"I got the whole thing up—there are six thousand. It's such a fine figure!" said Mrs. Gracedew.

He had sharply passed from her, to cover his mistake, and it carried him half round the hall. Then, as if aware that this pause itself compromised him, he came back confusedly and with her last words in his ear. "*Has* she a fine figure?"

But her own thoughts were off. "'She'?"

He blushed and recovered himself. "Aren't we talking——"

"Of Gossage? Oh, yes—she has every charm! Good-bye," said Mrs. Gracedew.

He pulled, at this, the longest face, but was kept dumb a moment by the very decision with which she again began to gather herself. It held him helpless, and there was finally real despair in his retarded protest. "You don't mean to say you're going?"

"You don't mean to say you're surprised at it? Haven't I done," she luminously asked, "what I told you I had been so mystically moved to come for?" She recalled to him by her renewed supreme survey the limited character of this errand, which she then in a brisk familiar word expressed to the house itself. "You dear old thing—you're saved!"

Clement Yule might on the other hand, by his simultaneous action, have given himself out for lost. "For God's sake," he cried as he circled earnestly round her, "don't go till I can come back to thank you!" He pulled out his watch. "I promised to return immediately to Prodmore."

This completely settled his visitor. "Then don't let me, for a moment more, keep you away from him. You must have such lots"—it went almost without saying—"to talk comfortably over."

The young man's embrace of that was, in his restless movement, to roam to the end of the hall furthest from the stairs. But here his assent was entire. "I certainly feel, you know, that I must see him again." He rambled even to the open door and looked with incoherence into the court. "Yes, decidedly, I *must!*"

"Is he out there?" Mrs. Gracedew lightly asked.

He turned short round. "No—I left him in the long gallery."

"You *saw* that, then?"—she flashed back into eagerness. "Isn't it lovely?"

Clement Yule rather wondered. "I didn't notice it. How *could* I?"

His face was so woeful that she broke into a laugh. "How *couldn't* you? Notice it now, then. Go up to him!"

He crossed at last to the staircase, but at the foot he stopped again. "Will you wait for me?"

He had such an air of proposing a bargain, of making the wait a condition, that she had to look it well in the face. The result of her doing so, however, was apparently a strong sense that she could give him no pledge. Her silence, after a moment, expressed that; but, for a further emphasis, moving away, she

195

sank suddenly into the chair she had already occupied and in which, serious again and very upright, she continued to withhold her promise. "Go up to him!" she simply repeated. He obeyed, with an abrupt turn, mounting briskly enough several steps, but pausing midway and looking back at her as if he were after all irresolute. He was in fact so much so that, at the sight of her still in her chair and alone by his cold hearth, he descended a few steps again and seemed, with too much decidedly on his mind, on the point of breaking out. She had sat a minute in such thought, figuring him clearly as gone, that at the sound of his return she sprang up with a protest. This checked him afresh, and he remained where he had paused, still on the ascent and exchanging with her a look to which neither party was inspired, oddly enough, to contribute a word. It struck him, without words, at all events, as enough, and he now took his upward course at such a pace that he presently disappeared. She listened awhile to his retreating tread; then her own, on the old flags of the hall, became rapid, though, it may perhaps be added, directed to no visible end. It conveyed her, in the great space, from point to point, but she now for the first time moved there without attention and without joy, her course determined by a series of such inward throbs as might have been the suppressed beats of a speech. A real observer, had such a monster been present, would have followed this tacit evolution from sign to sign and from shade to shade. "Why didn't he tell me *all*?—But it was none of my business!—What does he mean to do?—What should he do but what he *has* done?—And what *can* he do, when he's so deeply committed, when he's practically engaged, when he's just the same as married—and buried?—The thing for *me* to 'do' is just to pull up short and bundle out: to remove from the scene they encumber the numerous fragments—well, of what?"

Her thought was plainly arrested by the sight of Cora Prodmore, who, returning from the garden, reappeared first in the court and then in the open doorway. Mrs. Gracedew's was a thought, however, that, even when desperate, was never quite vanquished, and it found a presentable public solution in the pieces of the vase smashed by Chivers and just then, on the table where he had laid them, catching her eye. "Of my old Chelsea pot!" Her gay, sad headshake as she took one of them up pronounced for Cora's benefit its funeral oration. She laid the morsel thoughtfully down, while her visitor seemed with simple dismay to read the story.

VI

"Has he been *breaking*——?" the girl asked in horror.

Mrs. Gracedew laughingly tapped her heart. "Yes, we've had a scene! He went up again to your father."

Cora was disconcerted. "Papa's not there. He just came down to me by the other way."

"Then he can join you here," said Mrs. Gracedew with instant resignation. "I'm going."

"Just when I've come back to you—at the risk," Cora made bold to throw off, "of again interrupting, though I really hoped he had gone, your conversation with Captain Yule?"

But Mrs. Gracedew let the ball quite drop. "I've nothing to say to Captain Yule."

Cora picked it up for another toss. "You had a good deal to say a few minutes ago!"

"Well, I've said it, and it's over. I've nothing more to say at all," Mrs. Gracedew insisted. But her announcement of departure left her on this occasion, as each of its predecessors had done, with a last, with indeed a fresh, solicitude. "What has become of my delightful 'party'?"

"They've been dismissed, through the grounds, by the other door. But they mentioned," the girl pursued, "the probable arrival of a fresh lot."

Mrs. Gracedew showed on this such a revival of interest as fairly amounted to yearning. "Why, what times you have! *You*," she nevertheless promptly decreed, "must take the fresh lot—since the house is now practically yours!"

Poor Cora looked blank. "Mine?"

Her companion matched her stare. "Why, if you're going to marry Captain Yule."

Cora coloured, in a flash, to the eyes. "I'm *not* going to marry Captain Yule!"

Her friend as quickly paled again. "Why on earth then did you tell me only ten minutes ago that you were?"

Cora could only look bewildered at the charge. "I told you nothing of the sort. I only told you"—she was almost indignantly positive—"that he had been ordered me!"

It sent Mrs. Gracedew off; she moved away to indulge an emotion that presently put on the form of extravagant mirth. "Like a dose of medicine or a course of baths?"

The girl's gravity and lucidity sustained themselves. "As a remedy for the single life." Oh, she had mastered the matter now! "But I won't take him!"

"Ah, then, why didn't you let me know?" Mrs. Gracedew panted.

"I was on the very point of it when he came in and interrupted us." Cora clearly felt she might be wicked, but was at least not stupid. "It's just to let you know that I'm here now."

Ah, the difference it made! This difference, for Mrs. Gracedew, suddenly shimmered in all the place, and her companion's fixed eyes caught in her face the reflection of it. "Excuse me—I misunderstood. I somehow took for granted——!" She stopped, a trifle awkwardly—suddenly tender, for Cora, as to the way she had inevitably seen it.

"You took for granted I'd jump at him? Well, you can take it for granted I won't!"

Mrs. Gracedew, fairly admiring her, put it sympathetically. "You prefer the single life?"

"No—but I don't prefer *him*!" Cora was crystal-bright.

Her light, indeed, for her friend, was at first almost blinding; it took Mrs. Gracedew a moment to distinguish—which she then did, however, with immense eagerness. "You prefer someone else?" Cora's promptitude dropped at this, and, starting to hear it, as you might well have seen, for the first time publicly phrased, she abruptly moved away. A minute's sense of her scruple was enough for Mrs. Gracedew: this was proved by the tone of soft remonstrance and high benevolence with which that lady went on. She had looked very hard, first, at one of the old warriors hung on the old wall, and almost spoke as if he represented their host. "He seems remarkably clever."

Cora, at something in the sound, quite jumped about. "Then why don't you marry him yourself?"

Mrs. Gracedew gave a sort of happy sigh. "Well, I've got fifty reasons! I rather think one of them must be that he hasn't happened to ask me."

It was a speech, however, that her visitor could easily better. "I haven't got fifty reasons, but I *have* got one."

Mrs. Gracedew smiled as if it were indeed a stroke of wit. "You mean your case is one of those in which safety is *not* in numbers?" And then on Cora's visibly not understanding: "It *is* when reasons are bad that one needs so many!"

The proposition was too general for the girl to embrace, but the simplicity of her answer was far from spoiling it. "My reason is awfully good."

Mrs. Gracedew did it complete justice. "I see. An older friend."

Cora listened as at a warning sound; yet she had by this time practically let herself go, and it took but Mrs. Gracedew's extended encouraging hand, which she quickly seized, to bring the whole thing out. "I've been trying this hour, in my terrible need of advice, to tell you about him!" It came in a small clear torrent, a soft tumble-out of sincerity. "After we parted—you and I—at the station, he suddenly turned up there, and I took a little quiet walk with him which gave you time to get here before me and of which my father is in a state of ignorance that I don't know whether to regard as desirable or dreadful."

Mrs. Gracedew, attentive and wise, might have been, for her face, the old family solicitor. "You want me then to *inform* your father?" It was a wonderful intonation.

Poor Cora, for that matter too, might suddenly have become under this touch the prodigal with a list of debts. She seemed an instant to look out of a blurred office window-pane at a grey London sky; then she broke away. "I really don't know *what* I want. I think," she honestly admitted, "I just want kindness."

Mrs. Gracedew's expression might have hinted—but not for too long— that Bedford Row was an odd place to apply for it; she appeared for an instant to make the revolving office-chair creak. "What do you mean by kindness?"

Cora was a model client—she perfectly knew. "I mean help."

Mrs. Gracedew closed an inkstand with a clap and locked a couple of drawers. "What do you mean by help?"

The client's inevitable answer seemed to perch on the girl's lips: "A thousand pounds." But it came out in another, in a much more charming form. "I mean that I love him."

The family solicitor got up: it was a high figure. "And does he love *you*?"

Cora hesitated. "Ask *him*."

Mrs. Gracedew weighed the necessity. "Where is he?"

"Waiting." And the girl's glance, removed from her companion and wandering aloft and through space, gave the scale of his patience.

Her adviser, however, required the detail. "But *where*?"

Cora briefly demurred again. "In that funny old grotto."

Mrs. Gracedew thought. "Funny?"

"Half-way from the park gate. It's very *nice*!" Cora more eagerly added.

Mrs. Gracedew continued to reflect. "Oh, I know it!" She spoke as if she had known it most of her life.

Her tone encouraged her client. "Then will you see him?"

"No." This time it was almost dry.

"No?"

"No. If you want help——" Mrs. Gracedew, still musing, explained.

"Yes?"

"Well—you want a great deal."

"Oh, so much!"—Cora but too woefully took it in. "I want," she quavered, "all there is!"

"Well—you shall have it."

"All there is?"—she convulsively held her to it.

Mrs. Gracedew had finally mastered it. "I'll see your father."

"You dear, delicious lady!" Her young friend had again encompassed her; but, passive and preoccupied, she showed some of the chill of apprehension. It was indeed as if to meet this that Cora went earnestly on: "He's intensely sympathetic!"

"Your father?" Mrs. Gracedew had her reserves.

"Oh, no—the other person. I so believe in him!" Cora cried.

Mrs. Gracedew looked at her a moment. "Then so do I—and I like him for believing in *you*."

"Oh, he does that," the girl hurried on, "far more than Captain Yule—I could see just with one glance that *he* doesn't at all. Papa has of course seen the young man I mean, but we've been so sure papa would hate it that we've had to be awfully careful. He's the son of the richest man at Bellborough, he's Granny's godson, and he'll inherit his father's business, which is simply immense. Oh, from the point of view of the things he's *in*"—and Cora found herself sharp on this—"he's quite as good as papa himself. He has been away for three days, and if he met me at the station, where, on his way back, he has to change, it was by the merest chance in the world. I wouldn't love him," she brilliantly wound up, "if he wasn't nice."

"A man's always nice if you *will* love him!" Mrs. Gracedew laughed.

Her young friend more than met it. "He's nicer still if he 'will' love *you*!"

But Mrs. Gracedew kept her head. "Nicer of course than if he won't! But are you sure this gentleman *does* love you?"

"As sure as that the other one doesn't."

"Ah, but the other one doesn't know you."

"Yes, thank goodness—and never shall!"

Mrs. Gracedew watched her a little, but on the girl's meeting her eyes turned away with a quick laugh. "You mean of course till it's too late."

"Altogether!" Cora spoke as with quite the measure of the time.

Mrs. Gracedew, revolving a moment in silence, appeared to accept her showing. "Then what's the matter?" she impatiently asked.

"The matter?"

"Your father's objection to the gentleman in the grotto."

Cora now for the first time faltered. "His name."

This for a moment pulled up her friend, in whom, however, relief seemed to contend with alarm. "Only his name?"

"Yes, but——" Cora's eyes rolled.

Her companion invitingly laughed. "But it's enough?"

Her roll confessingly fixed itself. "*Not* enough—that's just the trouble!"

Mrs. Gracedew looked kindly curious. "What then *is* it?"

Cora faced the music. "Pegg."

Mrs. Gracedew stared. "Nothing else?"

"Nothing to speak of." The girl was quite candid now. "Hall."

"Nothing before——?"

"Not a letter."

"Hall Pegg?" Mrs. Gracedew had winced, but she quickly recovered herself, and, for a further articulation, appeared, from delicacy, to form the sound only with her mind. The sound she formed with her lips was, after an instant, simply "Oh!"

It was to the combination of the spoken and the unspoken that Cora desperately replied. "It sounds like a hat-rack!"

"'Hall Pegg'? 'Hall Pegg'?" Mrs. Gracedew now made it, like a questionable coin, ring upon the counter. But it lay there as lead and without, for a moment, her taking it up again. "How many has your father?" she inquired instead.

"How many names?" Miss Prodmore seemed dimly to see that there was no hope in that. "He somehow makes out five."

"Oh, that's *too* many!" Mrs. Gracedew jeeringly declared.

"Papa unfortunately doesn't think so, when Captain Yule, I believe, has six."

"Six?" Mrs. Gracedew, alert, looked as if that might be different.

"Papa, in the morning-room, told me them all."

Mrs. Gracedew visibly considered, then for a moment dropped Mr. Pegg. "And what *are* they!"

"Oh, all sorts. 'Marmaduke Clement——'" Cora tried to recall.

Mrs. Gracedew, however, had already checked her. "I see—'Marmaduke Clement' will do." She appeared for a minute intent, but, as with an energetic stoop, she picked up Mr. Pegg. "But so will yours," she said, with decision.

"Mine?—you mean *his*!"

"The same thing—what you'll *be*."

"Mrs. Hall Pegg!"—Cora tried it, with resolution, loudly.

It fell a little flat in the noble space, but Mrs. Gracedew's manner quickly covered it. "It won't make you a bit less charming."

Cora wondered—she hoped. "Only for papa."

And what was *he*? Mrs. Gracedew by this time seemed assentingly to ask. "Never for *me*!" she soothingly declared.

Cora took this in with deep thanks that gripped and patted her companion's hand. "You accept it more than gracefully. But if you could only make *him*——!"

Mrs. Gracedew was all concentration. "'Him'? Mr. Pegg?"

"No—he naturally *has* to accept it. But papa."

She looked harder still at this greater feat, then seemed to see light. "Well, it will be difficult—but I will."

Doubt paled before it. "Oh, you heavenly thing!"

Mrs. Gracedew after an instant, sustained by this appreciation, went a step further. "And I'll make him *say* he does!"

Cora closed her eyes with the dream of it. "Oh, if I could only hear him!"

Her benefactress had at last run it to earth. "It will be enough if *I* do."

Cora quickly considered; then, with prompt accommodation, gave the comfortable measure of her faith. "Yes—I think it will." She was quite ready to retire. "I'll give you time."

"Thank you," said Mrs. Gracedew; "but before you give me time give me something better."

This pulled the girl up a little, as if in parting with her secret she had parted with her all. "Something better?"

"If I help you, you know," Mrs. Gracedew explained, "you must help me."

"But how?"

"By a clear assurance." The charming woman's fine face now gave the real example of clearness. "That if Captain Yule should propose to you, you would unconditionally refuse him."

Cora flushed with the surprise of its being only that. "With my dying breath!"

Mrs. Gracedew scanned her robust vitality. "Will you make it even a promise?"

The girl looked about her in solid certainty. "Do you want me to sign——?"

Mrs. Gracedew was quick. "No, don't sign!"

Yet Cora was so ready to oblige. "Then what shall I do?"

Mrs. Gracedew turned away, but after a few vague steps faced her again. "Kiss me."

Cora flew to her arms, and the compact had scarce been sealed before the younger of the parties was already at the passage to the front. "We meet of course at the station."

Mrs. Gracedew thought. "If all goes well. But where shall you be meanwhile?"

Her confederate had no need to think. "Can't you guess?"

The bang of the house-door, the next minute, so helped the answer to the riddle as fairly to force it, when she found herself alone, from her lips. "At that funny old grotto? Well," she sighed, "I *like* funny old grottos!" She found herself alone, however, only for a minute; Mr. Prodmore's formidable presence had darkened the door from the court.

VII

"My daughter's not here?" he demanded from the threshold.

"Your daughter's not here." She had rapidly got under arms. "But it's a convenience to me, Mr. Prodmore, that *you* are, for I've something very particular to ask you."

Her interlocutor crossed straight to the morning-room. "I shall be delighted to answer your question, but I must first put my hand on Miss Prodmore." This hand the next instant stayed itself on the latch, and he appealed to the amiable visitor. "Unless indeed she's occupied in there with Captain Yule?"

The amiable visitor met the appeal. "I don't think she's occupied—anywhere—with Captain Yule."

Mr. Prodmore came straight away from the door. "Then where the deuce *is* Captain Yule?"

The amiable visitor turned a trifle less direct. "His absence, for which I'm responsible, is just what renders the inquiry I speak of to you possible." She had already assumed a most inquiring air, yet it was soon clear that she needed every advantage her manner could give her. "What will you take——? what will you take——?"

It had the sound, as she faltered, of a general question, and Mr. Prodmore raised his eyebrows. "Take? Nothing, thank you—I've just had a cup of tea." Then suddenly, as if on the broad hint: "Won't *you* have one?"

"Yes, with pleasure—but not yet." She looked about her again; she was now at close quarters and, concentrated, anxious, pressed her hand a moment to her brow.

This struck her companion. "Don't you think you'd be better for it immediately?"

206

"No." She was positive. "No." Her eyes consciously wandered. "I want to know how you'd value——"

He took her, as his own followed them, more quickly up, expanding in the presence of such a tribute from a real connoisseur. "One of these charming old things that take your fancy?"

She looked at him straight now. "They *all* take my fancy!"

"All?" He enjoyed it as the joke of a rich person—the kind of joke he sometimes made himself.

"Every single one!" said Mrs. Gracedew. Then with still a finer shade of the familiar: "Should you be willing to treat, Mr. Prodmore, for your interest in this property?"

He threw back his head: she had scattered over the word "interest" such a friendly, faded colour. She was either *not* joking or was rich indeed; and there was a place always kept in his conversation for the arrival of money, as there is always a box in a well-appointed theatre for that of royalty. "Am I to take it from you then that you *know* about my interest——?"

"Everything!" said Mrs. Gracedew with a world of wit.

"Excuse me, madam!"—he himself was now more reserved. "You don't know everything if you don't know that my interest—considerable as it might well have struck you—has just ceased to exist. I've given it up"—Mr. Prodmore softened the blow—"for a handsome equivalent."

The blow fell indeed light enough. "You mean for a handsome son-in-law?"

"It will be by some such description as the term you use that I shall doubtless, in the future, permit myself, in the common course, to allude to Captain Yule. Unless indeed I call him——" But Mr. Prodmore dropped the bolder thought. "It will depend on what he calls *me*."

Mrs. Gracedew covered him a moment with the largeness of her charity. "Won't it depend a little on what your daughter herself calls him?"

Mr. Prodmore seriously considered. "No. That," he declared with delicacy, "will be between the happy pair."

"Am I to take it from you then—I adopt your excellent phrase," Mrs. Gracedew said—"that Miss Prodmore has already accepted him?"

Her companion, with his head still in the air, seemed to signify that he simply put it down on the table and that she could take it or not as she liked. "Her character—formed by my assiduous care—enables me to locate her, I may say even to *time* her, from moment to moment." His massive watch, as he opened it, further sustained him in this process. "It's my assured conviction that she's accepting him while we stand here."

Mrs. Gracedew was so affected by his assured conviction that, with an odd, inarticulate sound, she forbore to stand longer—she rapidly moved away, taking one of the brief excursions of step and sense that had been for her, from the first, under the noble roof, so many dumb but decisive communions. But it was soon over, and she floated back on a wave that showed her to be, since she had let herself go, by this time quite in the swing and describing a considerable curve. "Dear Mr. Prodmore, why are you so imprudent as to make your daughter afraid of you? You should have taught her to confide in you. She has clearly shown me," she almost soothingly pursued, "that she *can* confide."

Mr. Prodmore, however, suddenly starting, looked far from soothed. "She confides in *you?*"

"You may take it from me!" Mrs. Gracedew laughed. "Let me suggest that, as fortune has thrown us together a minute, you follow her good example." She put out a reassuring hand—she could perfectly show him the way. "Tell me, for instance, the ground of your objection to poor Mr. Pegg. I mean Mr. Pegg of Bellborough, Mr. Hall Pegg, the godson of your daughter's grandmother and the associate of his father in their flourishing house; to whom (as *he* is to *it* and to *her*) Miss Prodmore's devotedly attached."

Mr. Prodmore had in the course of this speech availed himself of the support of the nearest chair, where, in spite of his subsidence, he appeared in his amazement twice his natural size. "It has gone so far as *that?*"

She rose before him as if in triumph. "It has gone so far that you had better let it go the rest of the way!"

He had lost breath, but he had positively gained dignity. "It's too monstrous, to have plotted to keep me in the dark!"

"Why, it's only when you're kept in the dark that your daughter's kept in the light!" She argued it with a candour that might have served for brilliancy. "It's at her own earnest request that I plead to you for her liberty of choice. She's an honest girl—perhaps even a peculiar girl; and she's not a baby. You over-do, I think, the nursing. She has a perfect right to her preference."

Poor Mr. Prodmore couldn't help taking it from her, and, this being the case, he still took it in the most convenient way. "And pray haven't I a perfect right to mine?" he asked from his chair.

She fairly seemed to serve it up to him—to put down the dish with a flourish. "Not at her expense. You expect her to give up too much."

"And what has she," he appealed, "expected *me* to give up? What but the desire of my heart and the dream of my life? Captain Yule announced to me but a few minutes since his intention to offer her his hand."

She faced him on it as over the table. "Well, if he does, I think he'll simply find——"

"Find what?" They looked at each other hard.

"Why, that she won't have it."

Oh, Mr. Prodmore now sprang up. "She *will!*"

"She won't!" Mrs. Gracedew more distinctly repeated.

"She *shall!*" returned her adversary, making for the staircase with the evident sense of where reinforcement might be most required.

Mrs. Gracedew, however, with a spring, was well before him. "She shan't!" She spoke with positive passion and practically so barred the way that he stood arrested and bewildered, and they faced each other, for a flash, like enemies. But it all went out, on her part, in a flash too—in a sudden wonderful smile. "Now tell me how much!"

Mr. Prodmore continued to glare—the sweat was on his brow. But while he slowly wiped it with a pocket-handkerchief of splendid scarlet silk, he remained so silent that he would have had for a spectator the effect of meeting in a manner her question. More formally to answer it he had at last to turn away. "How can I tell you anything so preposterous?"

She was all ready to inform him. "Simply by computing the total amount to which, for your benefit, this unhappy estate is burdened." He listened with his back presented, but that appeared to strike her, as she fixed this expanse, as an encouragement to proceed. "If I've troubled you by showing you that your speculation is built on the sand, let me atone for it by my eagerness to take off your hands an investment from which you derive so little profit."

He at last gave her his attention, but quite as if there were nothing in it. "And pray what profit will *you* derive——?"

"Ah, that's my own secret!" She would show him as well no glimpse of it—her laugh but rattled the box. "I want this house!"

"So do I, damn me!" he roundly returned; "and that's why I've practically paid for it!" He stuffed away his pocket-handkerchief.

There was nevertheless something in her that could hold him, and it came out, after an instant, quietly and reasonably enough. "I'll practically pay for it, Mr. Prodmore—if you'll only tell me your figure."

"My figure?"

"Your figure."

Mr. Prodmore waited—then removed his eyes from her face. He appeared to have waited on purpose to let her hope of a soft answer fall from a greater height. "My figure would be quite my own!"

"Then it will match, in that respect," Mrs. Gracedew laughed, "this overture, which is quite *my* own! As soon as you've let me know it I cable to Missoura Top to have the money sent right out to you."

Mr. Prodmore surveyed in a superior manner this artless picture of a stroke of business. "You imagine that having the money sent right out to me will make you owner of this place?"

She herself, with her head on one side, studied her sketch and seemed to twirl her pencil. "No—not quite. But I'll settle the rest with Captain Yule."

Her companion looked, over his white waistcoat, at his large tense shoes, the patent-leather shine of which so flashed propriety back at him that he became, the next moment, doubly erect on it. "Captain Yule has nothing to sell."

She received the remark with surprise. "Then what have you been trying to buy?"

She had touched in himself even a sharper spring. "Do you mean to say," he cried, "you want to buy *that*?" She stared at his queer emphasis, which was intensified by a queer grimace; then she turned from him with a change of colour and an ejaculation that led to nothing more, after a few seconds, than a somewhat conscious silence—a silence of which Mr. Prodmore made use to follow up his unanswered question with another. "Is your proposal that I should transfer my investment to you for the mere net amount of it your conception of a fair bargain?"

This second inquiry, however, she could, as she slowly came round, substantially meet. "Pray, then, what is yours?"

"Mine would be, not that I should simply get my money back, but that I should get the effective value of the house."

Mrs. Gracedew considered it. "But isn't the effective value of the house just what your money expresses?"

The lid of his hard left eye, the harder of the two, just dipped with the effect of a wink. "No, madam. It's just what *yours* does. It's moreover just what your lips have already expressed so distinctly!"

She clearly did her best to follow him. "To those people—when I showed the place off?"

Mr. Prodmore laughed. "You seemed to be *taking* bids then!"

She was candid, but earnest. "Taking them?"

"Oh, like an auctioneer! You ran it up high!" And Mr. Prodmore laughed again.

She turned a little pale, but it added to her brightness. "I certainly did, if saying it was charming——"

"Charming?" Mr. Prodmore broke in. "You said it was magnificent. You said it was unique. That was your very word. You said it was the *perfect* specimen of its class in England." He was more than accusatory, he was really crushing. "Oh, you got in deep!"

It was indeed an indictment, and her smile was perhaps now rather set. "Possibly. But taunting me with my absurd high spirits and the dreadful liberties I took doesn't in the least tell me how deep *you're* in!"

"For you, Mrs. Gracedew?" He took a few steps, looking at his shoes again and as if to give her time to plead—since he wished to be quite fair—that it was *not* for her. "I'm in to the tune of fifty thousand."

She was silent, on this announcement, so long that he once more faced her; but if what he showed her in doing so at last made her speak, it also took the life from her tone. "That's a great deal of money, Mr. Prodmore."

The tone didn't matter, but only the truth it expressed, which he so thoroughly liked to hear. "So I've often had occasion to say to myself!"

"If it's a large sum for you, then," said Mrs. Gracedew, "it's a still larger one for me." She sank into a chair with a vague melancholy; such a mass loomed huge, and she sat down before it as a solitary herald, resigning himself with a sigh to wait, might have leaned against a tree before a besieged city. "We women"—she wished to conciliate—"have more modest ideas."

But Mr. Prodmore would scarce condescend to parley. "Is it as a 'modest idea' that you describe your extraordinary intrusion——?"

His question scarce reached her; she was so lost for the moment in the sense of innocent community with her sex. "I mean I think we measure things often rather more exactly."

There would have been no doubt of Mr. Prodmore's very different community as he rudely replied: "Then you measured *this* thing exactly half an hour ago!"

It was a long way to go back, but Mrs. Gracedew, in her seat, musingly made the journey, from which she then suddenly returned with a harmless, indeed quite a happy, memento. "Was I *very* grotesque?"

He demurred. "Grotesque?"

"I mean—*did* I go on about it?"

Mr. Prodmore would have no general descriptions; he was specific, he was vivid. "You banged the desk. You raved. You shrieked."

This was a note she appeared indulgently, almost tenderly, to recognise. "We *do* shriek at Missoura Top!"

"I don't know what you do at Missoura Top, but I know what you did at Covering End!"

She warmed at last to his tone. "So do *I* then! I surprised you. You weren't at all prepared——"

He took her briskly up. "No—and I'm not prepared yet!"

Mrs. Gracedew could quite see it. "Yes, you're too astonished."

"My astonishment's my own affair," he retorted—"not less so than my memory!"

"Oh, I yield to your memory," said the charming woman, "and I confess my extravagance. But quite, you know, *as* extravagance."

"I don't at all know,"—Mr. Prodmore shook it off,—"nor what you *call* extravagance."

"Why, banging the desk. Raving. Shrieking. I over-did it," she exclaimed; "I wanted to please you!"

She had too happy a beauty, as she sat in her high-backed chair, to have been condemned to say that to any man without a certain effect. The effect on Mr. Prodmore was striking. "So you said," he sternly inquired, "what you didn't believe?"

She flushed with the avowal. "Yes—for you."

He looked at her hard. "For *me*?"

Under his eye—for her flush continued—she slowly got up. "And for those good people."

"Oh!"—he sounded most sarcastic. "Should you like me to call them back?"

"No." She was still gay enough, but very decided. "I took them in."

"And now you want to take *me*?"

"Oh, Mr. Prodmore!" she almost pitifully, but not quite adequately, moaned.

He appeared to feel he had gone a little far. "Well, if we're not what you say——"

"Yes?"—she looked up askance at the stroke.

"Why the devil do you want us?" The question rang out and was truly for the poor lady, as the quick suffusion of her eyes showed, a challenge it would take more time than he left her properly to pick up. He left her in fact no time at all before he went on: "Why the devil did you say you'd offer fifty?"

She looked quite wan and seemed to wonder. "*Did* I say that?" She could only let his challenge lie. "It was a figure of speech!"

"Then that's the kind of figure we're talking about!" Mr. Prodmore's sharpness would have struck an auditor as the more effective that, on the heels of this thrust, seeing the ancient butler reappear, he dropped the victim

214

of it as comparatively unimportant and directed his fierceness instantly to Chivers, who mildly gaped at him from the threshold of the court. "Have you seen Miss Prodmore? If you haven't, find her!"

Mrs. Gracedew addressed their visitor in a very different tone, though with the full authority of her benevolence. "You won't, my dear man." To Mr. Prodmore also she continued bland. "I happen to know she has gone for a walk."

"A walk—alone?" Mr. Prodmore gasped.

"No—not alone." Mrs. Gracedew looked at Chivers with a vague smile of appeal for help, but he could only give her, from under his bent old brow, the blank decency of his wonder. It seemed to make her feel afresh that she was, after all, alone—so that in her loneliness, which had also its fine sad charm, she risked another brush with their formidable friend. "Cora has gone with Mr. Pegg."

"Pegg has *been* here?"

It was like a splash in a full basin, but she launched the whole craft. "He walked with her from the station."

"When she arrived?" Mr. Prodmore rose like outraged Neptune. "That's why she was so late?"

Mrs. Gracedew assented. "Why I got here first. I get everywhere first!" she bravely laughed.

Mr. Prodmore looked round him in purple dismay—it was so clearly a question for him where *he* should get, and what! "In which direction did they go?" he imperiously asked.

His rudeness was too evident to be more than lightly recognised. "I think I must let you ascertain for yourself!"

All he could do then was to shout it to Chivers. "Call my carriage, you ass!" After which, as the old man melted into the vestibule, he dashed about blindly for his hat, pounced upon it and seemed, furious but helpless, on the point of hurling it at his contradictress as a gage of battle. "So you abetted and protected this wicked, low intrigue?"

She had something in her face now that was indifferent to any violence. "You're too disappointed to see your real interest: oughtn't I therefore in common charity to point it out to you?"

He faced her question so far as to treat it as one. "What do *you* know of my disappointment?"

There was something in his very harshness that even helped her, for it added at this moment to her sense of making out in his narrowed glare a couple of tears of rage. "I know everything."

"What do you know of my real interest?" he went on as if he had not heard her.

"I know enough for my purpose—which is to offer you a handsome condition. I think it's not I who have protected the happy understanding that you call by so ugly a name; it's the happy understanding that has put me"—she gained confidence—"well, in a position. Do drive after them, if you like—but catch up with them only to forgive them. If you'll do that, I'll pay your price."

The particular air with which, a minute after Mrs. Gracedew had spoken these words, Mr. Prodmore achieved a transfer of his attention to the inside of his hat—this special shade of majesty would have taxed the descriptive resources of the most accomplished reporter. It is none the less certain that he appeared for some time absorbed in that receptacle—appeared at last to breathe into it hard. "What do you call my price?"

"Why, the sum you just mentioned—fifty thousand!" Mrs. Gracedew feverishly quavered.

He looked at her as if stupefied. "*That's* not my price—and it never for a moment was!" If derision can be dry, Mr. Prodmore's was of the driest. "Besides," he rang out, "my price is up!"

She caught it with a long wail. "Up?"

Oh, he let her have it now! "Seventy thousand."

She turned away overwhelmed, but still with voice for her despair. "Oh, deary me!"

Mr. Prodmore was already at the door, from which he launched his ultimatum. "It's to take or to leave!"

She would have had to leave it, perhaps, had not something happened at this moment to nerve her for the effort of staying him with a quick motion. Captain Yule had come into sight on the staircase and, after just faltering at what he himself saw, had marched resolutely enough down. She watched him arrive—watched him with an attention that visibly and responsively excited his own; after which she passed nearer to their companion. "Seventy thousand, then!"—it gleamed between them, in her muffled hiss, as if she had planted a dagger.

Mr. Prodmore, to do him justice, took his wound in front. "Seventy thousand—done!" And, without another look at Yule, he was presently heard to bang the outer door after him for a sign.

VIII

THE young man, meanwhile, had approached in surprise. "He's gone? I've been looking for him!"

Mrs. Gracedew was out of breath; there was a disturbed whiteness of bosom in her which needed time to subside and which she might have appeared to retreat before him on purpose to veil. "I don't think, you know, that you need him—now."

Clement Yule was mystified. "Now?"

She recovered herself enough to explain—made an effort at least to be plausible. "I mean that—if you don't mind—you must deal with *me*. I've arranged with Mr. Prodmore to take it over."

Oh, he gave her no help! "Take what over?"

She looked all about as if not quite thinking what it could be called; at last, however, she offered with a smile a sort of substitute for a name. "Why, your debt."

But he was only the more bewildered. "*Can* you—without arranging with *me*?"

She turned it round, but as if merely to oblige him. "That's precisely what I want to do." Then, more brightly, as she thought further: "That is, I mean, I want you to arrange with *me*. Surely you will," she said encouragingly.

His own processes, in spite of a marked earnestness, were much less rapid. "But if I arrange with anybody——"

"Yes?" She cheerfully waited.

"How do I perform my engagement?"

"The one to Mr. Prodmore?"

He looked surprised at her speaking as if he had half-a-dozen. "Yes—that's the worst."

"Certainly—the worst!" And she gave a happy laugh that made him stare.

He broke into quite a different one. "You speak as if its being the worst made it the best!"

"It does—for me. You don't," said Mrs. Gracedew, "perform any engagement."

He required a moment to take it in; then something extraordinary leaped into his face. "He lets me off?"

Ah, she could ring out now! "He lets you off."

It lifted him high, but only to drop him with an audible thud. "Oh, I see—I lose my house!"

"Dear, no—*that* doesn't follow!" She spoke as if the absurdity he indicated were the last conceivable, but there was a certain want of sharpness of edge in her expression of the alternative. "You arrange with *me* to keep it."

There was quite a corresponding want, clearly, in the image presented to the Captain—of which, for a moment, he seemed with difficulty to follow the contour. "How do I arrange?"

"Well, we must think," said Mrs. Gracedew; "we must wait." She spoke as if this were a detail for which she had not yet had much attention; only bringing out, however, the next instant in an encouraging cry and as if it were by itself almost a solution: "We must find some way!" She might have been talking to a reasonable child.

But even reasonable children ask too many questions. "Yes—and what way *can* we find?" Clement Yule, glancing about him, was so struck with the absence of ways that he appeared to remember with something of regret how different it had been before. "With Prodmore it was simple enough. You see I could marry his daughter."

Mrs. Gracedew was silent just long enough for her soft ironic smile to fill the cup of the pause. "*Could* you?"

It was as if he had tasted in the words the wine at the brim; for he gave, under the effect of them, a sudden headshake and an awkward laugh. "Well, never perhaps *that* exactly—when it came to the point. But I had to, you see———" It was difficult to say just what.

She took advantage of it, looking hard, but not seeing at all. "You had to———?"

"Well," he repeated ruefully, "think a lot about it. You didn't suspect that?"

Oh, if he came to suspicions she could only break off! "Don't ask me too many questions."

He looked an instant as if he wondered why. "But isn't this just the moment for them?" He fronted her, with a quickness he tried to dissimulate, from the other side. "What *did* you suppose?"

She looked everywhere but into his face. "Why, I supposed you were in distress."

He was very grave. "About his terms?"

"About his terms of course!" she laughed. "Not about his religious opinions."

His gratitude was too great for gaiety. "You really, in your beautiful sympathy, *guessed* my fix?"

But she declined to be too solemn. "Dear Captain Yule, it all quite stuck out of you!"

"You mean I floundered like a drowning man——?"

Well, she consented to have meant that. "Till I plunged in!"

He appeared there for a few seconds, to see her again take the jump and to listen again to the splash; then, with an odd, sharp impulse, he turned his back. "You saved me."

She wouldn't deny it—on the contrary. "What a pity, now, *I* haven't a daughter!"

On this he slowly came round again. "What should I do with her?"

"You'd treat her, I hope, better than you've treated Miss Prodmore."

The young man positively coloured. "But I haven't been bad——?"

The sight of this effect of her small joke produced on Mrs. Gracedew's part an emotion less controllable than any she had yet felt. "Oh, you delightful goose!" she irrepressibly dropped.

She made his blush deepen, but the aggravation was a relief. "Of course—I'm all right, and there's only one pity in the matter. I've nothing—

nothing whatever, not a scrap of service nor a thing you'd care for—to offer you in compensation."

She looked at him ever so kindly. "I'm not, as they say, 'on the make.'" Never had he been put right with a lighter hand. "I didn't do it for payment."

"Then what did you do it for?"

For something, it might have seemed, as her eyes dropped and strayed, that had got brushed into a crevice of the old pavement. "Because I hated Mr. Prodmore."

He conscientiously demurred. "So much as all that?"

"Oh, well," she replied impatiently, "of course you also know how much I like the house. My hates and my likes," she subtly explained, "can never live together. I get one of them out. The one this time was that man."

He showed a candour of interest. "Yes—you got him out. Yes—I saw him go." And his inner vision appeared to attend for some moments Mr. Prodmore's departure. "But how did you do it?"

"Oh, I don't know. Women——!" Mrs. Gracedew but vaguely sketched it.

A touch or two, however, for that subject, could of course almost always suffice. "Precisely—women. May I smoke again?" Clement Yule abruptly asked.

"Certainly. But I managed Mr. Prodmore," she laughed as he re-lighted, "without cigarettes."

Her companion puffed. "*I* couldn't manage him."

"So I saw!"

"*I* couldn't get him out."

"So *he* saw!"

Captain Yule, for a little, lost himself in his smoke. "Where is he gone?"

"I haven't the least idea. But I meet him again," she hastened to add— "very soon."

"And when do you meet *me*?"

"Why, whenever you'll come to see me." For the twentieth time she gathered herself as if the words she had just spoken were quite her last hand. "At present, you see, I *have* a train to catch."

Absorbed in the trivial act that engaged him, he gave her no help. "A train?"

"Surely. I didn't walk."

"No; but even trains——!" His eyes clung to her now. "You fly?"

"I try to. Good-bye."

He had got between her and the door of departure quite as, on her attempt to quit him half an hour before, he had anticipated her approach to the stairs; and in this position he took no notice of her farewell. "I said just now that I had nothing to offer you. But of course I've the house itself."

"The house?" She stared. "Why, I've *got* it?"

"Got it?"

"All in my head, I mean. That's all I want." She had not yet, save to Mr. Prodmore, made quite so light of it.

This had its action in his markedly longer face. "Why, I thought you loved it so!"

Ah, she was perfectly consistent. "I love it far too much to deprive *you* of it."

Yet Clement Yule could in a fashion meet her. "Oh, it wouldn't be depriving——!"

She altogether protested. "Not to turn you out——?"

"Dear lady, I've never been *in*!"

Oh, she was none the less downright. "You're in *now*—I've put you, and you must stay." He looked round so woefully, however, that she presently attenuated. "I don't mean *all* the while, but long enough——!"

"Long enough for what?"

"For me to feel you're here."

"And how long will that take?"

"Well, you think me very fast—but sometimes I'm slow. I told you just now, at any rate," she went on, "that I had arranged you should lose nothing. Is the very next thing I do, then, to make you lose everything?"

"It isn't a question of what I lose," the young man anxiously cried; "it's a question of what I *do*! What *have* I done to find it all so plain?" Fate was really—fate reversed, improved, and unnatural—too much for him, and his heated young face showed honest stupefaction. "I haven't lifted a finger. It's you who have done all."

"Yes, but if you're just where you were before, how in the world are you saved?" She put it to him with still superior lucidity.

"By my life's being my own again—to do what I want."

"What you 'want'"—Mrs. Gracedew's handsome uplifted head had it all there, every inch of it—"is to keep your house."

"Ah, but only," he perfectly assented, "if, as you said, you find a way!"

"I *have* found a way—and there the way is: for *me* just simply not to touch the place. What you 'want,'" she argued more closely, "is what made you give in to Prodmore. What you 'want' is these walls and these acres. What you 'want' is to take the way I first showed you."

Her companion's eyes, quitting for the purpose her face, looked to the quarter marked by her last words as at an horizon now remote. "Why, the way you first showed me was to marry Cora!"

223

She had to admit it, but as little as possible. "Practically—yes."

"Well, it's just 'practically' that I can't!"

"I didn't know that then," said Mrs. Gracedew. "You didn't tell me."

He passed, with an approach to a grimace, his hand over the back of his head. "I felt a delicacy!"

"I didn't even know *that*." She spoke it almost sadly.

"It didn't strike you that I might?"

She thought a moment. "No." She thought again. "No. But don't quarrel with me about it *now*!"

"Quarrel with you?" he looked amazement.

She laughed, but she had changed colour. "Cora, at any rate, felt no delicacy. Cora told me."

Clement Yule fairly gaped. "Then she did know——?"

"She knew all; and if her father said she didn't, he simply told you what was not." She frankly gave him this, but the next minute, as if she had startled him more than she meant, she jumped to reassurance. "It was quite right of her. She would have refused you."

The young man stared. "Oh!" He was quick, however, to show—by an amusement perhaps a trifle over-done—that he felt no personal wound. "Do you call that quite right?"

Mrs. Gracedew looked at it again. "For *her*—yes; and for Prodmore."

"Oh, for Prodmore"—his laugh grew more grim—"with all my heart!"

This, then,—her kind eyes seemed to drop it upon him,—was all she meant. "To stay at your post—*that* was the way I showed you."

He had come round to it now, as mechanically, in intenser thought, he smoothed down the thick hair he had rubbed up; but his face soon enough gave out, in wonder and pain, that his freedom was somehow only a new predicament. "How can I take any way at all, dear lady———?"

"If I only stick here in your path?" She had taken him straight up, and with spirit; and the same spirit bore her to the end. "I won't stick a moment more! Haven't I been trying this age to leave you?"

Clement Yule, for all answer, caught her sharply, in her passage, by the arm. "You surrender your rights?" He was for an instant almost terrible.

She quite turned pale with it. "Weren't you ready to surrender *yours*?"

"I hadn't any, so it was deuced easy. I hadn't paid for them."

Oh that, she let him see,—even though with his continued grasp he might hurt her,—had nothing in it! "Your ancestors had paid: it's the same thing." Erect there in the brightness of her triumph and the force of her logic, she must yet, to anticipate his return, take a stride—like a sudden dip into a gully and the scramble up on the other bank—that put her dignity to the test. "You're just, in a manner, my tenant."

"But how can I treat that as such a mere detail? I'm your tenant on what terms?"

"Oh, *any* terms—choose them for yourself!" She made an attempt to free her arm—gave it a small vain shake. Then, as if to bribe him to let her go: "You can write me about them."

He appeared to consider it. "To Missoura Top?"

She fully assented. "I go right back." As if it had put him off his guard she broke away. "Farewell!"

She broke away, but he broke faster, and once more, nearer the door, he had barred her escape. "Just one little moment, please. If you won't tell me your own terms, you must at least tell me Prodmore's."

Ah, the fiend—she could never squeeze past *that*! All she could do, for the instant, was to reverberate foolishly "Prodmore's?"

But there was nothing foolish, at last, about *him*. "How you did it—how you managed him." His feet were firm while he waited, though he had to wait some time. "You bought him out?"

She made less of it than, clearly, he had ever heard made of a stroke of business; it might have been a case of his owing her ninepence. "I bought him out."

He wanted at least the exact sum. "For how much?" Her silence seemed to say that she had made no note of it, but his pressure only increased. "I really must know."

She continued to try to treat it as if she had merely paid for his cab—she put even what she could of that suggestion into a tender, helpless, obstinate headshake. "You shall never know!"

The only thing his own manner met was the obstinacy. "I'll get it from *him*!"

She repeated her headshake, but with a world of sadness added, "Get it if you can!"

He looked into her eyes now as if it was the sadness that struck him most. "He won't say, because he *did* you?"

They showed each other, on this, the least separated faces yet. "He'll never, never say."

The confidence in it was so tender that it sounded almost like pity, and the young man took it up with all the flush of the sense that pity could be but for *him*. This sense broke full in her face. "The scoundrel!"

"Not a bit!" she returned, with equal passion—"I was only too clever for him!" The thought of it was again an exaltation in which she pushed her friend aside. "So let me go!"

The push was like a jar that made the vessel overflow, and he was before her now as if he stretched across the hall. "With the heroic view of your power and the barren beauty of your sacrifice? You pour out money, you move a mountain, and to let you 'go,' to close the door fast behind you, is all I can figure out to do for you?" His emotion trembled out of him with the stammer of a new language, but it was as if in a minute or two he had thrown over all consciousness. "You're the most generous—you're the noblest of women! The wonderful chance that brought you here——!"

His own arm was grasped now—she knew better than he about the wonderful chance. "It brought *you* at the same happy hour! I've done what I liked," she went on very simply; "and the only way to thank me is to believe it."

"You've done it for a proud, poor man"—his answer was quite as direct. "He has nothing—in the light of such a magic as yours—either to give or to hope; but you've made him, in a little miraculous hour, think of you——"

He stumbled with the rush of things, and if silence can, in its way, be active, there was a collapse too, for an instant, on her closed lips. These lips, however, she at last opened. "How have I made him think of me?"

"As he has thought of no other woman!" He had personal possession of her now, and it broke, as he pressed her, as he pleaded, the helpless fall of his eloquence. "Mrs. Gracedew—don't leave me." He jerked his head passionately at the whole place and the yellow afternoon. "If you made me care——"

"It was surely that you had made *me* first!" She laughed, and her laugh disengaged her, so that before he could reply she had again put space between them.

He accepted the space now—he appeared so sure of his point. "Then let me go on caring. When I asked you awhile back for some possible adjustment to my new source of credit, you simply put off the question—told me I must trust to time for it. Well," said Clement Yule, "I've trusted to time so effectually that ten little minutes have made me find it. I've found it because I've so quickly found *you*. May I, Mrs. Gracedew, keep *all* that I've found? I offer you in return the only thing I have to give—I offer you my hand and my life."

She held him off, across the hall, for a time almost out of proportion to the previous wait he had just made so little of. Then at last also, when she answered, it might have passed for a plea for further postponement, even for a plea for mercy. "Ah, Captain Yule———!" But she turned suddenly off: the flower had been nipped in the bud by the re-entrance of Chivers, at whom his master veritably glowered.

"What the devil is it?"

The old man showed the shock, but he had his duty. "Another party."

Mrs. Gracedew, at this, wheeled round. "The 'party up'!" It brought back her voice—indeed, all her gaiety. And her gaiety was always determinant. "Show them in."

Clement Yule's face fell while Chivers proceeded to obey. "You'll *have* them?" he wailed across the hall.

"Ah! mayn't I be proud of my house?" she tossed back at him.

At this, radiant, he had rushed at her. "Then you accept———?"

Her raised hand checked him. "Hush!"

He fell back—the party was there. Chivers ushered it as he had ushered the other, making the most, this time, of more scanty material—four persons so spectacled, satchelled, shawled, and handbooked that they testified on the spot to a particular foreign origin and presented themselves indeed very much as tourists who, at an hotel, casting up the promise of comfort or the portent of cost, take possession, while they wait for their keys, with expert looks and free sounds. Clement Yule, who had receded, effacing himself, to the quarter opposed to that of his companion, addressed to their visitors a covert but dismayed stare and then, edging round, in his agitation, to the rear, instinctively sought relief by escape through the open passage. One of the invaders meanwhile—a broad-faced gentleman with long hair tucked behind his ears and a ring on each forefinger—had lost no time in showing he knew where to begin. He began at the top—the proper place, and took in the dark pictures ranged above the tapestry. "Olt vamily bortraits?"—he appealed to Chivers and spoke very loud.

Chivers rose to the occasion and, gracefully pawing the air, began also at the beginning. "Dame Dorothy Yule—who lived to a hundred and one."

"A hundred and one—ach *so!*" broke, with a resigned absence of criticism, from each of the interested group; another member of which, however, indicated with a somewhat fatigued skip the central figure of the series, the personage with the long white legs that Mrs. Gracedew had invited the previous inquirers to remark. "Who's dis?" the present inquirer asked.

The question affected the lovely lady over by the fireplace as the trumpet of battle affects a generous steed. She flashed on the instant into the middle of the hall and into the friendliest and most familiar relation with everyone and with everything. "John Anthony Yule, sir,—who passed away, poor duck, in his flower!"

They met her with low salutations, a sweep of ugly shawls, and a brush of queer German hats: she had issued, to their glazed convergence, from the dusk of the Middle Ages and the shade of high pieces, and now stood there, beautiful and human and happy, in a light that, whatever it was for themselves, the very breadth of their attention, the expression of their serious faces, converted straightway for her into a new, and oh! into the right, one. To a detached observer of the whole it would have been promptly clear that she found herself striking these good people very much as the lawful heir had, half an hour before, struck another stranger—that she produced in them, in her setting of assured antiquity, quite the romantic vibration that she had responded to in the presence of that personage. They read her as she read *him*, and a bright and deepening cheer, reflected dimly in their thick thoroughness, went out from her as she accepted their reading. An impression was exchanged, for the minute, from side to side—their grave admiration of the finest feature of the curious house and the deep free radiance of her silent, grateful "Why not?" It made a passage of some intensity and some duration, of which the effect, indeed, the next minute, was to cause the only lady of the party—a matron of rich Jewish type, with small nippers on a huge nose and a face out of proportion to her little Freischütz hat—to break the spell by an uneasy turn and a stray glance at one of the other pictures. "Who's *dat?*"

229

"That?" The picture chanced to be a portrait over the wide arch, and something happened, at the very moment, to arrest Mrs. Gracedew's eyes rather above than below. What took place, in a word, was that Clement Yule, already fidgeting in his impatience back from the front, just occupied the arch, completed her thought, and filled her vision. "Oh, that's my future husband!" He caught the words, but answered them only by a long look at her as he moved, with a checked wildness of which she alone, of all the spectators, had a sense, straight across the hall again and to the other opening. He paused there as he had done before, then with a last dumb appeal to her dropped into the court and passed into the garden. Mrs. Gracedew, already so wonderful to their visitors, was, before she followed him, wonderful with a greater wonder to poor Chivers. "You dear old thing—I give it all back to you!"

About Author

Henry James OM (15 April 1843 – 28 February 1916) was an American-British author regarded as a key transitional figure between literary realism and literary modernism, and is considered by many to be among the greatest novelists in the English language. He was the son of Henry James Sr. and the brother of renowned philosopher and psychologist William James and diarist Alice James.

He is best known for a number of novels dealing with the social and marital interplay between émigré Americans, English people, and continental Europeans. Examples of such novels include The Portrait of a Lady, The Ambassadors, and The Wings of the Dove. His later works were increasingly experimental. In describing the internal states of mind and social dynamics of his characters, James often made use of a style in which ambiguous or contradictory motives and impressions were overlaid or juxtaposed in the discussion of a character's psyche. For their unique ambiguity, as well as for other aspects of their composition, his late works have been compared to impressionist painting.

His novella The Turn of the Screw has garnered a reputation as the most analysed and ambiguous ghost story in the English language and remains his most widely adapted work in other media. He also wrote a number of other highly regarded ghost stories and is considered one of the greatest masters of the field.

James published articles and books of criticism, travel, biography, autobiography, and plays. Born in the United States, James largely relocated to Europe as a young man and eventually settled in England, becoming a British subject in 1915, one year before his death. James was nominated for the Nobel Prize in Literature in 1911, 1912 and 1916.

Life

Early years, 1843–1883

James was born at 2 Washington Place in New York City on 15 April 1843. His parents were Mary Walsh and Henry James Sr. His father was intelligent and steadfastly congenial. He was a lecturer and philosopher who had inherited independent means from his father, an Albany banker and investor. Mary came from a wealthy family long settled in New York City. Her sister Katherine lived with her adult family for an extended period of time. Henry Jr. had three brothers, William, who was one year his senior, and younger brothers Wilkinson (Wilkie) and Robertson. His younger sister was Alice. Both of his parents were of Irish and Scottish descent.

The family first lived in Albany, at 70 N. Pearl St., and then moved to Fourteenth Street in New York City when James was still a young boy. His education was calculated by his father to expose him to many influences, primarily scientific and philosophical; it was described by Percy Lubbock, the editor of his selected letters, as "extraordinarily haphazard and promiscuous." James did not share the usual education in Latin and Greek classics. Between 1855 and 1860, the James' household traveled to London, Paris, Geneva, Boulogne-sur-Mer and Newport, Rhode Island, according to the father's current interests and publishing ventures, retreating to the United States when funds were low. Henry studied primarily with tutors and briefly attended schools while the family traveled in Europe. Their longest stays were in France, where Henry began to feel at home and became fluent in French. He was afflicted with a stutter, which seems to have manifested itself only when he spoke English; in French, he did not stutter.

In 1860 the family returned to Newport. There Henry became a friend of the painter John La Farge, who introduced him to French literature, and in particular, to Balzac. James later called Balzac his "greatest master," and said that he had learned more about the craft of fiction from him than from anyone else.

In the autumn of 1861 Henry received an injury, probably to his back, while fighting a fire. This injury, which resurfaced at times throughout his life, made him unfit for military service in the American Civil War.

In 1864 the James family moved to Boston, Massachusetts to be near William, who had enrolled first in the Lawrence Scientific School at Harvard and then in the medical school. In 1862 Henry attended Harvard Law School, but realised that he was not interested in studying law. He pursued his interest in literature and associated with authors and critics William Dean Howells and Charles Eliot Norton in Boston and Cambridge, formed lifelong friendships with Oliver Wendell Holmes Jr., the future Supreme Court Justice, and with James and Annie Fields, his first professional mentors.

His first published work was a review of a stage performance, "Miss Maggie Mitchell in Fanchon the Cricket," published in 1863. About a year later, A Tragedy of Error, his first short story, was published anonymously. James's first payment was for an appreciation of Sir Walter Scott's novels, written for the North American Review. He wrote fiction and non-fiction pieces for The Nation and Atlantic Monthly, where Fields was editor. In 1871 he published his first novel, Watch and Ward, in serial form in the Atlantic Monthly. The novel was later published in book form in 1878.

During a 14-month trip through Europe in 1869–70 he met Ruskin, Dickens, Matthew Arnold, William Morris, and George Eliot. Rome impressed him profoundly. "Here I am then in the Eternal City," he wrote to his brother William. "At last—for the first time—I live!" He attempted to support himself as a freelance writer in Rome, then secured a position as Paris correspondent for the New York Tribune, through the influence of its editor John Hay. When these efforts failed he returned to New York City. During 1874 and 1875 he published Transatlantic Sketches, A Passionate Pilgrim, and Roderick Hudson. During this early period in his career he was influenced by Nathaniel Hawthorne.

In 1869 he settled in London. There he established relationships with Macmillan and other publishers, who paid for serial installments that they would later publish in book form. The audience for these serialized novels was largely made up of middle-class women, and James struggled to fashion serious literary work within the strictures imposed by editors' and publishers' notions of what was suitable for young women to read. He lived in rented rooms but was able to join gentlemen's clubs that had libraries and where

235

he could entertain male friends. He was introduced to English society by Henry Adams and Charles Milnes Gaskell, the latter introducing him to the Travellers' and the Reform Clubs.

In the fall of 1875 he moved to the Latin Quarter of Paris. Aside from two trips to America, he spent the next three decades—the rest of his life—in Europe. In Paris he met Zola, Alphonse Daudet, Maupassant, Turgenev, and others. He stayed in Paris only a year before moving to London.

In England he met the leading figures of politics and culture. He continued to be a prolific writer, producing The American (1877), The Europeans (1878), a revision of Watch and Ward (1878), French Poets and Novelists (1878), Hawthorne (1879), and several shorter works of fiction. In 1878 Daisy Miller established his fame on both sides of the Atlantic. It drew notice perhaps mostly because it depicted a woman whose behavior is outside the social norms of Europe. He also began his first masterpiece, The Portrait of a Lady, which would appear in 1881.

In 1877 he first visited Wenlock Abbey in Shropshire, home of his friend Charles Milnes Gaskell whom he had met through Henry Adams. He was much inspired by the darkly romantic Abbey and the surrounding countryside, which features in his essay Abbeys and Castles. In particular the gloomy monastic fishponds behind the Abbey are said to have inspired the lake in The Turn of the Screw.

While living in London, James continued to follow the careers of the "French realists", Émile Zola in particular. Their stylistic methods influenced his own work in the years to come. Hawthorne's influence on him faded during this period, replaced by George Eliot and Ivan Turgenev. 1879–1882 saw the publication of The Europeans, Washington Square, Confidence, and The Portrait of a Lady. He visited America in 1882–1883, then returned to London.

The period from 1881 to 1883 was marked by several losses. His mother died in 1881, followed by his father a few months later, and then by his brother Wilkie. Emerson, an old family friend, died in 1882. His friend Turgenev died in 1883.

Middle years, 1884–1897

In 1884 James made another visit to Paris. There he met again with Zola, Daudet, and Goncourt. He had been following the careers of the French "realist" or "naturalist" writers, and was increasingly influenced by them. In 1886, he published The Bostonians and The Princess Casamassima, both influenced by the French writers he'd studied assiduously. Critical reaction and sales were poor. He wrote to Howells that the books had hurt his career rather than helped because they had "reduced the desire, and demand, for my productions to zero". During this time he became friends with Robert Louis Stevenson, John Singer Sargent, Edmund Gosse, George du Maurier, Paul Bourget, and Constance Fenimore Woolson. His third novel from the 1880s was The Tragic Muse. Although he was following the precepts of Zola in his novels of the '80s, their tone and attitude are closer to the fiction of Alphonse Daudet. The lack of critical and financial success for his novels during this period led him to try writing for the theatre. (His dramatic works and his experiences with theatre are discussed below.)

In the last quarter of 1889, he started translating "for pure and copious lucre" Port Tarascon, the third volume of Alphonse Daudet adventures of Tartarin de Tarascon. Serialized in Harper's Monthly Magazine from June 1890, this translation praised as "clever" by The Spectator was published in January 1891 by Sampson Low, Marston, Searle & Rivington.

After the stage failure of Guy Domville in 1895, James was near despair and thoughts of death plagued him. The years spent on dramatic works were not entirely a loss. As he moved into the last phase of his career he found ways to adapt dramatic techniques into the novel form.

In the late 1880s and throughout the 1890s James made several trips through Europe. He spent a long stay in Italy in 1887. In that year the short novel The Aspern Papers and The Reverberator were published.

Late years, 1898–1916

In 1897–1898 he moved to Rye, Sussex, and wrote The Turn of the Screw. 1899–1900 saw the publication of The Awkward Age and The Sacred

Fount. During 1902–1904 he wrote The Ambassadors, The Wings of the Dove, and The Golden Bowl.

In 1904 he revisited America and lectured on Balzac. In 1906–1910 he published The American Scene and edited the "New York Edition", a 24-volume collection of his works. In 1910 his brother William died; Henry had just joined William from an unsuccessful search for relief in Europe on what then turned out to be his (Henry's) last visit to the United States (from summer 1910 to July 1911), and was near him, according to a letter he wrote, when he died.

In 1913 he wrote his autobiographies, A Small Boy and Others, and Notes of a Son and Brother. After the outbreak of the First World War in 1914 he did war work. In 1915 he became a British subject and was awarded the Order of Merit the following year. He died on 28 February 1916, in Chelsea, London. As he requested, his ashes were buried in Cambridge Cemetery in Massachusetts.

Biographers

James regularly rejected suggestions that he should marry, and after settling in London proclaimed himself "a bachelor". F. W. Dupee, in several volumes on the James family, originated the theory that he had been in love with his cousin Mary ("Minnie") Temple, but that a neurotic fear of sex kept him from admitting such affections: "James's invalidism ... was itself the symptom of some fear of or scruple against sexual love on his part." Dupee used an episode from James's memoir A Small Boy and Others, recounting a dream of a Napoleonic image in the Louvre, to exemplify James's romanticism about Europe, a Napoleonic fantasy into which he fled.

Dupee had not had access to the James family papers and worked principally from James's published memoir of his older brother, William, and the limited collection of letters edited by Percy Lubbock, heavily weighted toward James's last years. His account therefore moved directly from James's childhood, when he trailed after his older brother, to elderly invalidism. As more material became available to scholars, including the diaries of contemporaries and hundreds of affectionate and sometimes erotic letters written by James to younger men, the picture of neurotic celibacy gave way to a portrait of a closeted homosexual.

Between 1953 and 1972, Leon Edel authored a major five-volume biography of James, which accessed unpublished letters and documents after Edel gained the permission of James's family. Edel's portrayal of James included the suggestion he was celibate. It was a view first propounded by critic Saul Rosenzweig in 1943. In 1996 Sheldon M. Novick published Henry James: The Young Master, followed by Henry James: The Mature Master (2007). The first book "caused something of an uproar in Jamesian circles" as it challenged the previous received notion of celibacy, a once-familiar paradigm in biographies of homosexuals when direct evidence was non-existent. Novick also criticised Edel for following the discounted Freudian interpretation of homosexuality "as a kind of failure." The difference of opinion erupted in a series of exchanges between Edel and Novick which were published by the online magazine Slate, with the latter arguing that even the suggestion of celibacy went against James's own injunction "live!"—not "fantasize!"

A letter James wrote in old age to Hugh Walpole has been cited as an explicit statement of this. Walpole confessed to him of indulging in "high jinks", and James wrote a reply endorsing it: "We must know, as much as possible, in our beautiful art, yours & mine, what we are talking about — & the only way to know it is to have lived & loved & cursed & floundered & enjoyed & suffered — I don't think I regret a single 'excess' of my responsive youth".

The interpretation of James as living a less austere emotional life has been subsequently explored by other scholars. The often intense politics of Jamesian scholarship has also been the subject of studies. Author Colm Tóibín has said that Eve Kosofsky Sedgwick's Epistemology of the Closet made a landmark difference to Jamesian scholarship by arguing that he be read as a homosexual writer whose desire to keep his sexuality a secret shaped his layered style and dramatic artistry. According to Tóibín such a reading "removed James from the realm of dead white males who wrote about posh people. He became our contemporary."

James's letters to expatriate American sculptor Hendrik Christian Andersen have attracted particular attention. James met the 27-year-old Andersen in Rome in 1899, when James was 56, and wrote letters to Andersen that are intensely emotional: "I hold you, dearest boy, in my innermost love, & count on your feeling me—in every throb of your soul". In a letter of 6 May 1904, to his brother William, James referred to himself as "always your hopelessly celibate even though sexagenarian Henry". How accurate that description might have been is the subject of contention among James's biographers,   but the letters to Andersen were occasionally quasi-erotic: "I put, my dear boy, my arm around you, & feel the pulsation, thereby, as it were, of our excellent future & your admirable endowment." To his homosexual friend Howard Sturgis, James could write: "I repeat, almost to indiscretion, that I could live with you. Meanwhile I can only try to live without you."

His numerous letters to the many young gay men among his close male friends are more forthcoming. In a letter to Howard Sturgis, following a long visit, James refers jocularly to their "happy little congress of two" and in letters to Hugh Walpole he pursues convoluted jokes and puns about their relationship, referring to himself as an elephant who "paws you oh so benevolently" and winds about Walpole his "well meaning old trunk". His letters to Walter Berry printed by the Black Sun Press have long been celebrated for their lightly veiled eroticism.

He corresponded in almost equally extravagant language with his many female friends, writing, for example, to fellow novelist Lucy Clifford: "Dearest Lucy! What shall I say? when I love you so very, very much, and see you nine times for once that I see Others! Therefore I think that—if you want it made clear to the meanest intelligence—I love you more than I love Others." To his New York friend Mary Cadwalader Jones: "Dearest Mary Cadwalader. I yearn over you, but I yearn in vain; & your long silence really breaks my heart, mystifies, depresses, almost alarms me, to the point even of making me wonder if poor unconscious & doting old Célimare [Jones's pet name for James] has 'done' anything, in some dark somnambulism of the spirit, which has ... given you a bad moment, or a wrong impression, or a 'colourable pretext' ... However these things may be, he loves you as tenderly as ever;

nothing, to the end of time, will ever detach him from you, & he remembers those Eleventh St. matutinal intimes hours, those telephonic matinées, as the most romantic of his life ..." His long friendship with American novelist Constance Fenimore Woolson, in whose house he lived for a number of weeks in Italy in 1887, and his shock and grief over her suicide in 1894, are discussed in detail in Edel's biography and play a central role in a study by Lyndall Gordon. (Edel conjectured that Woolson was in love with James and killed herself in part because of his coldness, but Woolson's biographers have objected to Edel's account.)

Works

Style and themes

James is one of the major figures of trans-Atlantic literature. His works frequently juxtapose characters from the Old World (Europe), embodying a feudal civilisation that is beautiful, often corrupt, and alluring, and from the New World (United States), where people are often brash, open, and assertive and embody the virtues—freedom and a more highly evolved moral character—of the new American society. James explores this clash of personalities and cultures, in stories of personal relationships in which power is exercised well or badly. His protagonists were often young American women facing oppression or abuse, and as his secretary Theodora Bosanquet remarked in her monograph Henry James at Work:

> When he walked out of the refuge of his study and into the world and looked around him, he saw a place of torment, where creatures of prey perpetually thrust their claws into the quivering flesh of doomed, defenseless children of light ... His novels are a repeated exposure of this wickedness, a reiterated and passionate plea for the fullest freedom of development, unimperiled by reckless and barbarous stupidity.

Critics have jokingly described three phases in the development of James's prose: "James I, James II, and The Old Pretender." He wrote short stories and plays. Finally, in his third and last period he returned to the long, serialised novel. Beginning in the second period, but most noticeably in the third, he increasingly abandoned direct statement in favour of frequent

241

double negatives, and complex descriptive imagery. Single paragraphs began to run for page after page, in which an initial noun would be succeeded by pronouns surrounded by clouds of adjectives and prepositional clauses, far from their original referents, and verbs would be deferred and then preceded by a series of adverbs. The overall effect could be a vivid evocation of a scene as perceived by a sensitive observer. It has been debated whether this change of style was engendered by James's shifting from writing to dictating to a typist, a change made during the composition of What Maisie Knew.

In its intense focus on the consciousness of his major characters, James's later work foreshadows extensive developments in 20th century fiction. Indeed, he might have influenced stream-of-consciousness writers such as Virginia Woolf, who not only read some of his novels but also wrote essays about them. Both contemporary and modern readers have found the late style difficult and unnecessary; his friend Edith Wharton, who admired him greatly, said that there were passages in his work that were all but incomprehensible. James was harshly portrayed by H. G. Wells as a hippopotamus laboriously attempting to pick up a pea that had got into a corner of its cage. The "late James" style was ably parodied by Max Beerbohm in "The Mote in the Middle Distance".

More important for his work overall may have been his position as an expatriate, and in other ways an outsider, living in Europe. While he came from middle-class and provincial beginnings (seen from the perspective of European polite society) he worked very hard to gain access to all levels of society, and the settings of his fiction range from working class to aristocratic, and often describe the efforts of middle-class Americans to make their way in European capitals. He confessed he got some of his best story ideas from gossip at the dinner table or at country house weekends. He worked for a living, however, and lacked the experiences of select schools, university, and army service, the common bonds of masculine society. He was furthermore a man whose tastes and interests were, according to the prevailing standards of Victorian era Anglo-American culture, rather feminine, and who was shadowed by the cloud of prejudice that then and later accompanied suspicions of his homosexuality. Edmund Wilson famously compared James's objectivity to Shakespeare's:

242

One would be in a position to appreciate James better if one compared him with the dramatists of the seventeenth century—Racine and Molière, whom he resembles in form as well as in point of view, and even Shakespeare, when allowances are made for the most extreme differences in subject and form. These poets are not, like Dickens and Hardy, writers of melodrama—either humorous or pessimistic, nor secretaries of society like Balzac, nor prophets like Tolstoy: they are occupied simply with the presentation of conflicts of moral character, which they do not concern themselves about softening or averting. They do not indict society for these situations: they regard them as universal and inevitable. They do not even blame God for allowing them: they accept them as the conditions of life.

It is also possible to see many of James's stories as psychological thought-experiments. In his preface to the New York edition of The American he describes the development of the story in his mind as exactly such: the "situation" of an American, "some robust but insidiously beguiled and betrayed, some cruelly wronged, compatriot..." with the focus of the story being on the response of this wronged man. The Portrait of a Lady may be an experiment to see what happens when an idealistic young woman suddenly becomes very rich. In many of his tales, characters seem to exemplify alternative futures and possibilities, as most markedly in "The Jolly Corner", in which the protagonist and a ghost-doppelganger live alternative American and European lives; and in others, like The Ambassadors, an older James seems fondly to regard his own younger self facing a crucial moment.

Major novels

The first period of James's fiction, usually considered to have culminated in The Portrait of a Lady, concentrated on the contrast between Europe and America. The style of these novels is generally straightforward and, though personally characteristic, well within the norms of 19th-century fiction. Roderick Hudson (1875) is a Künstlerroman that traces the development of the title character, an extremely talented sculptor. Although the book shows some signs of immaturity—this was James's first serious attempt at a full-length novel—it has attracted favourable comment due to the vivid realisation of the three major characters: Roderick Hudson, superbly gifted but unstable and unreliable; Rowland Mallet, Roderick's limited but much more mature friend and patron; and Christina Light, one of James's most enchanting and maddening femmes fatales. The pair of Hudson and Mallet has been seen as representing the two sides of James's own nature: the wildly imaginative artist and the brooding conscientious mentor.

In The Portrait of a Lady (1881) James concluded the first phase of his career with a novel that remains his most popular piece of long fiction. The story is of a spirited young American woman, Isabel Archer, who "affronts her destiny" and finds it overwhelming. She inherits a large amount of money and subsequently becomes the victim of Machiavellian scheming by two American expatriates. The narrative is set mainly in Europe, especially in England and Italy. Generally regarded as the masterpiece of his early phase, The Portrait of a Lady is described as a psychological novel, exploring the minds of his characters, and almost a work of social science, exploring the differences between Europeans and Americans, the old and the new worlds.

The second period of James's career, which extends from the publication of The Portrait of a Lady through the end of the nineteenth century, features less popular novels including The Princess Casamassima, published serially in The Atlantic Monthly in 1885–1886, and The Bostonians, published serially in The Century Magazine during the same period. This period also featured James's celebrated Gothic novella, The Turn of the Screw.

The third period of James's career reached its most significant achievement in three novels published just around the start of the 20th century: The Wings of the Dove (1902), The Ambassadors (1903), and The Golden Bowl (1904). Critic F. O. Matthiessen called this "trilogy" James's major phase, and these novels have certainly received intense critical study. It was the second-written of the books, The Wings of the Dove (1902) that was the first published because it attracted no serialization. This novel tells the story of Milly Theale, an American heiress stricken with a serious disease, and her impact on the people around her. Some of these people befriend Milly with honourable motives, while others are more self-interested. James stated in his autobiographical books that Milly was based on Minny Temple, his beloved cousin who died at an early age of tuberculosis. He said that he attempted in the novel to wrap her memory in the "beauty and dignity of art".

Shorter narratives

James was particularly interested in what he called the "beautiful and blest nouvelle", or the longer form of short narrative. Still, he produced a number of very short stories in which he achieved notable compression of sometimes complex subjects. The following narratives are representative of James's achievement in the shorter forms of fiction.

- "A Tragedy of Error" (1864), short story
- "The Story of a Year" (1865), short story
- A Passionate Pilgrim (1871), novella
- Madame de Mauves (1874), novella
- Daisy Miller (1878), novella
- The Aspern Papers (1888), novella
- The Lesson of the Master (1888), novella
- The Pupil (1891), short story
- "The Figure in the Carpet" (1896), short story
- The Beast in the Jungle (1903), novella
- An International Episode (1878)
- Picture and Text
- Four Meetings (1885)
- A London Life, and Other Tales (1889)
- The Spoils of Poynton (1896)

- Embarrassments (1896)

- The Two Magics: The Turn of the Screw, Covering End (1898)

- A Little Tour of France (1900)

- The Sacred Fount (1901)

- Views and Reviews (1908)

- The Wings of the Dove, Volume I (1902)

- The Wings of the Dove, Volume II (1909)

- The Finer Grain (1910)

- The Outcry (1911)

- Lady Barbarina: The Siege of London, An International Episode and Other Tales (1922)

- The Birthplace (1922)

Plays

At several points in his career James wrote plays, beginning with one-act plays written for periodicals in 1869 and 1871 and a dramatisation of his popular novella Daisy Miller in 1882. From 1890 to 1892, having received a bequest that freed him from magazine publication, he made a strenuous effort to succeed on the London stage, writing a half-dozen plays of which only one, a dramatisation of his novel The American, was produced. This play was performed for several years by a touring repertory company and had a respectable run in London, but did not earn very much money for James. His other plays written at this time were not produced.

In 1893, however, he responded to a request from actor-manager George Alexander for a serious play for the opening of his renovated St. James's Theatre, and wrote a long drama, Guy Domville, which Alexander produced. There was a noisy uproar on the opening night, 5 January 1895, with hissing from the gallery when James took his bow after the final curtain, and the author was upset. The play received moderately good reviews and had a modest run of four weeks before being taken off to make way for Oscar Wilde's The Importance of Being Earnest, which Alexander thought would have better prospects for the coming season.

After the stresses and disappointment of these efforts James insisted that he would write no more for the theatre, but within weeks had agreed to write a curtain-raiser for Ellen Terry. This became the one-act "Summersoft", which he later rewrote into a short story, "Covering End", and then expanded into a full-length play, The High Bid, which had a brief run in London in 1907, when James made another concerted effort to write for the stage. He wrote three new plays, two of which were in production when the death of Edward VII on 6 May 1910 plunged London into mourning and theatres closed. Discouraged by failing health and the stresses of theatrical work, James did not renew his efforts in the theatre, but recycled his plays as successful novels. The Outcry was a best-seller in the United States when it was published in 1911. During the years 1890–1893 when he was most engaged with the theatre, James wrote a good deal of theatrical criticism and assisted Elizabeth Robins and others in translating and producing Henrik Ibsen for the first time in London.

Leon Edel argued in his psychoanalytic biography that James was traumatised by the opening night uproar that greeted Guy Domville, and that it plunged him into a prolonged depression. The successful later novels, in Edel's view, were the result of a kind of self-analysis, expressed in fiction, which partly freed him from his fears. Other biographers and scholars have not accepted this account, however; the more common view being that of F.O. Matthiessen, who wrote: "Instead of being crushed by the collapse of his hopes [for the theatre]... he felt a resurgence of new energy."

Non-fiction

Beyond his fiction, James was one of the more important literary critics in the history of the novel. In his classic essay The Art of Fiction (1884), he argued against rigid prescriptions on the novelist's choice of subject and method of treatment. He maintained that the widest possible freedom in content and approach would help ensure narrative fiction's continued vitality.

James wrote many valuable critical articles on other novelists; typical is his book-length study of Nathaniel Hawthorne, which has been the subject of critical debate. Richard Brodhead has suggested that the study was emblematic of James's struggle with Hawthorne's influence, and constituted an effort to place the elder writer "at a disadvantage." Gordon Fraser, meanwhile, has suggested that the study was part of a more commercial effort by James to introduce himself to British readers as Hawthorne's natural successor.

When James assembled the New York Edition of his fiction in his final years, he wrote a series of prefaces that subjected his own work to searching, occasionally harsh criticism.

At 22 James wrote The Noble School of Fiction for The Nation's first issue in 1865. He would write, in all, over 200 essays and book, art, and theatre reviews for the magazine.

For most of his life James harboured ambitions for success as a playwright. He converted his novel The American into a play that enjoyed modest returns in the early 1890s. In all he wrote about a dozen plays, most of which went unproduced. His costume drama Guy Domville failed disastrously on its opening night in 1895. James then largely abandoned his efforts to conquer the stage and returned to his fiction. In his Notebooks he maintained that his theatrical experiment benefited his novels and tales by helping him dramatise his characters' thoughts and emotions. James produced a small but valuable amount of theatrical criticism, including perceptive appreciations of Henrik Ibsen.

With his wide-ranging artistic interests, James occasionally wrote on the visual arts. Perhaps his most valuable contribution was his favourable assessment of fellow expatriate John Singer Sargent, a painter whose critical status has improved markedly in recent decades. James also wrote sometimes charming, sometimes brooding articles about various places he visited and lived in. His most famous books of travel writing include Italian Hours (an example of the charming approach) and The American Scene (most definitely on the brooding side).

James was one of the great letter-writers of any era. More than ten thousand of his personal letters are extant, and over three thousand have been published in a large number of collections. A complete edition of James's letters began publication in 2006, edited by Pierre Walker and Greg Zacharias. As of 2014, eight volumes have been published, covering the period from 1855 to 1880. James's correspondents included celebrated contemporaries like Robert Louis Stevenson, Edith Wharton and Joseph Conrad, along with many others in his wide circle of friends and acquaintances. The letters range from the "mere twaddle of graciousness" to serious discussions of artistic, social and personal issues.

Very late in life James began a series of autobiographical works: A Small Boy and Others, Notes of a Son and Brother, and the unfinished The Middle Years. These books portray the development of a classic observer who was passionately interested in artistic creation but was somewhat reticent about participating fully in the life around him.

Reception

Criticism, biographies and fictional treatments

James's work has remained steadily popular with the limited audience of educated readers to whom he spoke during his lifetime, and has remained firmly in the canon, but, after his death, some American critics, such as Van Wyck Brooks, expressed hostility towards James for his long expatriation and eventual naturalisation as a British subject. Other critics such as E. M. Forster complained about what they saw as James's squeamishness in the treatment of sex and other possibly controversial material, or dismissed his late style as difficult and obscure, relying heavily on extremely long sentences and excessively latinate language. Similarly Oscar Wilde criticised him for writing "fiction as if it were a painful duty". Vernon Parrington, composing a canon of American literature, condemned James for having cut himself off from America. Jorge Luis Borges wrote about him, "Despite the scruples and delicate complexities of James, his work suffers from a major defect: the absence of life." And Virginia Woolf, writing to Lytton Strachey, asked, "Please tell me what you find in Henry James. ... we have his works here, and

I read, and I can't find anything but faintly tinged rose water, urbane and sleek, but vulgar and pale as Walter Lamb. Is there really any sense in it?" The novelist W. Somerset Maugham wrote, "He did not know the English as an Englishman instinctively knows them and so his English characters never to my mind quite ring true," and argued "The great novelists, even in seclusion, have lived life passionately. Henry James was content to observe it from a window." Maugham nevertheless wrote, "The fact remains that those last novels of his, notwithstanding their unreality, make all other novels, except the very best, unreadable." Colm Tóibín observed that James "never really wrote about the English very well. His English characters don't work for me."

Despite these criticisms, James is now valued for his psychological and moral realism, his masterful creation of character, his low-key but playful humour, and his assured command of the language. In his 1983 book, The Novels of Henry James, Edward Wagenknecht offers an assessment that echoes Theodora Bosanquet's:

> "To be completely great," Henry James wrote in an early review, "a work of art must lift up the heart," and his own novels do this to an outstanding degree ... More than sixty years after his death, the great novelist who sometimes professed to have no opinions stands foursquare in the great Christian humanistic and democratic tradition. The men and women who, at the height of World War II, raided the secondhand shops for his out-of-print books knew what they were about. For no writer ever raised a braver banner to which all who love freedom might adhere.

William Dean Howells saw James as a representative of a new realist school of literary art which broke with the English romantic tradition epitomised by the works of Charles Dickens and William Makepeace Thackeray. Howells wrote that realism found "its chief exemplar in Mr. James... A novelist he is not, after the old fashion, or after any fashion but his own." F.R. Leavis championed Henry James as a novelist of "established pre-eminence" in The Great Tradition (1948), asserting that The Portrait of a Lady and The Bostonians were "the two most brilliant novels in the language." James is now prized as a master of point of view who moved literary fiction forward by insisting in showing, not telling, his stories to the reader. (Source: Wikipedia)

NOTABLE WORKS

NOVELS

Watch and Ward (1871)

Roderick Hudson (1875)

The American (1877)

The Europeans (1878)

Confidence (1879)

Washington Square (1880)

The Portrait of a Lady (1881)

The Bostonians (1886)

The Princess Casamassima (1886)

The Reverberator (1888)

The Tragic Muse (1890)

The Other House (1896)

The Spoils of Poynton (1897)

What Maisie Knew (1897)

The Awkward Age (1899)

The Sacred Fount (1901)

The Wings of the Dove (1902)

The Ambassadors (1903)

The Golden Bowl (1904)

The Whole Family (collaborative novel with eleven other authors, 1908)

The Outcry (1911)

The Ivory Tower (unfinished, published posthumously 1917)

The Sense of the Past (unfinished, published posthumously 1917)

SHORT STORIES AND NOVELLAS

A Tragedy of Error (1864)

The Story of a Year (1865)

A Landscape Painter (1866)

A Day of Days (1866)

My Friend Bingham (1867)

Poor Richard (1867)

The Story of a Masterpiece (1868)

A Most Extraordinary Case (1868)

A Problem (1868)

De Grey: A Romance (1868)

Osborne's Revenge (1868)

The Romance of Certain Old Clothes (1868)

A Light Man (1869)

Gabrielle de Bergerac (1869)

Travelling Companions (1870)

A Passionate Pilgrim (1871)

At Isella (1871)

Master Eustace (1871)

Guest's Confession (1872)

The Madonna of the Future (1873)

The Sweetheart of M. Briseux (1873)

The Last of the Valerii (1874)

Madame de Mauves (1874)

Adina (1874)

Professor Fargo (1874)

Eugene Pickering (1874)

Benvolio (1875)

Crawford's Consistency (1876)

The Ghostly Rental (1876)

Four Meetings (1877)

Rose-Agathe (1878, as Théodolinde)

Daisy Miller (1878)

Longstaff's Marriage (1878)

An International Episode (1878)

The Pension Beaurepas (1879)

A Diary of a Man of Fifty (1879)

A Bundle of Letters (1879)

The Point of View (1882)

The Siege of London (1883)

Impressions of a Cousin (1883)

Lady Barberina (1884)

Pandora (1884)

The Author of Beltraffio (1884)

Georgina's Reasons (1884)

A New England Winter (1884)

The Path of Duty (1884)

Mrs. Temperly (1887)

Louisa Pallant (1888)

The Aspern Papers (1888)

The Liar (1888)

The Modern Warning (1888, originally published as The Two Countries)

A London Life (1888)

The Patagonia (1888)

The Lesson of the Master (1888)

The Solution (1888)

The Pupil (1891)

Brooksmith (1891)

The Marriages (1891)

The Chaperon (1891)

Sir Edmund Orme (1891)

Nona Vincent (1892)

The Real Thing (1892)

The Private Life (1892)

Lord Beaupré (1892)

The Visits (1892)

Sir Dominick Ferrand (1892)

Greville Fane (1892)

Collaboration (1892)

Owen Wingrave (1892)

The Wheel of Time (1892)

The Middle Years (1893)

The Death of the Lion (1894)

The Coxon Fund (1894)

The Next Time (1895)

Glasses (1896)

The Altar of the Dead (1895)

The Figure in the Carpet (1896)

The Way It Came (1896, also published as The Friends of the Friends)

The Turn of the Screw (1898)

Covering End (1898)

In the Cage (1898)

John Delavoy (1898)

The Given Case (1898)

Europe (1899)

The Great Condition (1899)

The Real Right Thing (1899)

Paste (1899)

The Great Good Place (1900)

Maud-Evelyn (1900)

Miss Gunton of Poughkeepsie (1900)

The Tree of Knowledge (1900)

The Abasement of the Northmores (1900)

The Third Person (1900)

The Special Type (1900)

The Tone of Time (1900)

Broken Wings (1900)

The Two Faces (1900)

Mrs. Medwin (1901)

The Beldonald Holbein (1901)

The Story in It (1902)

Flickerbridge (1902)

The Birthplace (1903)

The Beast in the Jungle (1903)

The Papers (1903)

Fordham Castle (1904)

Julia Bride (1908)

The Jolly Corner (1908)

The Velvet Glove (1909)

Mora Montravers (1909)

Crapy Cornelia (1909)

The Bench of Desolation (1909)

A Round of Visits (1910)

OTHER

Transatlantic Sketches (1875)

French Poets and Novelists (1878)

Hawthorne (1879)

Portraits of Places (1883)

A Little Tour in France (1884)

Partial Portraits (1888)

Essays in London and Elsewhere (1893)

Picture and Text (1893)

Terminations (1893)

Theatricals (1894)

Theatricals: Second Series (1895)

Guy Domville (1895)

The Soft Side (1900)

William Wetmore Story and His Friends (1903)

The Better Sort (1903)

English Hours (1905)

The Question of our Speech; The Lesson of Balzac. Two Lectures (1905)

The American Scene (1907)

Views and Reviews (1908)

Italian Hours (1909)

A Small Boy and Others (1913)

Notes on Novelists (1914)

Notes of a Son and Brother (1914)

Within the Rim (1918)

Travelling Companions (1919)

Notebooks (various, published posthumously)

The Middle Years (unfinished, published posthumously 1917)

A Most Unholy Trade (1925, published posthumously)

The Art of the Novel : Critical Prefaces (1934)